ANARCHY

Book 3

SG Boudreaux

ISBN: 978-1-7361117-4-1 (Paperback)

ISBN: 978-1-7361117-5-8 (Digital)

SG Boudreaux

Printed in the USA

Sgboodro2@yahoo.com

www.SGBoudreaux.com

Cover Art, original art by Savannah King. Find more of her artwork @meadow_monarch on Instagram.

Glossary

Section with all CAPPED letters is the annunciated part of the word having inflection. Bold letters receive the long sound.

Praxtingen (PRAX tin jin) — Mid-size city, eastern territory.

Loradin (LOR a dun) — Large island city, eastern territory.

Martanzia (Mar TAN zee a) — Large city, northern territory

Bakrashan (Ba kru SHAN) — Large city, western territory

*Carpasmere (CAR pa **smear**)* — Mid-sized city, north-eastern territory, mostly housing based.

*Kabihan**xu** (Ka bi HAN **jew**)* — A massively large, four-legged, fire-breathing, bird, whose feathers are streaked in shades of red, yellow, orange, purple, teal, and gold. Its skin is like armor. Carnivorous. Slang term is **Firebird.**

*Monshok**to** (Mon SHOCK **toe**)* — A large, furry, long-haired creature, with a single horn in the middle of its head. Runs on all fours but walks on two legs. Eats fish and grass. Thrives in water and lives on the banks of the lake in pod groups.

Trefell (Tru FELL) — Smallish to medium sized ball of fur with sharp teeth. They can roll along at quicker speeds. Downs trees for their homes.

Tribhon (**TRI** *bun*)

Cross between a squirrel and racoon with a stinging tail and long, sharp retractable claws. Eats fruits and nuts.

Raisedback Vindaper
    (*R****AI****SED back VIN du pair*)

Resembles a wild boar. Has a short hair ridge down its spine a long whiplike tail and 6 legs. Tusks at the mouth and grows large enough to ride. Eats wild mushrooms, and table scraps. Can be very mean.

Yarequu (*YAR **a** koo*)

Resembles a very large horse. Eats fruits, berries, nuts, grasses. Has spikes at the knee joints which open to fans which allow it to glide through the air for short distances. Can camouflage to itself and its rider to their current environment when frightened.

*Pagorinx (PA **gor** inx)*

A massive, cat-like creature whose fur is so black It's almost purple. It has teal and white braided looking stripes from its ears to its rear haunches, sharp retractable clawsteal in color. Long, braided looking hair around its neck, long sabered teeth that protrude from the top lip. Carnivorous.

Zanchieth (*Zan **KEETH***)

Wealthiest people, Old world money.

Rhe Mines (Ray)

Mines with minerals known as Rhenium and Ruthenium. Highly sought

	after for their high melting point and used in weapons and armor against the Kabihanxu and Pagorinxes.
*Scaithers (**SKA** thers)*	Ruthless, lawless, band of people.
*Rhedon (**Ray** dawn)*	Zanchier's monetary system.
Brindelwren	A very large, kelpy-looking creature that resembles a seahorses head, an eels body, but with four large, kelpy, sinewy, flowing fins, and a long, poisonous tail that can produce spikes from beneath the flowing fins. It is bioluminescent and can turn translucent when needed.
Spiritflies	like butterflies, but longer, sweeping, wings that flow in the air like they were underwater. They also are multicolored and bioluminescent in different shades.
Jumpers	bioluminescent frog like creatures
Strikers	Snake-like creatures, vary depending on their environment.
MADS	Matter Arranging Devices, allowing the wearer to jump from one place to another.

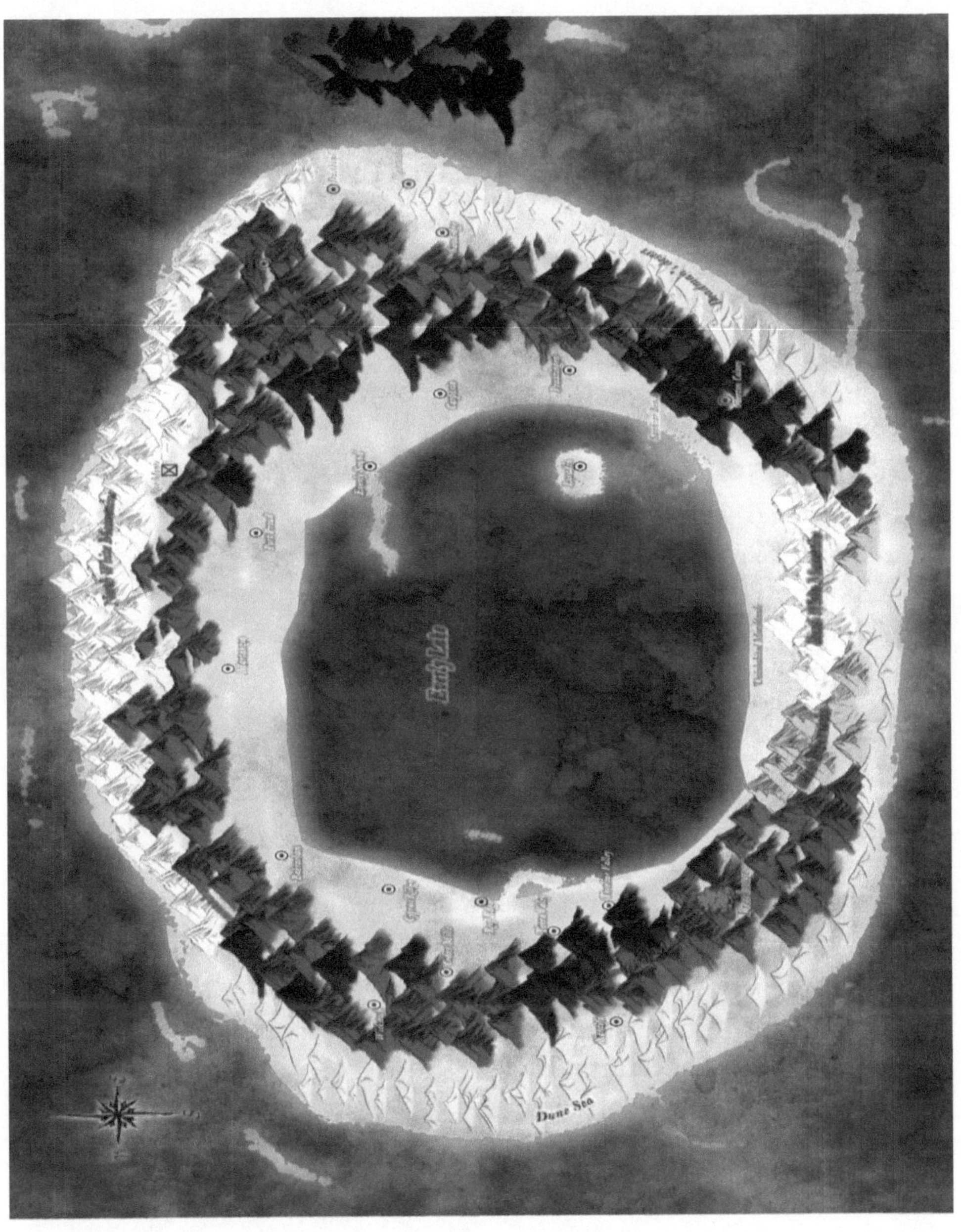

For a detailed view of the map, sign up for my email
list via my website; listed in the back of the book; on
the contact me page. As an email subscriber, you can
sign up to get free members only access to book-related
content for all my books.

Table of Contents

Chapter 1

War Torn

Wynne Brinley, now fourteen, sat aback the fully grown three-year-old Kabihanxu, Roamey, as they flew across the war-torn landscape of Zanchier patrolling the borders of Praxtingen, Carpasia, the city of Loradin and the many other outlying villages and territories. The brightly-colored, fire-breathing, four-legged bird was now more than twice the size of its juvenile beginnings. The last three years, since the initial outbreak of war, there had been on again, off again, battles that popped up here and there. The children of the Loradin Animal Rescue and Sanctuary, known as LARS, had continued to train with the animals in telepathic communications, and in learning how to use the animals and their remarkable abilities for the benefit of humanity. Wynne had been the first to make an unbreakable bond three years ago when she was only eleven and having just discovered her gift of animal communication. She and Roamey, then just a feathery-fluffed fledgling, had bonded so strongly that it had changed the course of the war. The children and their animals had aided in the three-army war and had helped to save the city of Rhamadon and secure the future of Zanchier after many deaths during the long month of fighting the Scaithers.

Unfortunately, the Scaithers had only grown in power and ruthlessness and were now the largest militaristic force in Zanchier. All the cities, what was left of them, are now loyal to Loradin and aid one another in the fight. However, many people still fear the Scaither's and their brutality.

Financially backed by the biggest crime syndicate in Zanchier and led by one Vonder Mortruff, the Scaithers had money, power, and weapons at their fingertips.

Riglan, Vonder's one and only son, now helped his father run the crime syndicate. Riglan Mortruff had always been a bully. Growing up in academy, Wynne's oldest brother Bain had many run-ins with Riglan, as they were around the same age and education level. Now that both boys were older, Riglan ran his father's crime syndicate and Bain was lead agent over a younger group of agents who had joined up with the Loradin Secret Society. After the war, many people pledged to continue to fight and protect their own livelihoods and those of their neighbors. Ever since, every service industry in Loradin and surrounding cities was packed with new recruits.

Since the age of sixteen, when young men and women graduated academy, Bain had been with the LSS. Their grandfather, Aaric Brinley, was head over the organization which was made up of many men and woman who served to protect the people of Loradin in secretive fashion. This society also included her father Wilkins, her mother Harper, and her Uncle Finn—her mother's oldest and dearest friend—and Aunt Paisley, Finn's wife. The LSS often led missions of the highest importance and answered only to the governor of Loradin, which at the moment was still Jasper Jeffries.

Jasper was a short, round, partly-balding man who had a large personality. He had served as governor of Loradin for many years before Wynne's family had moved there, and since the wars started, he had secured his place in the governor's office by taking the majority of the credit for being the man who had saved Zanchier. However, his service within the war was greatly exaggerated. It was the LSS, the Coastal Guard, the Loradin Air Patrol—which Wynne's other brother Seadon had served on—and the ordinary people of Zanchier who had taken up arms to protect their own, that had saved the city. The gifted telepathic children of LARS, under the tutelage of Dr. Patrice Barrister, had also played a large part in all of it as well. And since all of these entities were located within the border of the beautiful city of Loradin, and supposedly under the direction of the governor, Jasper Jeffries made out quite well as the leader of the rebellion, that had guided the forces, that had taken down the rest of the Zanchier armies and cities. Not only that, but he often spoke on how he had instructed the leading of the mission to overcome the now deceased Raif Martray—the once cruel leader and creator of the Scaithers, along with crime boss Vonder Mortruff, who had gladly taken Martray's place. Unfortunately, Vonder was still at large and causing trouble.

Roamey squawked loudly and shot a fireball into the air in front of them as they glided smoothly toward home. Wynne giggled at the bird, knowing he was feeling rather frisky on this beautiful cool morning. She reached down and patted his neck, ruffling his thick feathers.

"Let's head back, Roamey. Time for breakfast. I'm starving, what about you?"

Roamey squawked again and nodded his head in reply.

Wynne loved early mornings in the springtime. She smiled as the sun peeked over the horizon in the distance and bathed the land in a soft warm glow, warming her inside and out as the coolness of the air tingled against her bare arms and face.

Her smile soon turned to one of sadness as she looked down over the landscape below. Zanchier had once been a place of utter beauty and mystique. Sure the flowering trees in full bloom of spring shot color everywhere in the morning sunlight, but since the war began three years back, it was slowly decaying. The once beautiful thriving cities and towns mostly now reduced to rubble. The desert coastal city of Rhamadon had been one of the most beautiful and feared cities of all, but the once proud and skillful warrior people were shrinking away. Sickness and hunger due to the heavy hand of the Scaither organization was crumbling the once proud and strong walled city. And not just Rhamadon suffered, but all of Zanchier. Many cities no longer stood. Only a few of the outlying villages managed to keep the Scaithers at bay, and some only because the Scaithers feared the large carnivorous animals that roamed the mountains around those villages. The Shifts, sudden shifting of the Xantifal Mountains, also played a large part in their fear. No one but the locals knew how to navigate around the strange phenomenon of the rearranging mountain side. The people had learned to survive and live around the animals and with the Shifts, and they preferred dealing with them to Scaithers any day.

The fear the Scaithers instilled in people also increased their ranks on a daily level. People were offered freedom to do as they pleased as long as they pledged loyalty to the Scaithers. They robbed, raped, killed, kidnapped the women and the young, and destroyed anyone who tried to stand against them. The many other cities and towns throughout Zanchier were either too small to rally, or their council members and leaders were likely crooked and in the pocket of Vonder and Riglan Mortruff, and so their people suffered greatly for their treachery.

Out of the larger cities and villages, only Loradin, Praxtingen, and the surrounding villages were able to still stand firmly against the Scaithers. Over the last year there were less and less attacks. Wynne's father Wilkins told her that the lessening attacks were likely due to the fact the Scaithers controlled the rest of Zanchier and had plenty to keep them satisfied for now. However, he doubted that Loradin's respite from fighting would last long. Men who lusted after power were never satisfied until they had taken control of everything and everyone.

The city of Loradin came into view as they flew toward it. The LSS building was the tallest in the city and was made of mostly glass, like the city's massive bridge to the mainland. As they approached the city, the sun bounced off the rounded windows casting beams of light over the lower buildings like small beacons, rippling and changing what was highlighted below as they flew around the borders of the city.

Wynne breathed deeply of the cool morning air, reveling once more in the peace and tranquility her and Roamey's early morning rides afforded. It was basically the only time she was technically alone. Roamey was always there, but he understood her thoughts and needs like no one else could. That was what happened when you bonded with your creature. It gave you such a strong connection that you could sense what the other was feeling even if you were nowhere near each other. It traversed time and space and was a deeply emotional and unbreakable union.

Roamey soon touched down on the dock platform of the LARS building which sat on the southwestern coastal edge of Everly Lake. The LARS Institute, which was once a rehabilitation facility for injured animals and gifted children, was now the central location for the Loradin Animal Brigade. Dr. Barrister was trying hard to protect the gifted students from the Scaithers who tried regularly to abduct one of the Patrol Force to try and manipulate the use of the animals. Because of this, she had moved the school for the gifted to an undisclosed location within the Carpasian Mountains. The only people who knew where that was, included the Animal

Brigade, students of LARS, the LSS—which included only a few key people within that organization, and Captain James Donner and a handful of his most trusted Coastal Guard.

Kreelie, Bain, Seadon, Caislan, and Delmar all continued fighting with the resistance, and all worked for some organization or other, fighting on the front lines when necessary, and helping to keep the peace.

Harper and Wilkins had taken to keeping Adda safe from harm and kept to their home and inside the gates of Loradin for the most part. Harper mainly stayed at home for Adda, while Wilkins still worked as an LSS agent and was still searching for the mole from three years back that had gotten another agent killed.

Wynne, who was Brigade Captain, and Jerod the oldest boy and commander of the Patrol Force, were the leaders of the Animal Brigade. They all took turns scouting the Loradin borders and outer cities and villages with their creatures every morning and evening. After that, she and the other four younger students would return to the newly hidden Institute. Several of the older students had already graduated academy and worked full time at Patrol headquarters, living in the once boarding academy. Jerod Narta, now nineteen, was commander, and the handsomest boy Wynne had ever seen. He and Wynne liked one another and shared a casually comfortable relationship. Oudree Swywith, who was now eighteen, slim, tall, and darkly attractive, rode the Yarequu. A large four-legged animal standing eighteen hands high with grayish, teal-blue fur, a long nose, long mane and tail, curved fins at the knee joints, and had several very unique abilities. Matteo Ashwood was all of seventeen, overconfident and full of himself, and was still jealous of Wynne and Roamey's relationship. He often commanded the Raisedback Vindaper named Tusk. This six-legged animal had tusks, was large enough to ride, had short brownish-black hair that spiked from his head to his tail, decreasing in height at the front set of legs. It had three sets of tusks on its face—one that protruded from the bottom of its jawline at the back of the head and curved forward. The other two sets stuck upward from its mouth at the rear of the jaw. It had a long whip-like tail and was normally mean tempered. It had little fear of anything in the wild and often, comically so, stood its ground in front of Roamey, as if to say, 'try me.' The last of the gifted patrol riders was sixteen-year-old Kasin Merriweather. She and Wynne had become the best of friends over the years and as close as sisters. Kasin was the kindest and best of souls. She spoke very little, but when she did people often paid attention because what she said was often brilliant. Her bond animal was the Tribhon; a small to medium sized animal with long arms and tail. It swung from the trees and stung its victims with its long tail, temporarily paralyzing them. If feeling particularly threatened, they would also lash out at their adversaries with their long sharp talons. Since the Tribhon was too small to ride, Kasin had been given one of the LSS bi-mods for transport and patrolling. Because of this, Matteo was once again jealous, now of Kasin as well.

Wynne and the older riders were the only students who were allowed to stay longer at the Animal Brigade Headquarters at the LARS building. Even though she was the youngest of the independent patrol riders, Wynne was vastly intelligent, understood the creatures like no one else could, and was very independent and capable of commanding her own environment. Therefore, several nights a week she was allowed to stay at LARS with those that had now graduated. The rest of the younger original group of the Animal Brigade consisted of a thirteen-year-old girl named Jilly, an eleven-year-old boy named Naphin, and ten-year-old Eckshum, who was the bravest of them all at such an early age. He was fearless and had only been seven-years-old when he had fought in the wars three years earlier. He, Naphin, and Jilly were also inseparable friends.

Wynne stood at the docks and watched Jerod and Moshi—the hairy, four-legged, one-horned, water-loving Monshokto he had bonded with—return from scouting Loradin's and Everly Lake's watery borders.

Everly Lake was such a large body of water that it took at least five hours of straight hard flight to reach the other side. It was a vast round lake that sat dead center of Zanchier. It provided much of the country's food source and yet could be a very deadly place to navigate. Few people dared to venture into the water below the surface. Especially since the deadly, stinging, tentacle-covered Glowfish had begun to venture further into the lake waters and were beginning to become an invasive species. They had become such a problem that the Loradin government had commissioned people to fish and dispose of them as they were destroying other populations of fish. And, since Glowfish were attracted to things that sparkled in the sunlight, they were terrorizing the shoreline of the gleaming island city of Loradin.

Overton Colony, the southernmost city that was nearest Lumen Falls—the glowfish's spawning grounds—once fished for them regularly, using their poison, meat, flesh, and scales in their everyday life and for trading purposes. They had kept the population under control, but now that the city was no longer standing, and many of its people scattered across the land, the Glowfish population was out of control; just one more ill effect of war.

"Good morning Jerod," Wynne yelled, waving, and smiling brightly.

Jerod smiled back and waved from his position on Moshi's back. "Morning Wynne. How goes the patrolling?"

"Great," she said, as he began to climb off Moshi's back. "Nothing new to report, at least nothing menacing."

Jerod looked at her as her tone grew sad. He knew that she was depressed over the decline of the outer villages and cities.

"Well, at least we won't have to deal with Scaithers early today."

"No. I didn't see any activity at all around any of the outlying villages."

"Nor did I. Nothing happening on the water anywhere for at least ten miles out."

Wynne blanched at his answer, "You know if Dr. Barrister finds out that you are chancing going out that far on Moshi she will read you the riot act."

"Yeah well, she has the gifted to train and we have the Patrol to run. I am active commander and an adult. What she thinks is right, or wants, no longer comes in to play."

Wynne looked disapprovingly at him. "Jerod, if it were not for Patrice Barrister neither of us would be in this position now. You should show the woman some respect."

"I don't disrespect her. I just don't cling onto everything she says anymore. We know more about the animals and their abilities than she ever could. Besides, I don't fear anything when I'm with Moshi. You know exactly what I mean," he replied.

Wynne sighed. "Yes, I do know what you mean. Just make certain that you don't disrespect her in front of the other students. She technically is still in charge here. The Loradin Government may pay us a wage now for our efforts, but she still owns the property and graciously allows us to do this, even though she is firmly against using the animals in this way."

"Yeah, I know, Wynne. I just happen to think she is wrong about that. What other purpose could there be for our abilities if not to use the animals to help protect Loradin and its people?"

"I agree. I truly believe the Creator gave us our abilities for a very good reason. Just remember she spearheaded the LARS Institute, at the chagrin of many others, and at her own expense. She deserves everyone's respect, ours especially for recognizing our gifts and teaching us how to use them."

Jerod smile down at the fiercely outspoken young woman beside him. He reached out and threw an arm around her shoulder, "Yeah, yeah. I know you're right. You are my moral compass after-all."

She smiled up into his face, squinting into the brightening light of the sun as it rose higher in the sky. They joined Oudree and Matteo as they too were returning from their morning rounds. They all walked inside the LARS building, which was now the Animal Brigade Headquarters, to have a hearty breakfast before getting on with the rest of their day, which consisted of feeding and tending to the needs of the animals before the rest of the LARS students and Dr. Barrister showed up for their bi-weekly training sessions. The remaining Animal Brigade, Kasin and the younger students, would take the evening shift for patrols using Mods for transport since their animals were not the kind to be ridden, the younger three being chaperoned by the local armed Coastal Guard.

Chapter 2

Survival

Bain walked through the hidden, underground rooms of the Discovery Falls command center in search of Dr. Barrister. Discovery Falls had once, long ago, been a communications bunker for a rebellion from fifty years ago. When the most recent wars threatened all of Zanchier three years back, the communications bunker was reopened and had housed many refugees and soldiers and had been a central command center for the whole Loradian army. Shortly after the war had ended, the bunker was resealed and forgotten again; until Patrice Barrister asked to move the LARS students there for their own protection after the Scaithers tried several attempts to snatch the children right off the docks of the institute. Leaving the children locked up inside all the time, or under constant watch, had been cruel for them. So, with the protection and cover of the surrounding woods and waterfall, they would have more freedom by making the bunker their new home and academy. Not to mention that the children could walk to Treetop Village, a village in the tops of a neighboring forest still occupied after the destruction of many homes and villages during the war. They could take the underground tunnel and walk the few miles to get there and have access to all manner of creatures in the surrounding forest. Most of the military personnel for this outpost had been reassigned long ago, but now that the LARS students had taken up residency in the underground tunnels, members of the LSS agency were required to check on the doctor and her students at least once a week. And some of the Coastal Guard was stationed there permanently as protection, rotating different guards a week at a time.

Since Dr. Barrister had moved the gifted children out to the falls, the guards often had to bring supplies and even guard the students as they were transported back to the original LARS building for hands-on animal training. Dr. Patrice did have some smaller animals at the falls compound, but nothing like the larger animals back on Loradin Island. The training of adult, and uninjured creatures in the wild was proving to be harder than expected.

Bain rounded the corner and nearly ran over Raila Orman, his old girlfriend, whose arms were full of laundry.

"Bain! Watch where you're going will you?" Raila protested, nearly dropping the clean bundles of sheets, struggling to catch them before they hit the floor.

"Sorry, Raila, I didn't see you," he said, trying to help her.

"I noticed," she said sharply, "as usual." She quickly pulled back from him.

"What, Raila? What could I have possibly done now? I haven't seen or spoken to you in weeks," Bain asked. Her attitude toward him had become decidedly more harsh at every accidental meeting; which was quite often since he was usually the agent to escort the students to LARS. It was one of the few chances he got to visit with his sister Wynne *and* try to get Raila to speak to him. All he managed to do lately was torture himself, and her, with his bi-weekly visits.

Raila sighed heavily, "I'm fine." She tried pushing past Bain who put a hand on her arm to stop her.

"Raila, could you please just explain to me what it is I did that was so wrong? Why won't you talk to me?" he pleaded.

"Now you want to talk?" she said in disbelief. She looked at him with raised eyebrows, rolled her eyes at the dumbfounded look on his face, and stormed away.

Bain stood there and stared after her retreating back as she mumbled under her breath and made sharp movements, looking back at him once more before disappearing around a corner.

He really liked and cared for Raila, and he missed her. They had dated a few times early on after Bain had first moved to Loradin. Then, they had taken a break to explore growing up, only to come back together and date exclusively for a year. But, she had suddenly ended their relationship six months back without much explanation. He really didn't know what the problem was, but nowadays she usually avoided him like the plague. He shrugged his shoulders and continued his search for the doctor. He would have to pin Raila in a corner one of these days and hash out what the problem was. He couldn't take her regular intensifying animosity toward him much longer. He would see about speaking to his parents later and ask for their advice. They had been married for twenty years, minus the six years they spent separated by Raif Martray and the Scaither organization.

His father Wilkins had been conscripted to the military special operatives' team, and then a year later their brilliant, scientifically-minded mother, Harper, had been forcibly taken and forced to help others build a weapon. She eventually escaped capture, spent three years training herself to fight and aligning with people who could help her; like his unofficial Uncle, Finn Mobley; then spent the next six months to a year trying to find her children. She had been pregnant when they first took her and had been told that the baby had died after childbirth. When she found them all again, she discovered Adda, his youngest sister, then five years old. His parents had survived all manner of hell and torture and never stopped looking for each other or their children. They had a greater understanding of one another than any two people Bain knew. He respected his parents, and often witnessed the great love they shared. He wanted to find that kind of love one day, he just wasn't sure it existed anymore.

Bain entered the large underground central bunker that was built to house many war type vehicles at once. It also had a hidden ramp door at the forest's edge where the road just ended. The door hinged down into the underground room and then lifted back up into place, completely hidden as part of the forest floor.

"Dr. Barrister," Bain waved to the woman who turned at the sound of her name.

"Ah, good morning Bain." She smiled as he got closer. "The children are ready to go; I just need to get them into the transport mod."

"No hurry, I'm ready whenever you are. I just need to swing by Mother's to pick up Adda on the way to LARS. I promised her I would take her with me the next time I went."

"You're a good big brother, Bain. Adda must completely adore you."

"Thanks, but I think Adda just wants to ride the bi-mod and play with the animals."

They grinned at one another in understanding. Patrice turned to the children all scurrying around the animal pens at the far back of the room.

"All right, everyone, into the transport."

Twenty-three children piled into the large transport. Bain stood watching, amazed that there were so many new children these days. Not just any child could train with LARS, they had to have the gift of telepathy with animals and be able to bond with and command them.

Bain said, "It seems every few months you have a new added child to the ranks."

"Yes, well, as you know, since the war, parents contact me regularly asking if their untalented child could be gifted. We've had to set up a regular testing facility in one of the other rooms to handle the influx. Raila has taken over the testing for me since we are so busy training the newer children. Even Jerod has taken to coming here a few times a week to help with their training."

"So it's not just to see Wynne one more time after their every morning patrol?" Bain asked, a bit protective of Wynne.

Patrice laughed. "I can't answer assuredly 'no' to that, but he has been a tremendous help with training. He has a true gift for teaching."

"Yeah, well, him being four years older than my sister kind of makes it hard for me to truly like the guy."

"I completely understand, Bain," she grinned at his discomfort. "But your sister is the least likely girl to ever be taken advantage of in any way. She has a good head on her shoulders and sees things the way they truly are."

"Yeah, I know." Bain grinned at the doctor. Noticing that all the kids were loaded into the mod, he said, "Let's get this show on the road shall we?"

"We shall." Patrice walked over to the transport, got in and took the driver's seat while Bain straddled the bi-mod.

The large overhead ramp lowered into the underground and they left the bunker, taking the small dirt and grass road that led out of the forest alongside Discovery Falls for the forty-five-minute ride into Loradin. After crossing the glass skybridge into Loradin, the transport turned west, and Bain went east.

Bain pulled the bi-mod up to the curb of his old home and ran inside to grab Adda.

"Mother, I'm here," Bain said, walking toward the kitchen. Harper was standing at the bar and Adda was seated in one of the high stools.

"Bain!" Adda yelled excitedly and hopped down, throwing her arms around her big brother's waist.

"Hey kid," Bain smiled and hugged her back. "Are you ready to go? The transport should be at LARS pretty soon and I need to be there when they arrive."

"Yep! I'll get my sweater." Adda took off up the stairs.

Harper smiled at their relationship. "She adores you, and rightly so."

"Yeah well, the kid's got taste," Bain said, puffing out his chest and flexing his shoulders jokingly.

Harper giggled at him and walked over to give him a hug and a kiss on the cheek. "How are things going lately?"

Bain replied, "Great."

"Even with Raila?"

"Not so great. I would like to speak with you and father about that."

"Any time Son."

"Ready!" came the exuberant cry of Adda bounding down the steps.

Harper and Bain both laughed. "See you Mother," Bain said.

"Goodbye Mother!" Adda yelled as she bolted out the door.

Harper smiled as she watched two of her children interacting together, happy that her world was normal even for just a little while. She called after them, "Goodbye. You two be careful. Love you. And give Wynne a big kiss and hug from me as well!"

Bain waved from the seat of the bi-mod as Adda sat behind him, her arms wrapped tightly around his waist with a smile larger than life plastered on her face.

Harper's heart swelled with love and pride, grateful that she was able to enjoy her children after so long a separation. She had missed Bain, Seadon, and Wynne's early years; five whole years to be exact. The last three years had been a great healing for their family, and she had gotten the joy of raising the child she thought had died after childbirth. Adda had been her saving grace since her three eldest were nearly grown teenagers and had wonderful gifts and talents that gave their lives purpose, even at such young ages.

She decided that since she had the morning free she would drive out to the Praxtingen Airship Academy for an early lunch to see Seadon, her second child, now sixteen and soon to graduate academy; his future secure as the youngest airship pilot to date. She hadn't seen or spoken with him in nearly two weeks and it was time for a visit. She smiled at the thought of seeing her young airship captain. She grabbed her jacket, pulled the door closed and climbed into her mod for the hour-long drive into the eastern Carpasian Mountains, com-calling Seadon to let him know of her arrival.

"Seadon here," he answered the call without paying attention to who the caller was as he walked the academy halls.

"Morning my favorite pilot," Harper smiled into the com-device.

"Mother, good to hear from you," Seadon said with a smile himself.

"I'm headed that way. Can you take an early lunch with me?"

"Sure, classes don't start until eleven today, and anyhow, I'm acing them. So even if I miss it due to a long lunch with my favorite mother, it won't matter much."

Harper's smile enlarged at Seadon's words. "Great! I should be there in about an hour. See you soon."

"Looking forward to it. I miss you and everyone else, Mother. I'll be glad when I graduate and will have more time to see everyone."

"We miss you too, Son. See you soon."

The call disconnected and Harper had to push down the feeling of sadness that sometimes overtook her. Her children had been spread out all over Loradin and Praxtingen for the last three years. Yes, she still got to see them on a regular basis. Wynne and Bain more so than Seadon, but he had chosen to attend the Praxtingen Airship Academy two years earlier than most other kids. Flying was all he had ever wanted to do, and so they let him go earlier than normal. It put him farther away than Wynne and Bain, but he was happy. Soon, he could move into Loradin near the airship field and be much closer to home.

Bain made a quick scan of the LARS property with the heat detector, making certain that all visible persons were accounted for and no one was hiding out in the surrounding areas. Adda was bounding up and down beside him in anticipation of not only seeing her big sister Wynne, but Roamey as well. Adda, like Wynne, was drawn to the creatures. The two of them watched as the transport full of students walked into the institute and then followed them through to the back of the building. Bain's thoughts returned to Wynne, who would be returning on the transport to Discovery Falls later with the rest of them to continue her academy training because she still had a few years before graduating, but she was already far beyond what they were teaching her there. Because of that, she was given more leniency where lessons and classes were concerned.

"Wynne! Roamey!" Adda yelled excitedly. She ran to Wynne first and gave her a hug, then turned her attention to the firebird that cooed and clicked at the extra attention. Sometimes Bain thought that Adda could speak to the creatures as well, but it probably just appeared that way. The animals were so trained now that anyone could basically talk to them and feel as though they understood what you were saying.

"Hey Wynne," Bain said hugging her fiercely.

"Hey yourself big brother. Good to see you. I'm glad it's usually you, Uncle Finn, or Aunt Paisley who escorts the transport over. That way I get to see you all on a regular basis."

"That's why I do it, so I can torture my little sister." He smiled, grabbed her in a head lock, and knuckled her scalp with his other hand.

Wynne laughed as she slapped at him to stop. When she came up for a breath, she said, "I wish I could see Mother and Father more though. I mean, I see them at least once a week, but I kind of have some stuff to talk to Mother about."

"I promise, if you com-call her, she'll be here quicker than Roamey can fly."

Wynne giggled at the image his words conjured in her mind. "I know. I've just been busy, you know?"

"Yeah. Anything I can help you with?" Bain offered.

Wynne gazed in Jerod's direction then looked at her brother. Bain followed the direction her attention went then looked back at Wynne.

Wynne sighed a bit, "No. Thanks though."

Bain grew a tad serious yet kept it playful. "Do I need to beat anyone up or have a chat with somebody?"

Wynne giggled, "No, nothing like that. It's just girl stuff. Now that I have Mother back, girl stuff is easier to discuss. Grandmother Gracelynn was a bit foreboding and it was hard to talk to her about some things."

"Yeah, I remember." Bain grinned at her. "Come on you, let's go see to Adda before she climbs up on Roamey and takes off." But before they could turn around, Adda had done exactly that.

Bain screamed her name, waving her back to the ground. He turned to Wynne and asked, "I thought Roamey only flew with you?"

"Normally he does."

"Then why would he allow Adda to ride him alone?"

"I'm thinking because Adda can talk to him too."

"You mean like I can?" Bain stressed, worriedly.

"No. I mean like *I* can," Wynne stated plainly.

Bain groaned audibly and in frustration as he watched Adda and Roamey playing around in the sky above. "Not again. Every time I bring one of you girls over here you start talking to animals and Mother wants to wring my neck. She is not going to be happy that her youngest and last child is a telepath, and not just any telepath, but an animal talker."

Wynne blanched at his words, which made her feel like her mother might see her gift as a problem or nuisance. "Why would her having the same ability as I do make Mother upset?"

"Because she doesn't want her moving out early like you did," Bain clarified.

Wynne's next words caught Bain's attention. "That's not the only woman you're going to have to deal with. Dr. Barrister is coming this way. And I'm not sure what mood she is in. It's hard to tell from her expression."

Bain turned to see Dr. Barrister making a beeline for him and Wynne.

Chapter 3

Brothers In Arms

"Bain, why is Adda riding Roamey? We don't even let the new telepaths do things like that yet." Patrice said, coming to a stop beside him and Wynne, looking up to the sky.

"We did not let her do anything, Doctor. We turned around and up she went."

Patrice stood thoughtfully a moment. "Wynne, did you tell Roamey to take her up?"

"No ma'am. She just went over to say high to him while Bain and I visited."

Patrice smiled. "Well, it seems your gift runs in your family," she said to Wynne.

Bain groaned audibly and threw his hands over his face. "Mother is really going to kill me. Why me, it's always with me?" he said, sliding his hands down to his hips and staring up at the now descending firebird with his tiny eight-year-old sister sitting happily on its back.

They all watched as one very excited little girl jumped down and raced over to them.

Bain grabbed her by the arms, squatted down before her, and asked, "Adda, what were you thinking jumping on Roamey's back? You could have been hurt."

Adda's smiled faded a bit. "But Wynne rides him all the time."

"Yes, but he's Wynne's bond animal."

"I did ask him first."

"What do you mean you asked him?"

"I asked him, and he shook his head yes."

"So, you didn't hear him *say* yes, like in your mind?"

"Yes, but I wanted to make sure I understood him and asked again. That's when he shook his head."

Bain closed his eyes tightly as if in pain, while Wynne and Dr. Barrister smiled brightly between the two of them. Adda saw the smiles on their faces and smiled too. Then she looked at Bain's downcast figure.

"What's the matter, Bain? Aren't you happy that I can speak to the animals too, like Wynne?" she asked in a somber voice.

Bain looked at her and tried to bolster her a bit. He hadn't meant to make her sad. "I'm happy for you that you can talk to them. It's a really cool gift to have. You and Wynne are truly blessed. I'm just not certain how Mother will take the news."

Adda brightened. "She will be happy. We talk about Wynne's gift all the time and she always says how amazing Wynne is." Adda smiled brightly at her older sister who smiled back. Wynne's earlier injured feelings seeming silly at Adda's words.

Bain stood up and Dr. Barrister slapped him on the back. "Chin up, Bain. You told her once before and you can do it again."

"Yes, and it took them weeks to come to terms with Wynne's gift, and her wanting to live at the institute for training. Mother has really enjoyed having Adda around. I doubt she will let her leave the house. Wynne was almost twelve when she left. Adda is only eight."

"Well, if you remember, Naphin was eight and Eckshum was seven when they helped fight the wars. And they had already been living here for over a year training."

"Well, their parents aren't our parents. Mother didn't get to raise us like she is Adda. She missed our childhoods and I doubt she will want to miss hers."

"Either way, I'll leave it to you. It's not like we have a short supply of students, but apparently Adda's gift is as strong as Wynne's. I would hate for her to miss the opportunity of a lifetime."

"I'm sure she won't. It will probably just take several more years before Mother will let her train here."

Patrice smiled and walked back to the large group of students on the other end of the complex.

Bain turned to his sisters, a lost look on his face.

Wynne grinned at the obvious mental torment he was putting himself through. She looked down at Adda and took her hand. "Come along Adda, let's go over with the other students and join in the fun with the other animals."

"Yay!" Adda cheered.

Wynne patted Bain's shoulder as she past, remembering the chewing he received when he first told his parents about her gift. He gave her a crooked, tight-lipped grin. He stood there for a few seconds longer, took a deep breath and released it, then turned to follow his sisters.

The morning went quickly at LARS and they all went to have lunch inside the building. After which, all the students were loaded on the transport to be returned to Discovery Falls. By the time Bain followed the transport and returned Adda home, Harper had returned from her morning with Seadon.

Harper smiled as they entered the house. "Hey sweetie," she said to Adda as she embraced the happy girl in a hug. "You must have had a wonderful time, as always."

Adda smiled brightly up at her, "I can't wait to tell you what happened."

Bain quickly interrupted, "Uh, Adda, why don't you go to the kitchen and get us both a beverage."

"Sure Bain." With that, she skipped off happily from the room.

"Mother," Bain said pensively, "I need to tell you something."

Harper's face suddenly took on a curious, worried look.

Bain quickly said, "It isn't bad," and she relaxed a bit. "Adda has the same telepath gift that Wynne does."

"Oh." Harper thought for a minute. Her brows creased in concentration at the news. At that moment, Adda came running back into the living room with two beverages in hand.

"Mother," she said excitedly, handing Bain the drink. "I rode on Roamey today!"

"You what?" Harper looked up at Bain.

"I asked him to ride me, and he said yes."

Harper looked sideways at Bain who quickly threw his hands up in defense. "It wasn't my fault. Wynne and I were catching up and the next thing we knew she was in the air."

Adda watched the tension between Bain and Harper. "Mother," she said, pulling her attention back to herself, "I didn't get hurt. Besides, Wynne does it all the time and you don't get upset with her."

"I'm not upset with you, Adda," Harper softened. "It's just dangerous to ride things as large as Roamey when you don't really know how to do it properly."

"I can go to LARS and learn, like Wynne does."

Harper drew in a sharp breath and released it slowly. "We'll see sweetheart. That is something that your father and I will have to discuss first."

Adda smiled brightly, but Harper was heartbroken as she and Bain shared a look of apprehension.

Bain's bi-mod raced along the winding coastal road as he headed toward the LSS building in the center of the city. He felt badly for his mother, but no matter how much she might want it, she couldn't stop Adda from growing up. All of her siblings were out of the house and doing well with their chosen professions. Adda wanting to follow suit was bound to happen soon. As he parked the bi-mod in the garage of the LSS building his comm beeped. He looked down to see his best friend Kreelie Rintel calling.

"Kreelie," Bain answered happily, "Good to hear from you. It's been a few weeks."

Kreelie's voice held a smile. "Bain, Buddy. How are things going?"

Bain inhaled deeply, "Well, they are definitely interesting. How about with you?"

"Great. The boys are coming along nicely in their intensive policing training. I wasn't so sure about Caislan at first. He's kind of a tender-hearted fellow; but he's tough."

"What about Delmar?"

"He's a rough one. Tougher than nails and mean as a Sandstriker. No one around here calls him Delmar. He doesn't like his name so we go by his last, Bamerly."

"Good to know. It sounds like I should stay on his good side. Bamerly it is."

Caislan Harrington and Delmar Bamerly were all of twelve years old when Bain had first met them. They were conscripted into the war as sharpshooters by Raif Martray.

They were orphans when Kreelie first met them and they had clung to Kreelie and his protection back then. After the war, Kreelie, along with his father Durger Rintel, had taken them in. With Durger being the Policing Authority Captain, and Kreelie employed there as well, they had found the boys non-threatening positions on the force after the war basically ended. Not only had Kreelie—at the age of sixteen—taken to raising two young boys, but he also had to deal with his ailing father, and his own personal post-war demons. They all had those to deal with; everyone who served in the short but brutal month-long war.

"Smart man," Kreelie said.

Bain asked, "How's your dad, Kreelie?"

"A little better. He has some good and bad days. Mostly he just wanders around in his own world. When his bad days hit, he gets frantic and swears Raif Martray is still after us. I don't understand it, Bain, Father has always been a tough man. He never seemed afraid of anything in all the years of doing this job. Now, it's like he's afraid of his own shadow at times. I don't know what triggered this type of panic in him."

"I'm sorry, Kreelie. I wish I knew the answer to that question."

"Ah, it's life, right?" Kreelie stated, his manner becoming the same, good-ole, chipper, Kreelie that Bain had grown up with.

"Yeah it is," Bain smiled.

"Well, Bain, just a quick check in. I'll talk to you later buddy," Kreelie stated.

"Good hearing from you Kreelie. I'll com-call you later. Maybe we can meet up through the MADs some time and have a drink?"

"Sounds like a plan, man. Maybe I'll even come to Loradin for that? You have nicer places over that way."

Bain smiled. "Great, how about tonight then? Say around eight p.m.?"

"Sure, why not. See you then, Buddy."

Bain ended the call, glad that Kreelie sounded good. Their life-long friendship nearly ended during the war years ago.

They had come face-to-face in battle on opposite sides of the fighting. Kreelie had fought for Martanzia, where they had both grown up, and Bain had fought for Loradin, where he had just moved to only months before. Now, they were all brothers in arms. Everyone fought together on separate fronts against the Scaithers ongoing brutal attacks.

Bain was glad that travel with MADs—Matter Arranger Devices—was as simple as pushing a button and walking through to the other side. You could travel hours within seconds. MADs was a technology available all over Zanchier, but only the wealthier could afford them, or those higher up in important government positions. With Kreelie being a war hero promoted to a high-ranking position at such an early age, he also had a MAD. Bain had access to all manner of cool innovative technology since he worked for the Loradin Secret Society. They employed some of the most brilliant minds to be found anywhere, Maubrey Musippi, Cranston Astorph, Winnie Baker, and Kamsten Whitsler.

Bain entered the building and took the elevator up two stories to the tech department.

"Good morning you three brilliant people," Bain exclaimed, entering the room, greeting Maubrey, Cranston, and Winnie.

Maubrey looked up and smiled. "Bain, good morning. Have you been off to transport duty again today?"

"Yes, I have," Bain replied to the mousy looking man in his early thirties.

"You know they have other lower ranking agents who could do that task instead of you," Cranston put in. The man was always very straight forward and nonsensical.

"I know, but I enjoy it. I get to see my family more this way."

Winnie grinned up at him from her bent over position at a table. "And seeing Raila has nothing to do with that," she stated teasingly.

"Maybe a little," Bain said. "Not like it matters. She's still mad at me for something. She hasn't spoken a congenial word to me in over six months."

"You better figure it out soon before it's too late," Winnie offered, returning her attention to her work.

"It would help if she would actually tell me what it is," Bain mumbled. "But every time I get close to her, she just storms off, angrier than before."

"Sounds like whatever made her mad did so over a prolonged period of time. Like an unresolved issue," Winnie replied, her attention still on her work.

"Maybe." Bain thought about what Winnie said. He shrugged his shoulders. "Anyway, I need to get going. I'll see you all later. I have to see grandfather." Bain left the room and took the elevator to the highest floor where his grandfather Aaric Brinley's office was. Bain walked past Kinley Peters' desk, his grandfather's assistant. With a small wave he asked, "Hi Kinley, is grandfather in?"

She peered disapprovingly at him over her eyeglasses. "Yes, *Uncle* is in. Go right in."

Uncle was his LSS alias, and Kinley did not take to anyone calling him by anything else. She said it could become habit and someday compromise his cover. Bain opened the door to see his usually vibrant and healthy grandfather, not doing so well. Aaric Brinley was slumped over his desk, looking rather weak. Bain rushed to his side.

"Grandfather, are you all right?"

"Bain," Aaric suddenly stood up straighter and plastered a tired looking smile on his face. "Yes, yes son, I'm fine."

"Sorry, but you don't look fine. You look a bit haggard if you ask me."

Aaric looked shocked and unnerved by Bain's description. "Haggard is a bit strong don't you think?"

"Sorry," Bain smiled at his grandfather's pride. "How's a bit tired. Is that better?"

"Perhaps," Aaric looked at him sideways with a slight smirk to his lips.

"Seriously though, what's going on with you, Grandfather?"

Aaric breathed deeply, "I'm not totally certain. I'm just more tired as of late. With the ongoing skirmishes with the Scaithers, the rest of the LSS missions, and still trying to find the mole that got Mariska killed, I'm afraid my resolve is wearing thin. I'm not as young as I used to be and your grandmother Neitha has been on my case to take it easy, but that I'm afraid is impossible."

"Maybe it's time to retire from the LSS and pass the reins onto someone younger, like Father."

"Yes, I know you're right. Wilkins is a prime candidate for the position. But then again, so is Paisley. She's served this organization much longer than Wilkins and would do as good a job of running it."

"True, but with her being pregnant again, and having baby Joslyn to tend to, do you think she would continue to want the job?"

"It's something I need to consider. I would take her out of field work, which I'm certain she would be fine with now that she has Joslyn and another child soon on the way."

"Perhaps you should just create another position?" Bain suggested. You do take on way more than you should responsibility wise. Divide the work between Paisley and Father. Give Wilkins a more hands-on role and Paisley a more officiate role."

Aaric grinned at Bain's suggestion. "You have quite the mind for solving problems you know?"

Bain smiled brightly, "Well, that is where my talent lies. I was supposed to be creating tech with the three brainiacs downstairs."

Aaric chuckled at Bain's description. "It's truly a great suggestion. I'll think about it. Now, was there something you wished to discuss with me?"

"No. Just decided to come by and see my boss and grandfather. And I suggest you go down to the medical floor and have a good check up with the doctor. You still look pale."

"Yes, I suppose you're right. Would you like to walk with me?"

"Absolutely. I want to know what's going on with you as well."

"Bain, if they discover anything, just keep it between the two of us for now, all right?"

"Yes sir, as long as it isn't life-threatening."

"Deal," Aaric grinned.

Chapter 4

The Traitor Found

Wilkins Brinley rushed through the LSS building headed for his father Aaric's office. He had been years searching for the traitor who had gotten Mariska — one of the lead agents for the LSS — murdered three years back right before the war had broken out. It had taken him this long to find the person responsible due to destroyed paperwork, data-banks, war, and regular family life. But he was determined to not let this person slip through the cracks and had finally found success.

"Afternoon, Kinley, is Uncle in?" he asked the woman whose focus on her present task never wavered as she replied.

"No sir. He and Bain went down to the medical level."

"Is something wrong?"

"I don't believe so, Sir. Uncle was just feeling a little under the weather. But you didn't hear it from me, Sir," she said, glancing up at him from beneath her lashes.

Wilkins nodded his understanding. "Thank you, Kinley."

"Absolutely, Sir."

Wilkins went in search of Aaric and Bain on the medical floor level, finding them inside the doctor's office just as Aaric was finishing his tests.

"Father," Wilkins stated worriedly, "are you all right?"

Aaric breathed deeply and smiled at his only son. "Yes, yes, of course. I'm just tired and apparently over doing things a bit; nothing serious to worry about."

Wilkins looked at Bain for confirmation. Bain nodded. "That's what the doc said, Father."

"Well, what are you going to do about it then? If you're over doing things, then what things are you giving up to better take care of yourself?"

"Well, that is something we need to discuss tomorrow. I would like to meet with you and Paisley in my office first thing in the morning."

"That sounds rather official," Wilkins stated as they walked the hallway and the short distance toward the elevators to return to the top floor and Aaric's office.

"It is. Now, you came looking for me for a reason. Yes?"

"Yes. Then I found out you weren't feeling well."

"And how exactly did you find that out?" Aaric asked, knowing full well Kinley had let it slip. Aaric grinned; he knew they all meant well.

Wilkins cringed, "How doesn't matter. I was just concerned. Anyhow, I've found the mole."

Aaric turned to look at him, "Do you mean the mole from three years ago?"

"Yes. I know who the traitor was that opened the barrier walls to allow the Scaithers into Loradin. Not only that, but we have evidence to show that he also gave them a clue that Mariska was using the Image Enhancer to appear as Harper."

"Good grief. Not only is the man a traitor, but an accessory to murder as well. Excellent job, Son. Who is it we're going after?"

"Euwan Brinkhert."

"Jasper Jeffries' right-hand man?" Aaric asked, surprised.

"One in the same."

"However did you find this out?"

"A lot of digging, linking people's histories together, and figuring out who all had access to the pass-codes for entry points," Wilkins stated. "It shouldn't have taken me this long, but the war destroyed a lot of essential information. It was a chore to find and piece all the information together."

"And you're absolutely certain it was Euwan Brinkhert?"

"Yes sir. No doubt. Our monitoring department was even able to recover a piece of a video clip showing Brinkhert meeting with a known Scaither sympathizer right here inside Loradin."

"Well, I suppose we should grab a few enforcers and head over to city hall and have a chat with Governor Jeffries. This isn't going to bode well for him."

Wilkins nodded as they walked into Aaric's office. "No sir. This is going to likely end his illustrious career as Governor of

Loradin. He is ultimately responsible for Loradin's security and the wellbeing of its citizens. At least, he's the one who has taken all the credit for exactly that over the last four years."

"Yes," Aaric stated. "You have to know your people and who to trust. And what information is privileged and private. Unfortunately, Jasper has been so caught up in the praise and devotions of his loyal and unwavering constituents that he has overlooked some of the more important parts of being governor."

Aaric spoke into the comm device. "Kinley, call the enforcement department and have Captain Wrightman and some of his people come to my office will you? We need to make some arrests."

"Right away, Uncle," Kinley replied.

Within ten minutes, Aaric's office was flooded with Captain Wrightman and several other enforcement agents. Aaric explained the situation to the captain, who along with Aaric, Wilkins, Bain, and the other officers, headed out to make the arrest.

"Father, you don't have to come along," Wilkins stated.

"I feel I should. Jasper may be too trusting and a bit overwhelming at times, but he is a long-time friend. I feel I should be the one to explain the gravity of the situation."

Ten minutes later they arrived at city hall, their sudden appearance and the sheer number of agents surprised the entire office. Everyone watched them head straight for the governor's office. Once there, they didn't bother knocking; they just walked in and headed straight for Euwan Brinkhert, a spineless little man who coward when he realized their attentions were focused on him. The normally jovial Jasper Jeffries' face fell in confusion as he watched the agents begin to collect Euwan.

Jasper stuttered nervously as he gazed at the enforcement agents gathered in his office, quickly standing up behind his massive oak desk. "Aaric, what's the meaning of this? I don't understand what's going on here? Now look here," he turned to the agents arresting Euwan, "I don't know what you people think you're doing, but whatever it is, there must be some confusion."

Aaric stopped Jasper's protests. "No confusion, Jasper."

Jasper turned to look at Aaric. "There must be. What could Euwan possibly be guilty of? The man has been my right hand for more than ten years."

Aaric shook his head. "He's accused of treason and as an accessory to murder."

"Good heavens!" Jasper exhaled sharply and fell back into his heavily padded office chair. "How? Who?" Jasper stuttered.

"Three years back when Mariska Hartigan was murdered by Raif Martray while on a mission posing as my daughter-in-law, Harper. We have proof that Euwan was partly responsible for her death and for giving Loradin's barrier pass-codes to someone within the Scaither organization."

"But how…how could he have gotten the codes?" Jasper questioned.

"You tell me, Jasper. You are the only person here in city hall that has access to the codes."

Jasper's face went pale with fear. "Surely you don't think that I helped him?"

"No. There's no proof to that extent," Aaric replied as Jasper breathed a sigh of relief. "But you and you alone are responsible for keeping privileged information safely hidden. I have to say Jasper, that when word gets out about this, I'm afraid you'll have an awful lot of explaining to do; the council will likely call for your resignation."

Jasper leaned forward, his elbows on his desk and his hands covering his face in humiliation. "How could I have let this happen?" Jasper looked up at Aaric as he watched Euwan being led away, protesting fearfully, and proclaiming his innocence. "I'll call the lead council members as soon as everyone leaves my office. If they want me to submit my resignation, I'll do so first thing in the morning; along with a written apology to Miss Hartigan's family."

"I think that would be the best course of action. I'm afraid that if you tried to keep office after word gets out about this, you'd find it impossible to find support. I'm sorry, Jasper."

"Yes. I…I know you're right. Thank you for coming and telling me yourself, Aaric. I know it isn't part of your job description."

Aaric nodded and left the man's office.

Jasper could hear the commotion the arrest caused in the outer offices. He sat in silence and deep thought as regret washed over him.

The next morning, the arrest was all over the news followed by reports and questions as to whether Jeffries' would resign. Aaric watched as he waited on Wilkins, Harper, Paisley, and Finn to appear for the meeting he informed them of the afternoon before. It wasn't long before Paisley and Finn showed up, baby Joslyn in tow.

"Good morning Mobleys. How is everyone?" Aaric smiled as Joslyn happily toddled toward him. He scooped her into his arms.

"Good," Finn smiled, shaking Aaric's hand.

"Says you," Paisley smirked, placing her hands on her back, and stretching her round belly.

Aaric chuckled at her discomfort. "It should be over soon, yes?"

"Yes," she replied. "Another month and we'll have one more little Mobley running around Loradin."

They all smiled happily, playing with Joslyn when Wilkins, Harper, and Adda showed up. Adda took baby Joslyn with her out to Kinley's desk to visit and play while the adults talked.

Aaric began, "I called you all here to discuss my retirement."

"What?" Paisley stated, shocked. "Uncle, is something the matter?"

"No, no, nothing serious. I just need a change. My doctor informs me that my job is much too stressful for my aging body."

"Has something happened, are you ill?" Harper asked, worried.

"No, nothing like that. Neitha has been after me to take a less demanding role within the department for the last five years. After the issues with my blood pressure, and just a general tired feeling, I've decided that it's time for me to step down. Now, having said this, my decision on my replacement has been a tough one. Paisley, you have been my top agent and invaluable to the LSS for a very long time. But, with your growing family, I don't want to add too much to your plate.

So, I have decided to create two positions instead to replace my single one. Paisley, you; if you accept the position; will serve as Executive Director of LSS affairs on a more home-based front. Wilkins will take on the role of Missions Director, if he accepts it, and be more active out of office."

They were both a bit surprised and delighted at the news.

"Absolutely," Wilkins grinned broadly, shaking his father's hand.

Paisley said, "I'm honored, Uncle. Thank you. I only hope that I can do the job satisfactorily while raising my family."

"I'm fairly certain that you can. And I have no worries about your ability to handle the position. We can even take the conference room on the tenth floor and turn it into a nursery for you and any other LSS employees who might need it. We'll hire on some help as well."

"Goodness, what a benefits package," Paisley laughed.

"I just want to make the transition, and attractiveness of the offer, as easy as possible for you to accept."

Wilkins smiled, "Thank you, Father. I'm ready to do whatever you need me to; especially if it makes your life easier."

Aaric smiled. "Thank you, Son. I don't expect the two of you to share an office. I'll have the adjoining conference room turned into an office for Paisley since mine is a bit masculine. Paisley, you can get with Kinley and she'll give you the names of the remodeling agency and decorators so that you can personalize it to your own taste and needs."

"Wonderful. Thank you, Uncle."

"Does anyone have any questions or concerns?"

Everyone shook their heads no, replying in kind.

Wilkins asked, "Father, what are you going to do now?"

"Well, I've given it some thought, though unsuccessfully so. I'm sure your mother will have plenty to keep me busy for a while." They all chuckled with him.

"All right then. I will have Kinley send out a memo on the new company leadership, and we can spend the next few weeks going over some things you both need to know."

Bain walked into the office, knowing his parents would be there this morning.

They smiled as he walked over to them, sharing the news of Wilkins and Paisley's promotions.

"That's really great, Father. Not to change the subject, but did you two speak about Adda training at LARS yet? Every time she sees me she mentions me taking her back."

"Yes," Harper replied. She looked apprehensively at Wilkins. "She can train twice a week but she lives at home and will continue to attend academy as well the other three days. I've already spoken to the academy director and she has agreed to allow Adda to do this. She will *not*, however, be moving to the institute until she is much older."

Bain smiled. "I didn't think she would be. Dr. Barrister will surely agree to the terms, and Wynne and Adda will both be happy. Maybe you could allow her to spend *one night a week* at Discovery Falls with Wynne and the other children?"

"Don't push it, Bain," Harper chided teasingly. "I might eventually. It all depends on how things go."

"Why do you think Wynne and Adda have telepath gifts and Seadon and I don't?"

"I don't know," Harper said thoughtfully. "Maybe you do have the ability? Perhaps the girls just pay more attention to their feelings and their love of animals. Plus, Mother has the talent for premonitions. Perhaps some of what Wynne and Adda experience are along those lines?"

"Maybe. Do you ever have such things, Mother?"

"No. If I did, I could have avoided the majority of horrid things that I've experienced."

"True," Bain answered. "Well, see you both later. I have some things to take care of down in tech with the Brainiacs."

While Bain was on the way down to the technical department, one of the agents hurriedly entered the elevator, fully engrossed in whatever he was reading.

"Which floor?" Bain asked.

"Top please."

"Sorry, this one is going down."

He sighed heavily. "I need to get this to Uncle immediately.

"Why? What is it?"

The agent looked apprehensive at first, then realizing that Bain was Uncle's grandson and lead agent over the new recruits, he figured it would be okay to discuss the matter with him.

"Well, we have reports that the Scaither organization has designed and created a craft that can travel underwater."

"Really? Where did the information come from?"

"Since the war, Uncle instructed us to keep communications via the old radio towers open. Our allies in Martanzia report a lot of construction on the tech at the dock warehouse that Raif Martray owned before his death. Vonder Mortruff has, as you know, taken over Raif's assets and is financing the building of new weapons and spy equipment. This underwater vessel is the latest thing, and the reports say it is nearly finished and ready to be tested."

"Wow. What are the module's capabilities?"

"We aren't sure. None of our allies have been able to get that close to the project. Apparently, Vonder Mortruff isn't a very trusting man and is particular on who gets close to his more prized projects. But this thing could really be a problem. There's no way to see it coming or track it underwater."

"I see your point."

Once the elevator reached its destination, Bain pushed the button to return to the top floor. "I hope you don't mind my tagging along. I want to hear more about this, especially since I figure we'll be leading a mission on it soon.

Chapter 5

War Scouts

Aaric sat in his now empty office on a com-call meeting with the three highest ranking Zanchieths in the land, those who held positions of authority due to family connections and old-world money. The lead council members for all of Zanchier had requested an audience with Aaric after the Jasper Jeffries scandal.

"Aaric, we're all in agreement that you should take over the position of Governor of Loradin and the Carpasian territories."

"Council members, I've not even officially retired from the LSS yet. Besides, I'm no politician."

"Exactly, Aaric. After the Jasper debacle, and the backlash that we are already receiving from that, we need someone who will be more interested in Loradin security and the safety of its citizens than someone who is merely interested in the next gala, event, or Zanchieth soiree. We truly didn't know you were going to retire, we were just offering you the position, figuring you could handle both. But with this new development the timing couldn't be a mere coincidence."

"I'm flattered, truly, but I'm just not certain that I'm right for the position. I'm afraid I would likely run the city like I ran the LSS, more like that of a business and homeland security position."

"That's perfectly fine with us, Aaric. We expected as much to be truthful. Besides, we've also offered Kinley Peters the position of your secretary, and whatever, or whomever else you wish to make the move easier."

This irritated Aaric just a bit to know they went behind his back to try to entice him into the position, but wasn't that part of the politics? He wrestled his temper and controlled his tongue.

"As much as that last statement perturbs me, I'll say that I will give it some thought and get back with you all in a few days."

"Yes, well, we do need an answer as soon as possible. We have an urgent territory position needing filled," one pushy council member added.

"Then fill it already," Aaric stated bluntly.

"No, no, Aaric, sorry for any misconceptions there," another council member answered apologetically for the other's pushy statement. "The position is yours; we just need an answer as soon as possible."

"I understand the urgency, truly I do. Give me a day or two to weigh the pros and cons. I'll get back to you no later than the day after tomorrow."

"That will be fine, Aaric. Have a good day and thank you for your consideration to our request. We all truly believe that you are the only person for the job."

"Thank you for the high praise. Good day to you all." Aaric ended the call and decided to call Neitha to fill her in on the details of the councils offer. He had barely pushed her link when Kinley beeped in over the intercom.

"Uncle, Agents Prosper and Brinley are requesting to speak with you. Prosper says it's urgent."

"Give me just a second will you, Kinley, I've just called Neitha."

"Yes sir."

"Neitha, sorry, darling, I have some news to tell you about but something urgent has come up. Can I call you back shortly?"

"Is everything all right?"

"Yes, yes, nothing to worry about."

"Well then, certainly dear. Talk to you soon."

"Thank you, darling. Talk in a bit." Aaric ended the call. "Kinley, you can send them in now."

"Uncle's ready for you," she said to the agents.

Bain walked in smiling. "Kinley is all business. She will not let anyone pass her desk unless she notifies you first. Not even me or Father."

"Yes well, that's all about to change for your father," Aaric smiled. "Now, what's this urgent meeting about?"

"Intelligence reports from our allies in Martanzia, Sir."

"Oh, just a minute then, I believe Wilkins and Paisley both need to be here." Aaric pushed the button on his desk. "Kinley, call Wilkins and Paisley in here for an urgent meeting."

"Yes Uncle."

Within minutes, the two of them, followed by Finn and Harper entered the office.

Finn asked, "Do you mind if Harper and I stay?"

"Not at all. You'll likely be on this mission anyway, and Harper is considered an inactive agent."

Agent Prosper continued, "Mortruff and the Scaithers have built at least one underwater transport vessel."

"What does that mean exactly," Paisley asked.

"We aren't certain. But Mortruff is in the business of world domination and weapons trades. If he's built something like this we can only assume that it is a weapon, and an untraceable one at that."

Finn asked, "Is there just the one machine?"

"There hasn't been confirmation either way. Our informant has only listed one, but Mortruff is smart and sneaky."

Wilkins added, "We'll need to check this thing out. I'd like to see it with my own eyes. Get an idea about how it works. It sounds like something I saw those years I was traveling through time portals into other worlds, something called a submarine. It was a large ship that carried hundreds of men and floated below the surface of the water and carried bombs on board. They used something like a spyglass called a periscope to see above the water level. They could accurately target anything without anyone knowing they were even there."

"Well," Aaric said nervously, "let's hope that whatever Vonder Mortruff has built does not have those capabilities."

Paisley said, "There's only one way to find out."

"Right," Wilkins added. "Who's ready for an adventure?"

"I am," both Bain and Finn stated simultaneously.

"Great. Let's get started," Wilkins said.

Harper interjected, "Please be careful."

Wilkins leaned in and kissed her. "Don't worry, we will."

Harper and Paisley stood and watched as their husbands, Wilkins and Finn, and Harper's son Bain left the office for the tech department to get gear for the impromptu mission.

Harper sighed heavily, drawing Paisley's attention. Paisley asked, "Does it ever get easier, watching the ones you love take off on dangerous missions without you?"

"Nope," Harper answered honestly.

"I'm not sure I'm going to like this 'Executive Directors' position. I'm not used to staying put while others have all the fun."

"Well, your mission is those little ones now. They need their mother."

"Yes, and as much as I love the agent lifestyle, I love being a mother even more. I've had fifteen years as an agent. I'll gladly spend the rest working from here," Paisley said, lovingly rubbing her enlarged belly and looking down at Joslyn who played on the floor at their feet.

The women looked at one another and smiled. Harper's attention soon returned to the empty door where three of the most important men in her life had just exited in search of the biggest and most ruthless crime boss in all of Zanchier.

Seadon Brinley stood behind the steering wheel of the large airship leading training maneuvers. His sister Wynne flew out beside the ships on the large firebird.

The old captains used to tell stories of fighting off Kabihanxu attacks. It seemed odd that the same creature that his sister now rode upon, and commanded, was the same type of creature that used to terrorize the Zanchier skies and its people. The wild Kabihanxus still did of course, as well as the massive wild cats known as Pagorinxes, but with the gifted children now growing into adults who telepathically spoke with the animals of Zanchier, they could co-exist with the creatures without as much fear as they once had.

As the airships glided through the sky south of Loradin, past Sandbar Beach, they continued with their training maneuvers. Captain Matt Easton, the training commander for the Loradin Airship Academy, barked orders over the communications system to all ships from his central location on the bridge of the *Celeste*.

"Ready weapons and make certain your range is clear people. We don't want to take out any of our own ships or our allies. We might have used to fire on the Kabihanxu, but those days are now dwindling. Fire when ready."

The small ten ship fleet, testing their weapons, fired into the lake below to dispel the canon beams. Wynne watched as the water below splashed and rippled from the onslaught as every weapon on board every ship was tested. Wynne noticed a movement in the water to the south. Something large turned and swam away from the laser cannon fire. Wynne was surprised by the clarity of the lake waters this morning. She usually couldn't see much past the surface, but there was definitely something moving down there.

"Let's go, Roamey," she commanded, telepathically leading him toward the quickly moving mass.

"What could it be, boy?" she asked the bird, who only squawked in reply.

They continued their flight south, getting ever closer to the borders of the Marshlands. She had always been taught that nothing could live there. Beyond the Marshlands was nothing but sand for miles and miles. There was nothing there but death, with the White Mountains to the southeast, the Bleak Mountains to the west, and the Dune Sea and Deadman's Desert colliding to the south. No one ever went near them, and if they did, they were never heard from again. The gypsies often spoke of creatures that lived in those mountain ranges that were so vile, so starved by hunger that they would attack anything, no matter the size. Wynne tried to keep her eyes on the large moving mass, curious as to what it could be. It had to be an animal of some sort by the way it moved in the water, but as she continued to watch, the closer it got to the marshlands, it suddenly vanished completely. Wynne was curious how it could have just disappeared.

"Circle back around, Roamey." She scanned the water thoroughly with no luck.

"Hmm, nothing. There must be an underwater cavern in the lake somewhere. That might explain the brackish water here near the Marshlands. Perhaps it connects to the salt waters off the coast of Rhamadon to the east. But how would it get here, so far away? One day Roamey we're going to venture out past the mountains and deserts and see what else is out there. In academy and geographical class, regardless of what the gypsies say about the cursed lands, there must be life somewhere other than just here in Zanchier. Let's get back to the fleet before Seadon comes looking for us."

They turned back home toward Loradin and the direction of the airship fleet. As Wynne got closer she could hear the firing of the ship cannons still testing their weapons. She waved to Seadon as she got closer to his ship. He waved to her in return and the fleet, now finished for the day, turned toward home and the academy in the Praxtingen hillside. Wynne and Roamey took one last glance in the direction of the Marshlands, her curiosity getting the better of her.

"I'll be back to check out what you are," she said into the wind.

Wynne didn't see the creature return because of its ability to turn translucent. It stuck its head and neck out of the water, curious about the human who rode the flying beast. It watched as the two flew away, turning back one last time to look in its direction. After the flying beast and the human were out of sight, the beast dove back down into the lake waters toward the Marshlands once again.

When Wynne returned to Loradin, she decided to visit their old friend Silus Aersor, the Raisedback Vindaper butcher Bain met in the Praxtingen open-air market three years back. Silus was an older man who knew a lot of the much older men, who in turn knew a lot about Zanchier legend and folk-lore. If anyone knew anything about a creature that lived in the lake waters near the Marshlands, that person would be Silus.

Wynne and Roamey flew toward the market and landed in a grassy field just outside the city limits so Roamey wouldn't be in the way.

"Now stay here, Roamey. I'll bring you a nice big fish from the market. We don't want you running around without me and scaring people."

Roamey squawked his reply and bobbed his head. "Good boy," Wynne praised. As she walked away she turned to see him walk in a circle and plopped down in the grass, laying his head across his front paws, and closing his eyes. *Oh to be that secure in your own abilities to be able to fall asleep out in the open,* she thought with a smile, loving her life and the extraordinary things that she got to do.

She soon spotted Silus.

"Silus!" she yelled and waved her arms in the air high above the people who milled about.

"Miss Wynne," Silus called and waved back. As she drew nearer he asked, "Well bless my soul, what brings you out here this morning?"

"Well, I have a question for you. Have you ever heard the old-timers talk about a large creature that lives in the lake near the Marshlands?"

"Why do you ask?"

"Well, I saw something in the water today while out scouting."

"You were scoutin' out by the Marshlands?"

"Not exactly. I was hanging with the Airship fleet while they were testing weapons south of Sandbar Beach. When they let loose their weapons all at once into the lake, they stirred something beneath the water. I followed it for a bit and it headed toward the Marshlands."

"Well, first let me say that there isn't anything worth anything out in the Marshlands, so you steer clear of there, all right?" Wynne shook her head in understanding.

"But the old-timers do speak about a sea-beast that once lived in the lake waters out that way."

"I knew it!" Wynne said excitedly.

"Now hold on, Missy! Just because it's a creature and you and your friends can speak to them, doesn't mean this thing is real, *or* that you can communicate with it. Things that live in or near the Marshlands are evil creatures. Mark my words, they aren't fit for anything, not even food. The old-timers tell of the meat being so sour it smells rotten even after cookin'. There is nothing good about that area and beyond."

"I know. We learned about the area in academy. But I did see something moving in the water below."

"It could've been your own shadow on the water, or your eyes playing tricks," he discouraged her.

Wynne knew better but decided to change the subject. "So, what's beyond?" Wynne asked curiously, hearing him mention that area.

Silus answered carefully, "Nothing at all. No one that I ever talked to or heard about has ventured past the White Mountains. Old-timers called them 'the death mountains', and for good reason."

"I knew you would know more about everything. You're like a walking historical book." She smiled brightly at the man.

Silus beamed back. "Yes, well, when you've lived as long as I have and seen as much, it tends to stick with you." He turned and grabbed a couple of sandwiches. "You want some lunch?"

"Sure, thanks Silus." Wynne gratefully accepted his offer and sat down with him behind his market booth.

They sat and visited while he regaled her with more stories from his youth. Stories about small wars he helped to fight when he was very young, secret places throughout Zanchier, and mysteries concerning the mystique that surrounded their world. Wynne loved listening to the man and all the wisdom he would often share with her, her siblings, and anyone who was willing to listen.

Chapter 6

Discoveries

Finn, Wilkins, and Bain hit the transmit buttons on their MADs, walking through to an undisclosed location very near the warehouse on the eastern shoreline of Everly Lake in the southern Martanzian region of Port Proud.

Finn had been here before three years earlier when he and Paisley had led a mission to find Raif Martray and Vonder Mortruff. They had captured Raif, only to have to shoot the man dead before he could serve time in prison.

The massive waterfront warehouse was guarded by several of Mortruff's men.

Wilkins gave quiet instruction, "We stay together unless we need to split up."

Finn and Bain nodded. Wilkins led them toward the warehouse, sneaking in and around the large crates that decorated the docks and outside of the building.

The men managed to get into the building by way of an unlocked, and currently unguarded door in the building's side.

Finn took lead since he had been in the building before and knew the layout of the interior. Upon entering the building, they heard talking and quickly hid.

"I don't care about the problems; that's what I hired you for. Fix it," Mortruff's gruff yet steady voice instructed.

"But Victor, I told you, it isn't that easy. This is all new, untested, technology. The ship might just sink or collapse inward from the pressure as it sinks lower. We need to test it in a more shallow area where we can control what happens," a man argued.

Mortruff replied, "And where exactly is that supposed to be?"

Perhaps the smaller lake, Lake Pines, southeast of here just north of Fort Arvenguard."

"Isn't the fort still manned? Besides, why not test it right here, right outside off the docks?" Mortruff challenged.

"The fort is manned, but the lake is surrounded by large pines and trees. We should be able to test it in seclusion. If we test it here someone might see the machine."

"So what? Who am I afraid of in the city? I run this city and every other anywhere near here," Victor stated assuredly.

"Yes, but if the wrong person sees the machine, they could tell the others and you'd have the LSS on you in the blink of an eye."

"I'm not afraid of the LSS, but I suppose you're right. A sneak attack wouldn't be a surprise if they knew from where we might be coming."

"Great, I'll let the transports know that we are loading the underwater ship for off-site testing."

"Make it quick. I'm ready to see my weapon in action. It's been a long two years of building this thing."

Finn, Wilkins, and Bain all nodded to one another; slipping back outside the door through which they entered.

Wilkins whispered, "Let's see if we can find where they are loading the machine. Then, we'll jump over to Fort Arvenguard and see if we can see Lake Pines from there. If not, we'll go in closer and see exactly what their underwater ship can do."

They all pushed the MAD buttons and disappeared.

The Fort had not given them the ability to see from the safety of the high walls, so they jumped over to the lake. From their hidden positions amongst the thick trees that encompassed three sides of the small lake, they could see well. Thirty minutes after settling in, Mortruff's tarp-covered transport arrived with something large and egg-shaped strapped to the flat bed of the vehicle. They watched as the tarp was pulled back to reveal a shining copper-encased machine, with two small thick round windows on either side near the middle. The front had a glass window that curved around the sides, top and bottom, enough to allow the pilot to see all around him. As the transport crane lifted the machine up and off the back of the transport, lowering it into the water next to the dock, there was a hush as all of Victor's employees seemed to hold their breath. Once the machine touched water and floated, there was an audible release of breath, knowing they would all live to see another day. That is, if the machine actually did what it was supposed to do.

Wilkins said, as he peered through the telescope, "The man speaking to Vonder must be the pilot."

Finn replied, "Yeah, and the designer. Probably the same one we heard him talking to earlier."

"I know that man," Bain stated. "He was the scientific teacher at my old academy in Port Proud. Professor Yarbrough, a real intelligent man, kind of quirky, but super smart. His teachings were way above the level of most of the kids in his class; which is funny because it was the Port-Proud Academy for the Technically Advanced and Gifted. You had to be smart to be accepted to attend in the first place."

Finn and Wilkins looked at Bain. "Can you tell us anything about that machine since he was your teacher, and you were an academy student?"

Bain shrugged, "Well, you see the shape, it should glide through the water with ease, and the propellers on the front look as though they are on swivels, meaning they turn. It must be how the ship navigates the water. It also has rudders on the rear, which look as though they can maneuver up and down. Being made of copper, it has to be extremely heavy, which means it has an extremely powerful motor to propel it through the water. There are a set of lights at the top and bottom; and strangely enough the rear. There must be a camera somewhere near the back allowing for sight from behind, so there must be a screen display somewhere on board. And do you see the ports on the sides, where it looks like there are caps or covers? They likely move away to allow for firing capabilities. I sure would like to drive that thing," Bain said appreciatively.

The men stared at Bain, shocked that he could see and explain so much. He looked over at them and asked, "What? You did ask. And besides, I am my mother's son you know." He smiled broadly, grateful for the scientific abilities that he inherited from his equally, if not more so, brilliant mother Harper.

Finn grinned. "You're such a nerd," he teased.

"Yep," Bain replied. "And you're all the better off for it." He smiled at them and they both smiled back in return.

Wilkins beamed. "I'm proud to call you my son. And you're right, you *are* just like your mother."

The men watched in silence as Professor Yarbrough followed by another man, climbed down into the machine. They sealed the top hatch, and a few seconds later the machine whirred to life. A hissing sound could be heard and then the machine began to back up and sink below the water's surface. You could see the water turning and gurgling on the lake as the machine sank, dispelling air and circling beneath the surface. Vonder and his men moved away from the dock and building, watching the lake for movement. Soon, there was no sign of the machine. Nothing moved or was heard. Then, from the far end of the lake, they heard a faint clicking sound, followed by some sort of weapon fire that flew from beneath the water's surface. The small building that sat by the docks blew apart, shattering into thousands of pieces.

The group of people standing around the lake all cheered. Vonder Mortruff grinned menacingly.

Wilkins, Finn, and Bain all looked at each other with fear.

Wilkins asked Bain, "How many times do you think that thing can fire in succession?"

"I don't know. It depends on what sort of material they are using. I'm pretty sure it's not cannon balls because of the limited amount of storage. So it has to be something like liquid or much more compact."

Wilkins stated, "We're going to have to do something to dismantle that ship or destroy it. And let's pray he doesn't have more of them already in production. Let's get back to headquarters, inform the others, and make a plan."

They engaged the MADs and returned to Loradin by dinner time, planning a meeting for early the next morning in Wilkins new office as he took over the position of director of the LSS.

The next morning, Harper had dropped Adda off at LARS so that she could begin training then go to Discovery Falls with Wynne for the afternoon lesson. She and Wilkins had decided to allow Adda to begin training just a few days a week, but she would live at home.

Adda was excited to start her first day with her sister. Harper kissed Adda and gave her a warning.

"No jumping on the back of any animal alone, all right?"

"Yes Ma'am, I promise."

"I'll pick you up at three this afternoon," Harper smiled and stood up as Wynne approached.

"Good morning, Sweetheart," Harper said, pulling Wynne into a hug.

"Mother." Wynne smiled, staying in the hug a bit longer.

"Oh, how I miss all my children being home," Harper cooed.

"I miss you too, Mother." Wynne stepped back and leaned down to hug Adda, then said, "Are you ready for your first day as a LARS student?"

"Oh, Yes!" Adda beamed, jumping up and down in excitement. Harper and Wynne both chuckled at the girl.

"I'll let you go, I know you're busy," Harper said, waving to her daughters as they walked away, hand in hand. She shot up a small request to the Creator for the protection of all her children, before turning and walking back to her car to head to the LSS for the meeting with Wilkins.

Wynne and Adda walked over to Roamey's cage to let him out for the day's rounds.

"Wynne," Adda asked, "why do you still have to cage Roamey? Isn't he trained to stay here?"

"Well, yes, he is. The cage is as much for his protection as it is for everyone else. Besides, it's become his home, like your bedroom is to you."

"Yes, but I can leave my bedroom anytime I wish. Roamey must have permission."

Wynne grinned at Adda's assessment. "You're right. If there were another more appropriate place to keep the creatures that was as secure as the Loradin Animal Rescue and Sanctuary, I guess we could move them to give them more natural freedom. But with the Scaithers always hunting for Telepaths and creatures to steal, we must all stay as safe as possible." Her reply seemed to satisfy Adda's curiosity.

Wynne smiled at how Roamey took to Adda so quickly; just as he had with herself three years back.

"Hey, Adda, you want to take a ride with me to check something out?"

"Oh, yes, Wynne!" Adda answered cheerfully.

"All right, but remember to hang on to me."

"I did already fly with Roamey once, alone," Adda protested.

"Yes, but that was just right here. Where we are going is a bit of a distance."

"All right."

Wynne climbed on Roamey, and Adda followed, scooting in close to Wynne. The two took off toward the Marshlands and where Wynne saw the large water beast disappear.

Adda asked, "Wynne, where are we going?"

"I just want to see something."

"What?"

Wynne replied, "I thought I saw a new creature out here yesterday."

"Isn't that dangerous?" Adda asked.

"I don't think so, Adda. Just stay with me and hold on. Roamey will protect us if he needs to."

"All right," Adda replied, hesitantly.

Wynne scanned the water below, looking for the shape she saw yesterday. It did sort of resemble a striker with its long slithering movements in the water. But what she saw below the surface yesterday had been thicker toward the middle of the body and appeared to be a bit thicker in the tail area as well.

Roamey began to grow nervous, as if sensing something.

"What is it, boy?" Wynne questioned him. Roamey purred and clicked in reply.

"Where?" Wynne asked.

Roamey flew downward a bit and circled an area above the water.

Wynne scanned the water below but saw nothing. Adda let go of Wynne and leaned over to see better. Just at that moment, something unseen burst through the surface of the water and Roamey quickly turned, flying upward. Adda slipped from his back, falling toward the water below.

"Adda!" Wynne yelled, reaching back to try to catch her, but was unsuccessful.

"Roamey, get Adda!"

Roamey turned quickly, diving back down toward the water.

Adda hit the water, falling beneath the surface. While she swam upward, the creature appeared before her in the water, uncloaking itself. Adda became frightened and swam faster, but the creature disappeared again. She broke the surface, taking in a deep breath, terrified of what she saw, waiting for the creature to attack, but it didn't.

Wynne saw Adda and yelled, "Adda, reach up, we're coming."

But instead of doing as asked, Adda took a deep breath and dove below the surface once more, her fears suddenly subsiding. She swam down a little, scanning the water around her. She could sense that the creature was still there; almost like she could feel each watery breath it took. She waited patiently, kicking her arms and legs to turn herself in the water. She used her mind to reach out to the creature, unsure if it would even work. Suddenly, just about twenty feet away, the creature uncloaked once more. The two of them simply stared at one another in curiosity. Adda, turned her head one way, and the creature did the same. Adda grinned at the mocking gesture. The creature slowly approached her and she put her hand out, reaching for it. It was nearly touching her when a splash from above broke through the water directly in front of her. The creature disappeared once more, the force of water from the beast's retreat pushing her back.

Wynne grabbed Adda and pulled her up to the surface while Roamey reached down, grabbing Wynne around the torso, and pulling them both from the water.

"Wynne, wait!" Adda sputtered chokingly, looking back down at the water searching for the creature.

Wynne didn't speak, only held her sister tightly, swinging her up into Roamey's strong claws as he wrapped her tightly and securely within his talons. They flew toward home as the girls argued.

"Adda! I told you to hold on!" Wynne yelled over the force of the wind blowing in her face.

"But Wynne, I fell on accident!"

"Yes, because you weren't holding on! You could have been killed!"

"But Wynne, didn't you see her?"

"Yes, Adda! I saw 'her' coming at you in the water! I was scared it was going to eat you!"

"But she wasn't, Wynne! We were playing! She spoke to me!"

Wynne looked at her sister. "Are you sure, Adda? You aren't making it up?"

"No!" Adda protested with anger, crossing her arms clumsily over her chest as they rested on Roamey's paws.

"Sorry, I just know how badly you've always wanted to be like me. I mean, to have the gift that I have. I just have to make sure you can actually communicate with creatures."

"I can, Wynne."

"Perhaps, but not all of them are friendly, Adda. We don't know anything about that creature. She's never been studied to see how she would react with human contact. And she isn't a juvenile like most creatures that are brought to the institute for rehabilitation."

"I know she's called a Brindelwren," Adda smiled haughtily.

"She told you this?"

"Yes, when we were playing in the water. I asked her name right before you came splashing down and grabbed me."

Wynne sighed. "Adda, you *cannot tell* anyone else about this. We will both get into major trouble. Do you understand? We'll discuss how to handle this later, all right?"

Adda shook her head yes.

Wynne instructed Roamey to land north of Sandbar Beach so they could resume their place upon his back. At least the long windy flight had completely dried their hair and clothing. They didn't need people asking questions should they both return firmly clasped in his front talons.

Chapter 7

The Battle and the Brindelwren

Very early the next morning, the Loradin alarms began to blare before scouting rounds could even begin.

Jerod yelled to Wynne, "The alarms are going off all over, even on the outskirts of Praxtingen and Carpasmere."

"What do you think is happening?" Wynne replied, watching the other scouts run to ready their creatures.

"Must be an invasion," he answered, readying Moshi for exploration.

"Wouldn't we have seen the approach on rounds last night?"

"Not if they were out past our search area."

Wynne mounted Roamey and they took to the sky while Jerod and Moshi hit the water. She looked down to see Oudree and Yar, the Yarequu, take off across the land headed for the Coastal Guard station to question Captain James Donner, if he was still there and not already on board a ship.

Wynne and Roamey flew high to get the best view they could to try and see where the threat was coming from. Off to the northwest, she spotted a large armada of water-ships, and it appeared many airships, sailing their way from the direction of the Bakrashan and Martanzian border. They were closer than they should be. Why hadn't the alarms gone off before now?

Surprisingly, their own Loradian ships where moving quickly to face the Scaither army as far away from the land as possible. Not only were the ships moving out quickly, but she noticed, far back in the distance, the horizon to the east began to dot with airships called into action from the Loradin airstrip. They would likely be joined soon by the airships from the academy as well.

Wynne and Roamey, and Jerod and Moshi, were the front leaders on the fight. As they got closer, Roamey and Wynne swooped down, Roamey belching a line of fire upon the front line of ships, setting fire to the mainsails. Then they soared through the sky, slipping past airships, belching fire at them as well. Moshi and Jerod faced the ships in the water, Moshi's ability to bellow a deep reverberating sound that shook walls and created giant waves, rocked, and rattled the ships, slamming a few of them into each other.

The ships returned fire upon their attackers as Moshi threw up an electrical protective barrier from his horn that surrounded them both. They instantly dove beneath the water's surface as Moshi's bellow rattled the ships above them, his webbed underbelly that connected to his four hairy legs making navigation of the lake waters effortless.

Wynne and Roamey dodged fire from the laser cannons. Roamey's feathered armor-like skin protected him, but not Wynne, so as they flew, Roamey tried to put himself between Wynne and the ships around them.

The four of them continued their onslaught until the Loradin water ships and airships came into view and began to fire upon the Scaither armada. Wynne and Roamey turned back to take a more spectator approach now that the military had arrived. They would watch and wait to see if they were needed, attacking only when necessary.

The Scaither armada was large. There had to be thirty heavily armed ships in the water. The Loradin Coastal Guard did not disappoint however with nearly the same amount. Add the Loradin fleet of now forty plus airships and the Scaithers would think twice about attacking again; their smaller fleet of airships appearing to number less than twenty.

Wynne saw Jerod and Moshi surface to the southwest of her out of the range of fire. She and Roamey flew down toward them.

Just as she reached Jerod, Moshi and Roamey began to act strangely, wanting to head in the opposite direction toward Loradin.

"Moshi, what's gotten into you boy?" Jerod admonished the beast. "Stay your position."

Wynne remembered Roamey acting the same way yesterday. "Jerod, look around in the water. See if you spot anything strange."

They scanned the water's surface, and Wynne flew Roamey higher to scan from above. Sure enough, there it was; just south about three-hundred-feet of where Jerod and Moshi sat in the water. The Brindelwren, as Adda had called it, had been enticed from its lair by the sounds of weapon-fire. It must have already been swimming nearby in the lake to have gotten here so quickly. The Marshlands where she last saw it was hundreds of miles south.

"Jerod!" Wynne yelled down to him, trying to get his attention over the battle that was taking place a few hundred feet to the northwest. She yelled again, flying down toward her friends.

Moshi turned in the direction of the Brindelwren and began to bellow his deep reverberating sound. The water rippled outward toward the Brindelwren and the beast thrashed in the water, breaking the surface, and shaking its massive head in aggravation, shrieking in pain.

Jerod's eyes grew large, and Moshi, sensing his distress, engaged his protective electrical shield.

Wynne and Roamey reached Jerod and Moshi, and flew stationary next to them, ready to take a fighting position if needed. The Brindelwren stared at the group of four, recognizing the two that hovered over the water. It quickly dove back beneath the water's surface, headed for the Marshlands.

Wynne and Roamey took off after it.

"Wynne!" Jerod yelled, as he and Moshi followed in pursuit as well.

They followed the beast for as long as Wynne could keep sight of it. But before long it vanished again. Jerod and Moshi slowed in the water below her as she and Roamey came to a stop in the air; hovering above as Wynne scanned the waters below.

"Wynne! What do you think you're doing? Are you crazy? You did see the size of that thing, right?"

Wynne ignored his rant and simply answered, "Yeah."

"And?" Jerod insisted, finally getting her full attention. "Adda and I encountered it yesterday. Adda said it told her it was a Brindelwren."

"How did Adda get close enough to speak to it?"

Wynne flinched and prepared for the chewing out that she knew was coming, as she related the details of yesterday's scouting mission.

"Are you crazy! You know you aren't allowed to take newbies on scouting missions."

"I know that, but...Adda is not just some newbie, Jerod, she's my sister."

"Even more reason why you should have been more careful."

"Are you going to report me?"

Jerod thought for a second and replied, "No. Only because I know you normally wouldn't disregard direct orders; and because you're my girlfriend. But, if it happens again, Wynne, I will have to report it, regardless of the consequences."

Wynne smiled at his reply, "I understand. Thank you Jerod." Wynne was giddy inside at his confession of their budding relationship. He had actually called her his girlfriend.

Jerod sighed heavily, "Now let's get back to the battle. They might need some help; especially if there are men in the water."

They traveled back toward the battle as quickly as possible. The battle continued for hours until the Loradin fleet finally sent the remaining Scaither ships retreating.

What Wynne and Jerod hadn't noticed before they took off after the water-beast, was the underwater ship that had followed them beneath the surface when its captain, one Vonder Mortruff, had witnessed the Monshokto's interaction with the massive beast.

"Did you see what I saw Professor?" Vonder asked his first-mate.

"Yes, I did! Quite a remarkable creature."

"I say we follow it."

"But Vonder, what about the battle?"

"They'll handle it. This is a once in a lifetime opportunity."

Vonder had heard of the water-beast in lore and legend but thought it just that. If he could capture that creature, and snatch one of the telepathic children, he would have an undefeatable weapon. There might even be more than one of them.

Vonder left his fleet of ships to fend for themselves and pursued the creature through the water. The children finally gave up their pursuit when it had vanished, but Vonder would not give up so easy. He kept the water-ship pointed in the direction the creature had swum. After several hours of pursuit, Vonder came upon a large opening to an underwater cavern which sat on the bottom of the lake. The size of the hole was plenty large enough for the water-beast to have disappeared into, and he bet that was exactly where the thing had been hiding.

Vonder said, "What say you, Professor? Are you up for a little exploration?"

Professor Yarbrough answered nervously, "We don't know what that thing is or where this tunnel leads? It could be dangerous. Not to mention, we are unsure about what the water ship can do. The pressure inside might be greater than what it can handle. There's no one to help if we should get into trouble."

"So that's a yes, then." Vonder grinned at the Professor's discomfort, taking the ship into the hole in the bottom of the lake.

Professor Yarbrough nervously answered, "Yes, Vonder, whatever you wish," as he silently prayed for deliverance from Vonder's newest venture.

An alarm sounded on the machine's control panel.

"What's that, Professor," Vonder asked irritably.

"The fuel is at the halfway mark. If we continue, we won't make it back to Port-Proud."

Vonder seethed, "Looks like we need to upgrade the tank to a larger one. After which, I will be back to explore this tunnel."

"We can try to upgrade Vonder, but there might not be room for such a thing. The ship is already very compact."

"What do you suggest then Professor?"

"Transporting the underwater ship to the shoreline of Treeline Valley and putting in there. It would make the trip shorter and easier than traveling the entire way underwater from Port-Proud."

"Sandbar Beach is closer," Vonder replied.

"Yes, but then you would have to transport the underwater ship past Fort Arvenguard, and through Carpasia and Praxtingen. You wouldn't get through without drawing attention and possibly losing your cargo. Then the enemy would have our invention."

"True," Vonder said as he held the ship still, staring into the inky darkness of the long, deep cavern.

"Um…Vonder, you really should turn the ship around. The longer we sit here, the more fuel we lose."

Vonder turned the ship around and left the cavern, pointing the ship toward Port-Proud.

"We need to give our little invention a name, Professor, instead of referring to it as the underwater ship."

"Well," the Professor answered with a clearing of his throat, "When drafting the plans for the build, I called it the Professor Ephrem Hezikiah Yarbrough's Ground-breaking Revolutionary Underwater Exploration Transportation Module."

Vonder thought a moment, "A bit windy there eh, Professor. I think I'll call it UWEM, an acronym for Under Water Exploration Module."

"Why not the PYEM?" the Professor suggested with a nervous chuckle. "for Professor Yarbrough's Exploration Module."

"Nah," Vonder shot down. "I like UWEM. It has a nice ring to it."

The professor nodded, sighing over losing all claim and rights to yet another of his inventions. What did he expect when getting mixed up with Raif Martray five years ago? Now he had to answer to Vonder Mortruff in Raif's place. What he wouldn't give to be rid of the man. Vonder controlled nearly every move he made, and claimed every invention he came up with, with very little compensation for his trouble and time. Sure Vonder had financed the building of the underwater-ship, so he supposed Vonder did have some claim to it. The man had even insisted on piloting the machine at the last minute, having no idea how to do so or any experience with the sensitive equipment. The Professor had to give him a crash course in the controls right before they disembarked on today's trial run and war attack. To which, they never even fired the first shot from the UWEM after Vonder spotted the sea-beast. Yarbrough's nerves were shot, especially since he had to spend hours in the UWEM with Vonder and his short temper. At least the man was thoroughly enjoying himself instead of screaming threats his way.

A smiling Vonder piloted the UWEM home while the Professor wiped the nervously acquired perspiration from his forehead, watching the fuel gauge and praying they would make it back without sinking to the floor of Everly Lake to a watery grave.

After the skirmish was over, the airships returned to Loradin, unable to be of further aid to anyone.

The prisoners were rounded up from the lake waters and placed under lock and key on-board the Loradin ships. The dead, those who could be found anyway, were also pulled into dinghies launched by the Loradin ship captains. The bodies of the Loradin crews were recovered and returned to the families for proper burial, families whose lives were now forever changed. Those belonging to the Scaithers were wrapped in cloth and given a burial at sea.

Wynne and Jerod spent that time lashing mooring ropes between the wrecked and damaged ships to the ones that were still maneuverable. After an hour of plucking people from both sides from the water and securing the disabled ships to others, the large group and their prisoners began the long return to Loradin.

Wynne watched as the last of the sinking ships and burning debris finally sunk to the bottom of Everly Lake. Some of those ships belonging to Loradin. She turned her attention toward the Marshlands once more, curiosity about the beast that had fled taking over her every thought. Jerod noticed her distracted behavior.

"Wynne, we can go back another time and check it out."

She smiled at Jerod who knew her so well. "I plan on doing so this afternoon. I'm going to let Roamey rest for a while. He's been flying for hours with very little break."

"How about we both go and take Moshi instead. The creature is likely hiding out underwater anyway. Roamey can't swim."

"Yes he can," Wynne protested.

"You know what I mean. Not underwater, and certainly not long enough to hold his breath, like Moshi."

"True. Do you promise to take me back?" she asked, unsure he was being truthful.

"Yes. Besides, I want to check it out too. It could have killed us all if it had wanted too, and for some reason it didn't. It's the biggest thing I've ever seen. It was twice the size of

Roamey and Moshi, and three times longer than Roamey, including his long tail-feathers. I mean, the thing…"

"Brindelwren," Wynne corrected.

"Yeah, Brindelwren, had to be fifty feet long from what I could tell."

"At least I know you'll keep your word," she replied. "You're even more excited about it than I am."

They shared a laugh and turned to follow the floating mass of partially crippled ships back to Loradin. They took the quickest route and beat the slow-moving ships a full half-an-hour, excited to return quickly to explore the edges of the Marshlands.

Chapter 8

A New World

Wynne, Jerod, and several of the older students were busy feeding and tending to the needs of the animals currently housed at LARS when Jerod walked over to Wynne.

He whispered in her ear, "Wynne, are you ready to go?" Dr. Barrister was conducting class with the newer telepath students, one of whom was Adda.

"Do you think we can sneak away without being questioned?" Wynne whispered back.

"She doesn't question us much these days. Besides, there isn't anything you can learn in these early morning classes. Plus, if anyone asks, we can just say we are ramping up our rounds because of the Scaither attack this morning."

Wynne nodded her reply and the two of them slipped away unnoticed by all except Adda. She followed them quietly; slipping away while Dr. Barrister's back was to the class. She quickly tiptoed after them, sneaking around the LARS building toward the docks. When out of earshot of the rest of the class, Adda called to Wynne.

"Wynne, wait. Where are you going?"

Wynne turned abruptly, "Adda, what are you doing away from the rest of the class? You need to get back or Dr. Barrister will come looking for you."

"I want to go with you and Jerod."

"You can't, Adda, especially not after the sneak attack by the Scaithers this morning. It's not safe."

"But you're going!" Adda protested.

"Yes, Adda, I am. It's my job to patrol and keep Loradin safe from invaders."

"You and Jerod already did patrol early this morning," she noted, snidely.

Wynne sighed in frustration. "We are ramping up our efforts,"

"But you aren't taking Roamey," Adda pointed out. Then realization set in. "You're going after the Brindelwren! I want to go, Wynne! I spoke to her first!"

"Shh…keep you voice down Adda. Look, where we are going and why, is none of your business. Besides, taking you with me is not safe. I promise to take you with me another day."

"I want to go now! I'll tell Dr. Barrister what you're up to," Adda threatened.

"First, you don't know what we are up to, not really. And second, if you do tell, I'll never take you with me again. Now, go back to class or I'll tell Mother that you aren't participating the way you should and aren't mature enough for this program," Wynne threatened in return.

Adda crossed her arms over her chest in defiance. "Fine, but I'm *not* going to be happy about it." She stomped off, turning occasionally to throw a look of animosity in Wynne's direction.

Jerod stated, grinning, "She's going to be a handful sooner rather than later."

Wynne grinned back. "You have *no* idea. She's likely the most head strong of us all, and that is saying a lot."

They both climbed on Moshi's back and took off across the water, Wynne turning back to make sure that Adda was not trying to take Roamey. Wynne decided to instruct Roamey telepathically to not take Adda anywhere. Now that that was taken care of, she turned back to her present adventure as Moshi swam quickly across the water for the more than four-hour swim to the shores of the Marshlands.

As they got closer to the Marshlands, Jerod stayed in tune to Moshi's emotional state. The last time they got close to the Brindelwren, Moshi acted nervous, so maybe that would let them know if they were close. However, Moshi showed no signs of distress in any way.

"There's no sign of the beast anywhere, Wynne. Maybe we should just call it quits. We've already been looking for an hour."

"We have plenty of daylight left. We are past where I saw it disappear. Why don't we dive down and see if there is anything below?"

"All right, Moshi, shield up," Jerod instructed. Moshi threw up the shield encompassing them both fully as it dove effortlessly beneath the surface.

Wynne spoke while they searched. "Moshi is an amazing creature, Jerod. You're lucky to have been the one to bond with him."

"Yeah, I agree. I'm still finding out stuff he's capable of doing. Nothing like what they told us about in animal study classes, that's for sure."

"I didn't know he could hold his breath underwater for so long."

"Yeah. A whole fifteen minutes normally, but I think he can go even longer. I timed him once at nearly twenty minutes."

Wynne suddenly spotted something long and tube-like on the lake floor. "Jerod, look," she pointed at the large tunnel.

Jerod whistled, "I never knew that was there."

"That's because everyone is scared to come out here to explore. The old-timers say the Marshlands are haunted, and the gypsies say they are cursed."

Jerod swallowed hard, "You sure you want to keep exploring, Wynne?"

"We'll be fine, Jerod. Moshi will protect us. Besides, he doesn't appear the least bit worried," she said petting Moshi's thick, furry, back.

Moshi swam up the long dark tunnel, uncertain where they were going. Jerod and Wynne couldn't make out much. The deeper they got the darker it became. Moshi could see where he was swimming due to his eyesight adjusting to the inky darkness of the large wide cavern.

The mere size of the cavern was the only thing that lent what little light they still had, filtering in from the massive opening behind them. As it grew so dark that Jerod and Wynne's ability to see became nonexistent, they began to rethink their exploration.

"Jerod, maybe we should go back. We can't see a thing. We're just relying on Moshi's range of sight and he has no idea what he's looking at, or for."

"True, but at least he isn't skittish," Jerod replied, "meaning we aren't in any type of danger. But you're right. We should have brought a few torch-lights to see with."

"Jerod, look!" Wynne pointed, seeing a strange bluish green glow ahead of them.

"I see it," Jerod replied, whispering.

"Let's check it out," Wynne said, whispering back.

"Why are we whispering?" Jerod asked her.

"I don't know," she stated. "You started it," she defended.

They sat in silence as Moshi silently glided through the tunnel.

Wynne asked, "How are we doing on air?"

"About seven minutes or so left."

"Maybe we should return to the surface."

"If Moshi needed air, he would. We'll be okay. It's almost like he knows where he's going."

The glow grew brighter as they got closer, and as they rounded a small bend in the cavern an entire ecosystem of bio-luminescent water life came into view. Long, finger-like coral glowed a bright blue, as another finger-like plant swayed in the undercurrent, its color a bright green. The coral, though some appeared to be illuminated by the bio-luminescence of nearby plants, glowed bright in reds, purples, oranges, blues, greens, and yellows. The entire reef line on both sides of the cavern glowed brightly, lighting up the underwater world.

Wynne and Jerod were in awe of the beauty of the entire area. They had never before seen such plants and life before. There were even several types of fish with bio-luminescence as well, never before seen in Everly Lake. The tunnel seemed to split with a deeper section trailing off to the right, but Moshi turned left and began swimming upward. The light from the glowing underwater world began to dim as they broke the surface of the water into an underwater air pocket. Moshi's protective shield shut off, and Wynne and Jerod breathed deeply of the damp salty air.

Moshi moaned lowly as he ambled up on the rocky and sandy shoreline. Wynne and Jerod slid from his back onto the ground, looking around at the still darkness, lit only by the glow of the underwater ecosystem behind them that emanated upward through the water's surface.

Moshi shook his fur violently, sending water flying all around them. Wynne and Jerod laughed as they were pelted with water. Then, Wynne suddenly noticed the blink of more bioluminescent life as the water spray from Moshi's fur landed all around the dark cavern, making lights in various colors blink for a brief moment. Wynne touched Jerod's arm and pointed to the phenomenon.

"What..." he began to say, but Wynne silently hushed him. She stepped further into the open-air cavern, followed by Jerod and Moshi. As they slowly walked, dim light began to appear all around them. More bioluminescent life slowly came into view, their glowing forms beginning to light the now visible massive cavern.

Mushrooms in varying colors of purple, yellows, and oranges glowed brightly. Trees teemed with brightly colored jumpers, leaping back and forth between branches. Flying creatures whirled about, glowing as they flew all around them, seemingly unbothered by their presence. Beautiful, winged, creatures that resembled the spiritflies from the surface world floated by, ambling throughout the unusual bushes and plants that were loaded with glowing flowers. Some appeared to have some type of fruit on them. They noticed that the glowing of the flowers seemed to wane to a lesser glow as they turned to fruit.

Wynne and Jerod were dumbstruck by what they were seeing. They didn't speak a word, only wandered deeper into the glowing underground forest. Large vines, some spotted and some lined, hung down around them. Wynne ran her hands along them as she passed by. One of the vines felt different and glowed stronger when she touched it. The vine suddenly pulled itself straight up into a curling position around the branch from where it sat. Wynne watched in awe at the offended creature, realizing that the other end had a head with glowing yellow eyes that peered down from its place amongst the branches above her. She smiled as the creature peered down at her.

"So sorry," she said to it. The creature replied with a nod and watched them curiously.

"Jerod," Wynne now whispered excitedly.

"Yeah," he whispered back.

"They can understand us."

"Good to know. Wait, where's Moshi?"

Jerod looked around and didn't see him anywhere. "Moshi," he called as loudly as a whisper would allow.

Moshi lowly bellowed from a stand of bushes off to the side; poking his head through the branches and leaves to look at them.

"What?" Jerod asked audibly, as he and Moshi stared at one another. "Okay, we're coming."

"Come on Wynne." Jerod motioned for her to follow.

"Where are we going?"

"Not sure. Moshi just said for us to follow him. Didn't you hear him?"

"No, sorry. I'm sort of absorbed into this incredible world we've just discovered."

"We've been gone a long time. We should probably get back before Patrice sends the coast guard searching for us."

"She's likely back at Discovery Falls by now," Wynne distractedly replied.

"Yes. And you're not. You still live there most nights with the other students, remember?"

"Oh yeah," she replied still distracted by all that was around her.

Jerod grabbed her by the hand to pull her along behind Moshi.

"Where are you taking us boy?" Jerod asked, as they seemed to climb upward higher and higher. They had to climb over and around some rocks, duck through a few other smaller tunnels, and curve and wind their way ever upward. The higher up they went, the dimmer the glow from the bioluminescent plants below became, until they were completely no more. Not long after the darkness set in, they could make out a dim light filtering down through the much smaller cavern. It was beginning to get so tight that Jerod feared that Moshi might get stuck, but the beast ambled on upwards, climbing the rocks on his two hind legs, and using his front paws like hands to pull himself up and squeeze between boulders.

They suddenly broke through the end of a cavern, right in the middle of nowhere. Jerod looked around at the array of large boulders and rocks that surrounded them, unable to see much more than rocks and dead trees in the dimming light of dusk.

Wynne stepped out, surveying the area where they stood. "Wow, it's getting late. I didn't realize we were down there that long. But I think I know where we are."

"Good, because I have no clue."

"Rock City; you know the rocky area west of Cactus Valley and the Marshlands."

"You really think we are that far over?"

"Yeah, I think so. It makes sense."

"Well, let's find the shoreline and get back to the water. We are going to be in a lot of trouble getting back so late."

"We'll think of something to tell everyone. But let's not mention the underwater world just yet. We need to decide how much to tell about that if anything at all."

"Right, come on Moshi," Jerod called. The beast ambled over on its hind legs and dropped to all fours. Jerod and Wynne climbed up onto his back, and Moshi began heading northeast.

"He must know where he's going," Wynne stated.

"He also must know this area well since he led us up the cavern to the surface. Do you think anyone else knows about this place?"

"I doubt it. I don't think anyone else comes here," Wynne stated.

Five minutes later, Moshi dropped into the water at the shoreline of the Marshlands. Wynne stuck her hand into the water and wiped her face with the cool liquid.

"Hmm…the water is salty here. Why do you think that is?"

"Not sure. I didn't think any part of Everly Lake was salty."

"Apparently it is here near the Marshlands."

As they swam toward the east side of Everly Lake, a small group of beasts; fierce and gnarled by the harsh elements of the Bleak Mountains—the place they called home; stood and watched the intruders glide away through the water from their perch on the distant mountain top. They watched the lost meal move away, snarling and gnashing their teeth at one another, howling mournfully into the dimming light of the night air.

Wynne and Jerod both turned at the eerie sound falling down over the lake from somewhere behind. Darkness now began to swallow the light, and they watched as the glow of the Marshlands bathed the air around it in an eerie orange-green glow.

"Well, at least we now know what the spooky glowing of the Marshlands is from," Jerod replied, "all the bioluminescent plant and animal life."

"Yeah, but what sort of creature makes a sound like that?" she asked, spooked by the now fading calls that drifted out in the distance. Wynne thought about the gypsy stories from childhood and wondered if the creatures called Hunger-hounds were responsible for the sound.

"I don't know, and I sure don't want to find out," Jerod answered.

They made it back to LARS in record time, Jerod pushing Moshi to travel as quickly as possible. It was already well past dark and approaching the midnight hour.

"What are you going to tell Dr. Barrister?" Jerod asked.

"I'll just say that after this morning's unexpected attack, we decided to expand our border patrol area by a hundred miles or so. I won't be lying. We are planning to expand our patrol area."

"You think she'll buy it?"

"Why not?"

"What about Adda?" he looked at her questioningly.

"I doubt she mentioned the Brindelwren, which I am disappointed at not seeing. Besides, she knows not to push me or I'll act on my threat."

"How are you going to get back to Discovery Falls tonight?"

"I'll have Roamey fly me, but you'll have to come along and return him to his cage, just to make sure he doesn't get distracted and take off elsewhere for a while."

Jerod agreed, and after caging Moshi, they uncaged Roamey and mounted him.

Jerod stated, "I don't think I've ever ridden on Roamey with you before now."

"Really, how odd. This should be a new experience then."

"Yes, and quite a romantic one."

Wynne smiled broadly at his remark. They sailed through the night air, the moon shining upon the trees and buildings below, casting shadows here and there. The night was quiet and cool as they rode in silence, taking in the beauty of the shadowy landscape below. They reached the hidden base in the falls in about twenty minutes. Roamey sat down, allowing Wynne to climb off easily.

"See you tomorrow, Wynne," Jerod said, staring down into her eyes.

"Goodnight, Jerod." Wynne smiled, giving Roamey a pat. She stood watching them fly away against the pale light of the moon. As she turned to open the hidden doorway, Dr. Barrister stepped out from the darkness.

Wynne jumped at seeing her. "Goodness, Dr. Barrister, you frightened me."

"Wynne." Dr. Barrister addressed her. "Would you mind telling me where you've been? I've been very worried, and unable to reach either you or Jerod on the com-calls. What exactly have you two been up to?"

Wynne grinned at the doctor, nervous about what she should say. The doctor was no fool and could often see a lie a mile away.

Bain and Kreelie met at one of the local restaurants for a meal and a drink, wanting to catch up with one another. It had been a while since they had been able to get together and just visit. Life was busy, and with the war, they never knew when the Scaithers would attack and so had to always be on guard.

Kreelie walked into the establishment, meeting up with Bain who already waited at the bar.

Bain smiled as he watched his friend enter the building and stood to greet him.

"Kreelie," he smiled broadly, pulling him into a hug.

"Bain, buddy," Kreelie replied in kind.

"It's good to see you, Kreelie."

"You too man. Let's grab a table and get a bite." Bain led the way across the room, settling into a booth that sat against the wall.

They ordered their meal and drinks and caught up on each other's most recent events while waiting for their food to arrive. When the waiter brought their food, they ate their dinner in relative silence. When done, they ordered a few more drinks as they settled into the booth, leaning back against the wall, and spent the rest of the evening catching up and reliving academy days and adventures.

Bain asked, "So how's your father doing?"

"Not so good Bain. He seems to slip away more and more each day. It would be better for him to leave this world. He has no quality of life at all. He stays inside nearly all the time, and lives in a completely other world."

"Well, if it's any comfort, no one really has a quality of life anymore. I feel like we spend every moment in expectation of war. At every turn, every waking day we could face a Scaither attack."

"True, which makes it even harder on Father," Kreelie stated. "With me being gone so much tending to all the skirmishes, I hardly ever see him during his more normal episodes. One of our neighbors, an elderly widow, tends to him for me. I pay her for her services a little just to help her out."

"Sorry man. That's tough. It's hard to imagine Durger like that at all."

Kreelie nodded in reply and then asked, "What about you and Raila? How's that going?"

Bain's eyebrows rose as he inhaled and exhaled quickly. "Not good. You know she broke it off about six months ago." Kreelie nodded in reply. "Well, she refuses to talk to me. No matter how hard I try, she gets mad and runs off."

"You must have done something pretty bad," Kreelie teased, chuckling lowly.

"That's just it, Kreelie. I have no idea what I did."

"Well, then maybe you should pay more attention to what goes on between the two of you."

"What do you mean?"

"If she broke it off without an explanation, and it has nothing to do with another guy being in the picture, then maybe it has to do with communications between the two of you?"

"I guess. I know that I've been really busy with LSS missions, training of the new recruits, and the war efforts over the last three years. Perhaps I've overlooked her or taken her for granted without realizing it?"

"Good luck with figuring that out, Bain. I'm glad I don't have to worry about such things right now."

"No women in your future?" Bain asked with a grin.

"No way. Between my job, worrying about Father, Caislan, and Bamerly, my hands are beyond full," Kreelie said with a chuckle.

They chatted for a while longer before Kreelie stated that he had to get back to check on his father. They said their goodbyes and parted ways, glad to have had the chance to catch up and have this small snippet in time to live like things were normal once again.

Chapter 9

Destruction

Wynne stood straight, lending a light smile to her features before answering. "Sorry, Dr. Barrister. Jerod and I extended our patrol boundaries this evening because of the Scaither attack this morning. The alarms were a bit late signaling danger, so we thought we should start checking several more miles out. I guess the distance interfered with our reception. I never even heard my comm go off."

"That still doesn't explain such a late return."

"I guess we just got caught up talking," Wynne tried as an excuse.

Patrice cocked an eyebrow at her, unsure of her story. "Wynne, Jerod is a young man of a certain age, and I know the two of you like one another in more than just friendship. Be careful, all right? If anything should happen to you, your parents would really come down hard on me. I would also have to send you home."

"Oh! Dr. Barrister! It's nothing of the sort, I assure you. Jerod and I haven't even so much as kissed," Wynne protested with a shudder. "We just like spending time together. I'm not ready for any serious relationships. I am only fourteen. I like my life here at LARS, well, the falls," she corrected with a shrug and a wave of her hand.

"Good. Because I would hate to lose a gifted student like yourself only a few years before graduation. You have your whole life ahead of you. Don't mess up the few years you have left to just be a kid," Patrice stated with heartfelt care. "Now, off to bed with you."

Wynne nodded her understanding and went straight for her bunk in the large dormitory style room that all the female students shared. As she lay down, she breathed a sigh of relief that Patrice hadn't asked too many questions. She wasn't sure what else she could have come up with off the cuff.

Fortunately, she had drawn her own conclusions, incorrect ones, but they had provided Wynne an out none the less. Her active mind and all she had witnessed today would not allow her to relax, and sleep did not come quickly. She lay there thinking about what they had seen and experienced out beneath the Marshlands. It took hours before sleep would actually claim her for the few precious hours before morning rounds would begin.

The next several days were busy for Wynne and the others. First, her grandfather Aaric had accepted the Zanchieth council's offer to be Governor of Loradin and the surrounding territories, and so the city was having a ceremony to officially commission his office position. Anyone from all the territories was invited, but the Policing Authorities, LSS agency employees, Coastal Guard, and any agencies in connection with that, were expected to attend; which included the Loradin Animal Brigade.

On top of family stuff and government office re-quirements, the Animal Brigade had extra workloads to tend to. The Coastal Guard ships and the airships needed repairing from the battle they had fought, so Jerod and Moshi were on recovery duty for any reusable parts that were laying on the lake floor. He and Moshi would pull them up, and Wynne and Roamey would fly them to the shipyards. Oudree and Matteo would pull parts to wherever they were needed using her Yarequu, Yar, and his Raisedback Vindaper, Tusk.

Recovery wouldn't be necessary if the cities access to the minerals in the mines were as plentiful as it once had been, but since the Scaither's powerful reach had grown so extensive, they couldn't get the minerals from the mines like they used to. Lumber was readily accessible from the mountains and forests all around the outlying cities, but the Rhenium and Ruthenium from the Rhe Mines, prized for its high melting point qualities and strength under intense pressure, was currently unattainable. The mines lay north of Martanzia, and the Scaithers pretty much controlled nearly all the northern and most of the western territories. The only cities still holding out on Scaither takeover to the west were Wickstock Fortress, Cypress Ridge, Treeline Valley, and the Xantifa Tribe Village.

Most of those western cities were far enough away from Bakrashan to avoid much Scaither activity. They were the only four cities large enough to be able to hold their own. Oddly enough, the governor and council members over Cypress Ridge, the city once heavily allied with the Scaithers in the war three years back, had turned sides and allied with Loradin after an attack on their ships by their very own allies. Their governor hadn't liked taking orders from then commander, Raif Martray, and his cruel ways. But from what Wynne had heard through the rumor-mills, contrary to the majority vote in Cypress Ridge, there was much unrest in the city. It was having its own civil war so to speak. Half of its population wanted to just allow the Scaithers to do what they wanted to end the fighting. The other sensible half knew that letting the Scaithers have their way meant the end of their fair and beautiful city as they knew it. They still fought for their own rights and freedoms over peace and a one organization rule. But their city was growing weaker because of the constant unrest within their own walls. Her father, Wilkins, said they couldn't stand strong for much longer under such conditions.

Wynne and Roamey circled overhead as Jerod and Moshi pulled the last of the recovery items from the water below. They grabbed the items and flew them back to the nearby shipyard on the shoreline of Loradin very near the LARS institute. The men waved their appreciation to her as she flew off to the brigade headquarters, ready for some lunch. Jerod met up with her there.

They sat in the cafeteria with dozens of others piled all around them, quietly and hungrily eating their meal.

Jerod whispered, "Wynne, when do you think we'll get the chance to go back out on our extended rounds?" he asked. Careful to use words that wouldn't attract too much attention from listening ears.

"Soon I hope. I really want to keep tabs on activity out that way," she carefully responded.

"How about after lunch? We have the rest of the day to go check it out. There's no hurry to get back either since tonight is one of the nights you stay here at headquarters. We can go as far as necessary."

"Sounds good to me," Wynne put in.

"I want to go," Adda said, sitting down with her tray of food.

Wynne sighed, "Adda, it's too dangerous."

"You promised me that you would take me with you. If you don't take me this time, I'm going to tell Dr. Barrister about the Brindelw…"

"Sh…," Wynne and Jerod both hushed her. They exchanged a look with each other, Jerod shrugged his shoulders and Wynne exhaled loudly, defeated.

"Fine. But you have to promise to listen to me, and, to keep your mouth shut about what you see. Tell no one, understand?"

Adda beamed, shaking her head yes happily. "I'll see if I can clear taking you with me with Dr. Barrister after lunch. But Adda, I'm very serious about what I said."

"I promise Wynne, I won't tell a soul. And I'll listen," she added when Wynne gave her a sideways look. "Did you see it again when you went out the other day?" she asked quietly.

"No. But we did find something else. You'll see when we get there. Now eat up and quit asking questions before someone hears you."

Adda quickly ate, excited about the adventure she was about to go on with her big sister and Jerod, the Animal Brigade Commander. She felt rather important indeed.

"Vonder, are you certain you want to go into that cavern? We don't know what's inside or where it might take us," Professor Yarbrough nervously stated, taking in the size and depth of the underwater cave.

"Professor, for a scientist, you sure are a whiny, frightened, fella'," Vonder replied.

"It's just, the size of the creature we saw; we wouldn't stand a chance against it should it decide to attack."

"We have the other five UWEM's we finished. Between the six ships firing capabilities, I'd say we stand a very good chance. Besides, I want to use the creature, like those kids do at LARS. And, if I can get my hands on one of those telepaths, I'd have it made. No city could stand against us."

"Yes, but we don't have a gifted child yet, and you're already going after the animal. Isn't that putting the cart before the wheel so to speak?"

"Relax Professor; you're really starting to get on my nerves. I can man this thing without you if necessary," Vonder stated, looking at the Professor over his shoulder.

Professor Yarbrough cleared his throat, swallowing hard, understanding Vonder's meaning quite well. He nodded his concession, and quietly turned to monitor the UWEM's control panels.

The six UWEMs quietly whirred their way into the long, dark cavern toward the underwater world that lay a few miles deep inside.

"Professor, do you see some sort of light coming from up that way?"

"Yes, I believe so. Shut down the on-board lights for a moment," the Professor instructed.

Vonder did as asked, his eyes growing large as the bioluminescent ecosystem came into view.

"What do you make of this Professor?" he asked in awe.

Professor Yarbrough gasped at what he saw. "Well, I never expected to see such a sight here. The Glowfish and their spawning ground, Lumens Falls, were thought to be the only bioluminescent life on Zanchier. This is utterly amazing! No one has ever discovered this before. I'll...I'll be famous! I just wish I could get out and take some samples."

"There's another tunnel out that way," Vonder said, pointing to the right. He radioed back to the other five UWEMs. "Four of you take that tunnel and see where it goes. If it branches off again, stay in pairs of two. Carver, you follow me. We're gonna' see about all this glowing stuff here."

"Right Boss," came several replies over the radio.

As Vonder and the other sub traveled forward, the Professor said, "It appears we are rising in elevation. The lake floor seems to be going upward, which means that we might actually surface somewhere soon."

"Meaning what?" Vonder asked.

"Perhaps there's an air opening nearby?"

"Like a cave where we can breathe air?"

"Quite possibly."

"Well then Professor, you might get to take your little samples after all," Vonder stated, as the UWEM's top began to break the water's surface; the other UWEM directly behind them.

It was darker above the water as the machines systems shut down, and they dropped the anchors. The Professor hurriedly opened the hatch to exit the UWEM, grabbing the test tubes he always carried with him just for such a situation. As the four of them climbed out of the two vessels, the world above the water slowly began to come to life. With each sudden noise the glowing would disappear and the area would be thrown into darkness once again.

The Professor instructed, "Shh…try to be as quiet as possible. And shut off those torchlights."

The other two men looked at him, then at Vonder questioningly. Vonder shrugged and nodded and the three of them did as they were told.

Almost immediately the world around them began to glow. Little by little, more things came to light. Gleaming plants and flowers lit the underworld. Strange little creatures whizzed by in splendid color, as others floated by gracefully. Sounds permeated the large open cavern as chirps and croaks reverberated off the walls and high ceiling, and other animal sounds came from somewhere deeper inside the large cavern.

The Professor was overcome with emotion, his senses overwhelmed by all he saw and heard.

Vonder's voice boomed, "Would you look at this, boys?" And the world quickly darkened.

"What happened?" Vonder asked loudly.

The Professor shushed him again, which Vonder didn't take kindly to.

"Watch it Professor. You're skating on thin ice."

"I'm just trying to get you to be quiet," the Professor whispered. "Apparently the life down here is startled easily and goes into camouflage mode when frightened."

"Okay, I'll be quiet," Vonder said a bit too loudly.

They all stood still, being as quiet as possible, and the world around them slowly began to glow again. The Professor excitedly and carefully as he could, began snipping small samples off some of the glowing plant life. He even was able to capture a few flying bugs into one of his sample jars.

Vonder and the other two men wandered around the cavern looking at all the creatures. One grabbed at a vine and jerked on it, only to end up with a striker-like creature around his neck. He yelled in fear, making the cavern partially dim once again. He threw the offending creature as far as he could and shivered at the thought of what had landed on him, careful to not touch anything else. As they walked further into the lush forest with the wide lane cut through the center, they all heard a faint roar from somewhere deeper, the sound bouncing off the cavern walls.

They all stopped what they were doing and looked at one another. Soon the ground beneath their feet began to shake. They turned and began running back toward the UWEMs. The Professor completely caught up in his task, kept busy with his collecting.

The roar grew louder, and suddenly the Professor felt the ground vibrate beneath his feet. He watched as the three men ran, scampering into the UWEMs, and quickly pocketed his samples.

"Vonder," he called, "wait for me!" he pleaded, knowing the man could care less if he was left behind or not. He barely made it inside before Vonder secured the hatch. They hurriedly started up the engines and the vibrant life faded instantly at the intrusive foreign sound, plunging the cavern in darkness yet again. The roar became louder as the Brindelwren came out of hiding. It was suddenly so loud that it shook the vessels and the water in which they sat. Vonder quickly flipped on the outboard lights to the UWEM and the beast came into view.

The Brindelwren's long outstretched neck made it appear to be at least fifty foot tall on all fours. It had a head and body like a seahorse, but a longer neck. The torso had four, long, flipper-like fins, with sinewy kelpy looking hair that swayed around the part of the fin that attached to the body. Its tail was long and tapered down to a point at the tip and had the same sinewy hair that was around the flippers, swinging and swaying with every swish of the beast's tail. It roared at the intrusion to its underwater lair, stomping and snorting, threatening the intruders.

All four men in the two separate mods gasped, trying to quickly maneuver the UWEMs backward and out through the cavern. Victor hailed the other four UWEMs with a mayday signal.

"We need you four to head back! We need your assistance! We're under attack!" Vonder yelled over the radio.

"Vonder, the creature hasn't made any attempts to harm us, just to frighten us off," the Professor exclaimed.

"Well, I'm not waitin' around for it to kill me first. Let's hit it with some firepower."

"Vonder, wait, you'll destroy the entire ecosystem down here!"

"Better it than me." Vonder hailed the other UWEMs. "Fire at will boys. Let's take it down."

The Professor protested again, "But I thought you wanted to capture it!"

"I think it's a lot bigger than I originally thought. Besides, did you bring a net?" Vonder asked incredulously.

Balls of fire shot from the two UWEMs, striking the Brindelwren. It roared in pain as it turned and swung at the machines. It's long tail producing spikes as it slammed into the other one. The spike penetrated the hull of the machine, and the Brindelwren picked it up and smashed it down into the water and the bottom of the shallow cavern floor. The force of the impact shook Vonder's UWEM, the waves pushing it further out into the cavern, giving him a head start. He turned the machine quickly, maneuvering the underwater ship at top speed back through the tunnel toward Everly Lake. The other four UWEMs appeared from the other tunnel and fell in behind Vonder's, pushing the modules to top speed as the beast came into sight. The Brindelwren dove into the water in pursuit of the machines, grabbing the closest machine in her powerful jaws and slinging it into the underwater cavern wall. The angry animal roared loudly, vibrating the water around the UWEMs, and sending shock waves that momentarily disrupted the machines operations. They were only a mile from the opening, but the Brindelwren was closing in quickly. The UWEMs ducked and maneuvered around anything they could to escape the Brindelwren's wrath. It stretched out one long flipper and slapped another of the machines into a large rock, causing it to explode. Vonder and the other two UWEMs exited the tunnel at top speed, their fuel burning faster than expected. One UWEM had a leak in the hull near the fuel supply from shrapnel from the last explosion. The machine slowly came to a dead stop just as the Brindelwren slammed into it, sending it into a spin and bouncing it off the edge of the cavern's entrance. Large pieces of broken rock fell quickly from above, disabling another of the UWEMs. As the Brindelwren attacked the last two modules, tearing them apart, only Vonder and the Professor were left. Vonder steered the UWEM toward the shore as quickly as possible.

"Vonder, what are you going to do?" the professor asked nervously.

"The only thing I can do. Run aground as fast as possible, climb out of this thing and onto dry land."

"We can't outrun that thing!" the Professor said, fear making his voice shrill.

"Well, there isn't anywhere out here to hide. Plus we're running out of fuel."

Vonder sped to the nearest shoreline, that being the Marshlands.

"We can't land here, Vonder! The Marshlands are as dangerous as that beast!"

"Professor, quit your whinin' and hold onto something! After we run aground, open that hatch as fast as you can and get out!"

The Professor grabbed onto the inside of the UWEM as it ran aground on the edge of the Marshlands and Cactus Valley. It hit hard, throwing them both forward into the ships glass. They shook off the impact and threw open the hatch, climbing over the hull and sliding into the water, hunkering down in between the canals, and hiding amongst the thick Mangrove trees that ran through the Marshlands.

The Brindelwren breached the water's surface with a loud roar and brought her large body down on the UWEM, smashing it to bits and burying it down into the mud of the lake bottom.

Vonder and Professor Yarbrough, lay as quiet as possible in the marsh, hoping the Brindelwren thought them destroyed with the machine.

Chapter 10

Deadly Explorations

Wynne, Jerod, and Adda, wrapped in an air bubble on Moshi's back, glided through the entrance to the cavern tunnel toward the recently discovered underwater world. Jerod pointed to the newly fallen rock from the top of the cavern entrance.

"What do you think caused that?" he asked Wynne.

"I wouldn't know," she answered.

Adda was in awe of what she was experiencing until she noticed some sort of strange underwater module smashed on the rocks, a line of air bubbles floating upward toward the cavern ceiling. Wynne noticed it too.

"Jerod, what is that? It wasn't here last time."

"It looks to be some sort of underwater module."

"Mother told me about this. Vonder Mortruff was building some sort of underwater ship."

"Apparently he made more than one," Jerod clarified.

"What?"

Jerod pointed to another such module, also smashed to bits on the opposite side of the cavern.

"Oh my," Wynne stated worriedly. "Vonder must have somehow found the cavern too. What do you think he was looking for?"

Jerod answered, "Well, the Scaithers *have* been trying to snatch one of us. Perhaps he's also seen the Brindelwren and tried capturing it; unsuccessfully by the look of his ships."

Wynne asked, "Moshi, please hurry to the open-air cavern." Moshi obediently swam faster. As they approached the area where the land went upward, some of the bioluminescent life that once glowed closer to the surface no longer did so. They discovered why once they got closer. Another one of the underwater modules was smashed against the coral and lodged firmly in the ground beneath by a large spike that protruded upward. Adda nervously tapped Wynne on the shoulder, her voice shaky and frightened.

"Wynne, there's a dead man inside that module."

Wynne turned as best she could from her seated position and hugged her little sister, looking at where Adda's attention was taken.

They soon broke the surface and Moshi lumbered up on shore. He knelt down and the three riders dismounted. Moshi didn't move to stand. He lay there moaning in sadness. They all three surveyed the horrible damage with heavy hearts. Much of the bioluminescent life there at the mouth of the open-air cavern had been destroyed. Smoke still billowed from several different areas. One large tree off to the side still smoldered with fire, as did several other plants along the wide path area.

Wynne was shocked and saddened by what she witnessed.

Jerod spoke. "This just recently happened. It wouldn't still be smoking and burning in these areas if not."

"Like, how recently?" Wynne asked.

"Within the last thirty minutes or so."

Wynne grew nervous. "You don't think there is anyone else still down here do you?"

"I can't be sure, but from the look of the destruction of the underwater modules coming in, I doubt anyone that was here is still alive."

"Wynne, I can feel her pain, and hear her moans," Adda said, her anxiety growing.

"Who, Adda?" Wynne asked.

"The Brindelwren. She's hurt," Adda said, turning to look at her sister. "We have to help her, Wynne."

"How Adda? Do you know how to treat an injured creature? Especially one we know nothing about?"

"No, but I can comfort her," Adda stated.

"Adda, do not go looking for her. If she is injured, she is likely frightened and angry. She might attack us; especially since we are of the same species that has already intruded on her world and damaged it."

"I understand, Wynne," Adda answered softly. "But, surely, since we are here, we are going to look for her?"

"Maybe, but we need to proceed with caution. We probably shouldn't try to interact with her today if we do find her."

Adda shook her head in understanding, taking Wynne by the hand. The three of them, with Moshi ambling behind, followed the wide worn area apparently made by the Brindelwren, making their way toward the interior of the underwater world.

Vonder and the Professor slowly and carefully made their way through Cactus Valley, keeping the lake shoreline in sight to their right. As long as they stayed near the lake, they wouldn't get lost or turned around. They had been walking for the last thirty minutes, headed toward Treeline Valley and the first sign of civilization.

As they walked, they spoke very little, every now and then each one releasing an occasional yelp as they brushed by an offending cactus plant.

Vonder exhaled heavily in aggravation. "How much longer do we have to walk through these things, Professor?"

"I'd say at least another fifteen minutes before we are completely out of them."

"What's after that?"

"Rock City."

"Is that the rocky area south of the Xantifal Plains?"

"Yes. It's more than just rocky I'm afraid. The rocks and boulders can be quite large, and everything there is completely dead. No water or life for miles."

"So maybe we should get some fresh water from the lake before we head too much further."

"Well, that depends on whether the water is fresh. Back at the marsh, I noticed it had become very salty."

"It might not taste good, but it drinks all the same."

"Unfortunately, Vonder, your assessment is incorrect. You can't drink saltwater. It will dehydrate you."

"Oh. Well, let's go see if the water has changed anyway."

They walked toward the shoreline, trying to avoid the larger cactus that grew nearer the water. They eventually came to the edge of the valley where it began to mingle with the large rocks and boulders of Rock City. Once out of the cactus, they bent to taste the water. It was finally beginning to turn back to the fresh waters of Everly Lake, but still had too much salt to actually drink.

The Professor said, "I think the water will be good enough to drink a few more miles up."

"Good. I'm dying of thirst here. I haven't walked this much since I was a kid running around our village."

"Shh…" the professor stated.

"What?" Vonder asked irritably. Then he heard the distant woeful howl too. The two men looked at one another, each one ducking behind the large rocks, trying to peer around them to see what manner of creature made the mournful sound.

"Professor, what was that?"

"I'm not sure."

"What do you mean you're not sure? Don't you study this kind of stuff?"

"Yes, but no one has ever studied the creatures of Bleak Mountain. Those who have tried were never heard from again."

"Don't you think that was something you should have mentioned earlier?" Vonder seethed angrily, as fear gripped them both.

"Why? Would it have somehow *changed* our course? We're *stuck* out here because *you* decided to take on the legendary *sea-beast*!" the Professor whispered forcefully and irritably. "If we *die* out here, Vonder, it's *your* fault!"

"Watch it, Professor…"

"Or what, Vonder? Is there anything worse that you can do to me at this point in my life? Very soon we may be running for our lives; trying desperately to outrun whatever horrid, native, creature lives here, probably without even the *smallest chance* of success. Now, we need to move as quickly and as *quietly* as possible here. Keep your eyes open, Vonder, and your mouth shut!" Professor Yarbrough seethed as quietly as possible.

"Fine," Vonder replied, shocked at the Professor's sudden finding of his backbone. Vonder wasn't used to being afraid of anything, but right now, with the way the Professor was acting and what the man had just said, he was terrified.

The two men traveled as fast as they could, squeezing between the rocks and boulders; having to climb up and over some, trying not to expose themselves to the sight line of the mountains off in the distance. Neither of them was certain that they hadn't already been seen.

Another eerie howl was heard, and it sounded as if it were growing closer. The men scrambled, trying to move faster if that were even possible. The lake grew closer and closer, and the area finally opened up into an easier pathway with less rock to maneuver around, but it also left them completely exposed with no hiding place.

The Professor glanced back over his shoulder and fear gripped his entire being. A large animal stood on all fours on top of a tall boulder just a stone's throw away from them. Its snout long and hairless, fangs larger and longer than one of his hands, protruded down out of its mouth. It was hideous, and he could smell the scent of death permeating the air. The creature's fur was short around its head and legs and shaggy and matted in other areas. Its paws were larger than the Professors head with long, razor-like nails. Its fur was dull in color and grayish-brown; much like the colors of the rocks surrounding it.

The professor took off as fast as his legs could carry him, jumping into Everly Lake, hoping the beast wouldn't follow, sinking down below the surface and holding himself underwater for a few seconds to see if anything followed. As he came back up to the surface for air, he heard screaming. His attention was drawn over to Vonder Mortruff who was being attacked by three of the beasts, his cries of pain ringing in the Professor's ears. He swam out further into the lake, hoping that no creature was following him. Daring to stop swimming and turning around, he saw that two of the creatures were pacing the border of the lake, foaming at the mouth and gnashing their horrible, long, blood-stained teeth in his direction, but not daring to enter the water.

He felt he was finally safe, but poor Vonder was not. His cries for help had stopped as several beasts tore him apart. The Professor was so shaken he began to shiver in the water. He decided he had better get moving and began trying to pace himself as he swam along the shoreline, breast-stroking his way further north. The creatures followed him for a short way along the shore, howling and growling their dismay. They soon gave up, deciding there was a ready meal they were leaving behind and turned to fight for their share.

The professor swam for nearly an hour, his body bone tired from exhaustion over the whole ordeal. Finally deeming himself safe at last, he swam toward the shore. Before he could reach the water's edge, something wrapped around his ankle, stinging him. He cried out in pain, kicking with his other foot at what he assumed was a Glowfish. In agonizing pain, he pulled himself out of the lake and onto the shore just north-east of the Xantifal Plains grasslands. He crawled out of the water and onto land, getting as far from the water as he could before passing out from exhaustion and pain. The poison of the Glowfish began to take its toll on his body as his ankle began to swell, his flesh marred with the tentacle shaped suckers of the Glowfish.

"Adda, where are you going? Slow down," Wynne called to her, trying to keep up with the quickly moving girl.

Adda pushed through the thick glowing plant-life of the underwater cavern toward the Brindelwren. Adda could feel her pain as if she were calling to her. The closer Adda got the more anguish she felt, until she soon began to cry in empathy for the beast. Her emotions were so raw, her whole being felt the creatures sorrow.

Wynne could hear Adda as she began to weep audibly. "Adda, are you all right?" Wynne became worried, as she moved faster to try to reach her, unable to actually see her due to the height and thickness of the plants. She and Jerod moved quickly in the direction Adda went, trying to catch up to her.

"Adda!" Wynne yelled, now worried for her sister.

"Over here," Adda yelled, from a south-east position. They quickly made their way through the underbrush, coming out to an opening directly behind Adda. They all stood there in awe of the Brindelwren. The creature lay curled up in a ball at the edge of the cavern wall. It seemed to be sleeping; its breathing sounding labored, with soft moans here and there as it exhaled, its powerful breath stirring the leaves of nearby plants.

Adda slowly moved forward, and Wynne reached out, grabbing her arm to halt her progression.

"Adda, what do you think you're doing?" Wynne whispered forcefully.

"She won't harm me, Wynne," Adda's tear-stained face looked up at her.

"You say that, but you don't know this creature. Adda, she's absolutely huge! She could step on you without even knowing that you're there!"

"You had the same connection with Roamey, remember?" Adda questioned.

"Roamey was a fledgling when we first met; a brand-new baby which basically took to me as his mother. The Brindelwren is a fully grown creature. At least, I think she is; which is what I mean by not knowing anything about her. Her kind isn't in any of our academy or historical house books, except in legend. And legend says they are destructive beasts that only kill."

Jerod put in, "I've read about them too, Adda. It's only hear-say mind you, but the lore and legend books talk of how they often attack sailing ships for no reason."

Adda replied, "Yes, books written by men and how they see things. Perhaps men initiated the attacks on her kind first, and then reaped the repercussions of those attacks. Like Vonder and his men."

Wynne and Jerod looked at each other, trying to come up with a way to sway Adda from running to the Brindelwren's side.

Suddenly the Brindelwren moved; her long tail unwinding from around her greenish blue, smooth-looking flesh. Her torso lifted off the ground as she sat partially up on her front flippers. She shook her head, and her long billowy mane of kelpy-looking hair flew about behind her. She bellowed a painful sound as she turned and licked the burnt flesh on the right side of her torso and front flipper, trying to soothe the burnt flesh. She startled when she saw the three of them and Moshi standing at the clearing's edge. She roared at them in a warning not to come closer.

Adda stepped forward toward her, and Wynne reached out, grabbing her but stumbling forward as well. Adda spoke to the creature.

"Hello. Do you remember me?" Adda asked as she inched ever closer, Wynne trying to hold her back without too much motion for fear of startling the creature whose attention they now fully held. She was failing miserably as a determined Adda pulled her forward with her.

The Brindelwren gave a throaty bellow and nodded her head up and down just once. Wynne wasn't sure if that was a reply to Adda's question or just her imagination. Her question was soon answered.

Adda slapped at Wynne's hands as she broke free, slowly stepping forward. Wynne and Jerod close behind her every step, waiting to intercede should they need to.

"I'm sorry you're hurt. I wish there was some way I could help you, but I can't, I'm just a little girl. All I can offer you is my sympathy and comfort."

The Brindelwren sat still and watched them approach cautiously. It never moved, only watched them. Adda was very near the creature now, only about twenty feet away from her body. She continued speaking to it.

"My name is Adda. I remember you told me that you are a Brindelwren. Is that right?"

The creature shook its head up and down once again, bellowing as if in a small answer.

"May I call you Wren?" Adda asked, once again getting a nod from the Brindelwren.

Adda grinned. She looked up at the creatures burns, and tears came to her eyes and streaked down her cheeks. "I'm so sorry you're hurt. Shame on those evil men! I wish there were some way to help you to heal."

The Brindelwren stretched its long neck down toward Adda. Wynne and Jerod grew nervous, not sure of the creature's intentions. But the Brindelwren only nudged Adda, as if trying to comfort the girl in her emotional state. Adda reached up and hugged the beast's long snout, rubbing her soft slightly slimy-feeling skin. Wren gurgled softly, releasing a puff of air from her nostrils, and sending Adda's hair and clothes into a momentary billowy flight. Adda giggled slightly at the sensation it caused. She turned to Wynne and Jerod waving them over toward Wren.

Wynne and Jerod slowly walked toward them both, placing a hand on the creature's snout. They both smiled brightly as Wren nudged against the movement of their hands on her flesh.

Wynne said, "Perhaps Dr. Barrister has something back at LARS to help her flesh to heal quicker."

Jerod stated, cautiously, "I'm not so sure we should bring Wren back to LARS. It might cause a panic."

"Why?" Wynne replied. "It wouldn't likely cause any more of a panic than any of the other creatures did years ago. Besides, Dr. Barrister is the one who started treating animals long before telepaths were even discovered. I'm sure she could help. Adda, see if she will trust us and come to LARS where we can treat her burns?"

Adda spoke to the Brindelwren asking it to follow them. It refused. Anxious since most of its interactions with the human race had been negative.

"We'll protect you, I promise," Adda begged her.

Wren simply laid her head over her fins, tucking it back underneath her rear flippers, steadfastly refusing to move.

Wynne laid a hand on Adda's shoulder. "I don't think you'll convince her to come. We can get the medicine and bring it back here to her. "

"But, Wynne, she's hurting and we can't come back tonight."

"She'll be all right until we can get back here tomorrow. Come on, it's time for us to go."

Adda looked at Wren, now curled up and sleeping. "I'll see you tomorrow girl."

The three of them climbed up on Moshi's back and he lumbered toward the water. The four of them swam through the cavern back toward Loradin. Adda and Wynne would gather whatever supplies and medicines they might need to treat Wren's burns. The three of them made plans to return to the cavern early the next morning, planning to make the long journey to the Marshlands once again. It would make it much easier if they could convince the Brindelwren to return to Loradin with them, but she was understandably reluctant.

Chapter 11

Retribution and Revenge

The Professor faded in and out of consciousness. He could see dim streaks of light and feel the bump and sway of movement beneath him. The scent of spices and herbs filled the air around him along with the low chanting voice of someone. The searing pain in his left ankle throbbed occasionally, and he was grateful for sleep because the pain was nonexistent at that point.

The gypsy woman known as Aliyah, tended to the wounds of the man they had found lying by the shoreline a few hours ago. They had realized he was still alive and had pulled him into the back of the wagon and placed him on one of the cots. She applied healing herbs and wraps to the stings and swollen skin. They had ripped the man's pants up to the hip to see if the poison had already entered the blood-stream. Unfortunately, the telltale bluish-purple lines that traveled up the veins from the sting below were proof that the man would likely perish.

Aliyah worked to ease the man's pain and tried to draw out the poison through an incision she had made just above the swollen skin. She packed the poultice around the incision and also covered the tentacle-marred, swollen, ankle as well, hoping to draw out the poison there too. The man would groan in pain here and there, and when he would briefly wake, he would mumble something about Vonder and beasts.

Aliyah had some idea of what he might be mumbling about. They had been traveling from their furthest camp site in the Xantifal Plains about twenty miles from Rock City. On a clear night, when the southern winds blew across the plains, they could hear the very distant, mournful howls of the creatures that lived in the Bleak Mountains. The gypsies called them the Hungerhounds, for every tale that ever came from lore and legend about the Bleak Mountains spoke of vicious creatures driven crazy with hunger; for nothing good or plentiful came out of the Bleak Mountains. They, the Gypsy people, never went anywhere near those mountains, or the

Marshlands for that matter. The Marshlands were a cursed land, in fact the whole region of the Bleak and White Mountains south of the Marshlands was as well; full of death and evil spirits

She held up the samples encased in glass tubes and jars that she had found in the man's long, white coat; curious where he found such strange glowing creatures and plants on this side of Zanchier. Lumens Falls was the only place to exhibit such lifeforms, and she had never before witnessed anything like what was in these jars.

Her patient stirred once more, crying out in anguish, waking in a sweat as he tossed and turned.

"Here now. Take a sip of this," Aliyah stated, holding his head up and putting the cup to his lips. "This will help to take away the pain. There you go, a bit more. That's fine, now lay yourself back and try to rest. I know the wagon ride is a bit bumpy on these old dirt roads, but you're in the best hands around. If anyone can help you to heal, it's old Aliyah."

The Professor swallowed the bitter tasting liquid. He blinked several times, trying to make out the wrinkled and blurry face of someone as he passed out, unconscious once more.

Riglan Mortruff yelled orders at the men in the communications room. "What do you mean you've lost contact with all the UWEMs? How is that even possible? If it's a tower issue then get it fixed, now!"

"Riglan, it isn't an issue with the towers. We've already checked them all," one tech replied.

"Then get some modules or ships out there and locate our UWEMs, and my father."

"I'm sure Vonder and the others are fine…"

"You can see the future, can you?" Riglan interrupted, standing nose to nose with the man.

"No, sir, I can't. But Vonder and the men he took with him this morning are all capable of handling any situation."

"If you argue with me one more time, I'll shoot you where you stand," Riglan stated bluntly.

"Yes sir," the man replied. He got on the communicators and commanded, "Gather a search team and send them out toward the southwestern shoreline where the UWEMs disembarked this morning."

"Yes sir," came the reply across the com.

"Contact our teams in Cedar Mills and have them launch a few ships as well. There may be a problem with the UWEMs."

"Right away, sir."

"Now, that wasn't so hard, was it?" Riglan cockily asked.

The man didn't reply, just turned around and got back to doing his job.

"I asked you a question!" Riglan screamed.

Vonder's right hand man, Everin, stepped forward and placed a hand on Riglan's shoulder to calm him.

"Riglan, I know you're worried about your father. Come with me and let's go have a drink. Maybe it'll calm you down a bit until we find out what's going on, okay?"

"Fine. Maybe you're right. I need a drink," Riglan stated. The two of them left the room and went to Vonder's office where a fully stocked bar waited.

When Jerod, Wynne, and Adda returned to LARS, the girls' brother, Bain, was waiting on them.

"Bain," Wynne said joyfully, wrapping her brother in a hug, Adda doing the same.

"Hey," Bain replied, returning the hugs. "What have you three been up to this afternoon?"

Wynne and Adda looked at one another. "What do you mean? Rounds as usual," Wynne stated innocently.

"It's more than that," Bain stated, following behind the girls as they walked.

"What more could there be to rounds, Bain? You just ride and monitor."

"True, but you're not riding Roamey, and I spoke to Seadon about your rounds and the airship weapons trials the other day. He said you took off after something in the water."

Wynne's head snapped up to look at him. Bain caught the reaction.

"What do you mean?"

"Wynne, Seadon saw whatever it was you took off after. Now, are you going to tell me what's going on, or do I ask Jerod or Dr. Barrister?"

"Fine," Wynne said in a hushed voice, "but you can't tell anyone. No one, Bain," she threatened.

"All right, I promise. As long as whatever it is you're doing isn't dangerous."

The three of them walked to a secluded corner to chat, making sure no one else was within earshot. She told him all about her scouting find that day, the underwater cavern full of life, where it was located, and their venture that afternoon where they discovered Vonder's destroyed underwater modules and the injured Brindelwren.

"Adda bonded with it, Bain. I truly believe it's her creature."

"Wynne are you nuts! Not everything in Zanchier can be tamed! Not to mention the dangers of the Marshlands!" Bain stressed, trying to keep his temper in check and his voice low.

"Bonding with creatures is what we do, Bain," Wynne said, looking at Adda and motioning to all the others working with creatures at LARS. "The Brindelwren is a gentle creature; at least she was with us. She's also injured and needs medical attention. I plan on getting medicine and going back early tomorrow morning, right after patrol rounds."

Bain looked at her, then scanned the complex grounds. "Fine, but I'm going with you, and Adda has to stay here."

Adda and Wynne both protested. "She can't, Bain. If the Brindelwren bonded with her, then we need her there. I can communicate with the creature, but only Adda holds her full trust."

Bain nodded in concession, not liking the situation one bit. "How do we all get there? I doubt Moshi can carry all of us."

"Well, you and I can ride on Roamey and take the land pass from Rock City. Jerod and Adda can take Moshi through the water cavern."

"What land pass? And what are you doing exploring Rock City?" he asked agitated.

"Moshi showed us a way out and in from Rock City."

Bain shook his head in agitation and surprise that they were taking such risks.

"All right, but we need to make it quick, Wynne. I've heard stories about the creatures that live in the Bleak Mountains. I don't want to draw any attention from whatever it is that lives out there. I sure don't want them following us into an underground cavern and trapping us there."

"I don't think that will be an issue. I think fear of the Brindelwren must keep them out of the cavern. I'm telling you, Bain, the world down there is magnificent, peaceful, and beautiful; wholly undisturbed. Well, except for the damage those men and their underwater modules did."

"All right. I'll meet you back here at eight in the morning. That should give us time to get out there, treat this Brindelwren, and get Adda back before I have to take her home."

They agreed, and Wynne went in search of medical supplies while Adda joined the group of students still in classes, tending to and bonding with the other creatures at LARS. Adda asked Dr. Barrister questions about how to treat injured animals, especially burns on water creatures. Dr. Barrister, answered joyfully, unaware that Adda had an underlying reason for such a question.

Professor Yarbrough woke slightly, realizing that the swaying and bouncing of movement had stopped. He appeared to be in a room. He was sweating profusely and the pain in his leg was causing it to throb. It felt as though the swelling was moving further up to his thigh. He tried to sit up to see what the damage was to his lower limb but couldn't manage it. He looked around the room, trying to see through his still blurry vision. It looked to be a boarding room of some kind. There was a chair near the bed, a small wash basin, and a bathroom off to his right. Another chair and a table sat tucked beneath a window to his left. The entry door sat directly at the foot of the bed where he now lay. As he lay there, the door opened and in walked an old gypsy woman; her wild gray hair sticking out beneath her colorful hair-wrap that encircled her forehead and tied on the side. Her dress was just as colorful, and jewelry dangled from her ears, wrists, and adorned several fingers. She entered the room and sat down in the chair next to the bed. She pulled a pan of water and a rag from a bedside nightstand he hadn't noticed before.

She spoke. "Glad to see you are awake. I've tended your wounds as best I could, but I'm afraid there isn't much more I can do for you."

Ephrem nodded his understanding. "Thank you for your help," he said with labored breath.

"We couldn't just leave you lying out there in the open. What were you doing way out there by yourself?"

"Underwater exploration. And I wasn't alone. All though, I am now. My companion was attacked and killed by wretched creatures in Rock City."

"Do you mean the Hungerhounds?" the gypsy woman offered.

"Is that what they're called?"

"It's what we gypsy folk call them. Vicious beasts with no sense of loyalty, driven by hunger and pain from the time they are birthed. Sorry for your friend. What a horrible way to meet the Creator."

"Well, not to speak ill of the dead," he continued laboriously, "but I doubt Vonder was headed in that direction to begin with."

The gypsy woman startled at the mention of Vonder's name. "You mean to say Vonder Mortruff was eaten by the Hungerhounds?"

"Yes. I only escaped by leaping into Everly Lake and swimming out of their reach. That's how I got stung by the Glowfish."

"Yes, well, you might have done better by taking your chances with the Hungerhounds," she said, giving him a look that told him he likely wouldn't make it.

"So, you can't heal me then?" Ephrem asked.

"I'll do what I can, but I think if we had found you earlier, then you would have had a better chance at surviving this. The poison has already gotten into your bloodstream. I'm trying to draw it out, but I'm not sure I can get it all."

"I understand," the professor said, laying his head back into the pillow and staring at the ceiling, a lump forming in his throat.

"Can I ask where you got the unusual samples I found in your coat pockets?"

"We found a large underwater cavern below the Marshlands. A wonderful, bioluminescent ecosystem."

"Hmm…that explains your fate. The Marshlands are a cursed place. You should have never ventured there."

He made no attempt to answer.

She wiped his head a bit, gave him another draught of medicine and stood to leave. She looked down at him again. "I'm not trying to take away any of your hope here, but I suggest that you make things right with the Creator before it is too late. I'm still holding out hope that you'll pull through this, but just in case, take care of your afterlife." With that, she left the room, pulling the door closed.

Ephrem Yarbrough had never been one to believe much in a Creator. Science could explain most everything. But the Gypsies were wise people, and if he was going to die then he wanted and needed to make atonement for his dismal life. He lay there talking to the Creator before the pain medicine caused him to doze off.

Sometime later, Ephrem woke to someone yelling angrily. The voices outside the door, somewhere nearby, were muffled and indistinguishable.

"Look, gypsy woman, I want to know where you got your information?" one Scaither asked.

"I told you. We found a man dying out by the lake; someone who traveled with Vonder Mortruff. He said that Vonder had been attacked by Hungerhounds in Rock City. He then jumped into the water to safety, although that has proved a deadly decision for him."

"I want to speak to this man personally," the Scaither ordered.

"Fine. But I tell you now, he is dying a slow and painful death from the Glowfish sting. Keep your questions short and nonthreatening. Allow him a peaceful death or I shall curse you where you stand."

The man nodded in agreement, swallowing a lump of fear at her threat. He and two others followed her through the inn and back to one of the rooms.

Aliyah opened the door to Ephrem's room and stepped inside followed by the man who questioned her. When the Scaither men saw the Professor's condition, they winced in visible empathy, one getting nauseous and turning from the room, unable to handle the horrid condition of the Professor's swollen, tentacle-marked, oozing, leg.

"Professor Yarbrough?" the guard asked as he entered the room.

The professor looked up into the face of one of the Scaither men he slightly recognized. He nodded through the sweat and pain.

"Professor, this woman tells us that Vonder Mortruff is dead. Is that true?"

The professor nodded, swallowing hard, his words now harder to get out. "Beasts attacked him."

"What about the others? There were ten other men in UWEMs. Where are they?"

"Dead. Destroyed…by the…sea-beast."

"Sea-beast? That old legend? I've never seen such a creature," one of the other men added.

The first Scaither continued, "You mean to say that all of the UWEMs and men are gone?"

"Yes," the professor breathed out heavily. "Cavern, bio…lum…" his words broken by labored breathing. He winced in pain and Aliyah stepped over.

"I think you have enough. Leave him be now."

The Scaither stood, nodded his understanding and he and the other two men left. They would reluctantly return the information to Port Proud headquarters, knowing that Riglan Mortruff would not be happy.

"Dead?" Riglan asked Everin again. "You're sure that's what the guard said?"

"Yes. They got the information from Professor Yarbrough himself."

"I want to see for myself," Riglan said, anger and hurt controlling his emotions and lack of sense.

"No," Everin stated.

Riglan turned abruptly. "How dare you tell me no!" he seethed.

"I will tell you no when you act irrationally. I used to do the same for your father. It's my job to keep you safe now. Those were Vonder's orders to me when he brought you into the organization."

"Well he isn't here anymore. I'm in charge now, and you will do as I say."

"Riglan, if you have a death wish and want to travel out to Rock City and take on a bunch of wild Hungerhounds, then go ahead, but good luck getting your men to follow. Just, don't do anything rash right now. Take some time to mourn your father and get your head on straight. You have a huge responsibility now to run your father's organization."

"You think I don't know that! I'm twenty years old and leader of the Scaithers. I've had ideas for years now and father would never listen. He'd tell me, 'watch and learn boy'. He never took me seriously. Well, now all of Zanchier will take me seriously. They'll all learn that there's a new leader in town. I'm tired of playing at war and only hitting these small villages and cities. I say we go all in and take over all of Zanchier. It's time Loradin and all those cities that think they are above Scaither rule see things in a different light."

"Riglan, you need to do things the smart way, not off the cuff. Taking on the larger cities, especially Loradin, is a big mistake. They have the Animal Brigade, remember? We can't compete against the telepaths and their creatures."

"Maybe not, but we can take a whole lot of everything and everyone else around instead. The Council and city leaders thought my father was ruthless? Well, they haven't seen anything yet!"

Chapter 12

Anarchy

Wynne and Bain flew low over the water as Roamey kept near to Moshi. Jerod and Adda bounced along the water below. As the Marshlands came into view, Moshi soon engaged his protective barrier and dove below the water's surface. Roamey flew straight for the underground opening, guided by Wynne.

Bain could see several creatures scurrying about off in the distance toward the Bleak Mountains. They looked miniscule from this distance, but just the fact that he could see them told him otherwise. He tapped Wynne on the shoulder and pointed at them.

She nodded, understanding that there was danger nearby. "Quickly Roamey, we might have visitors."

Roamey dove down toward the large opening and after letting Wynne and Bain down, sat upon one of the higher rocks, his eyes trained toward the Bleak Mountains.

Wynne watched him and how focused he was. He had never been a wild bird, but instinct tended to kick in and he knew danger when he sensed it.

"You be careful now, Roamey. Understand?" she said, looking up at the massive adult Kabihanxu.

Roamey returned her gaze and squawked ever so slightly.

"Let's go, Wynne," Bain instructed. "He'll be fine. It's us I'm worried about. We definitely need to be out of here way before nightfall."

Bain pulled out his torchlight, and the two of them followed the path that Moshi had shown them last time, down into the underground world deep below.

Alarms were sounding all over Zanchier as city after city sent out distress calls. Reports of Scaither movement came from everywhere. The brutality of the attacks was unexpected as Scaithers tore through every smaller village and town, slaughtering anyone who stood in their way.

Word had reached Aaric at the Loradin Governor's office that Vonder Mortruff was dead and Riglan Mortruff was now the new leader. Vonder had been cruel, but smart. Riglan was proving to be even more ruthless than his father had been but apparently he wasn't as smart. Bain had told Aaric once that Riglan would cut off his own nose to spite his face, and obviously he was doing just that. The boy had no idea how destroying everything in his path would affect not only the entire future of Zanchier, but his own lively-hood.

Aaric called upon Dr. Barrister and the Animal Brigade to come out in full force.

"Governor Brinley," Dr. Barrister addressed, "two of our leaders, Wynne and Jerod, are not here at the moment. They should be out on scouting rounds."

"Then they are likely doing their jobs already. I just pray that Zanchier, and its people, can survive this unsolicited attack."

"I'll let Oudree, Matteo, and the others know of the dangers." Patrice hung up the com-call with Governor Brinley. She didn't like or approve of using the telepaths and the creatures, but if what Aaric said was true and the reports coming from the west were correct, they would all likely be bearing arms soon. She shot up a prayer to the Creator as she left her office to prepare the children and return them quickly to the safety of Discovery Falls.

Bain watched in amazement at the intensely glowing life teeming in the underwater cavern. He also watched nervously as his sister's and Jerod approached the massive creature curled up at the rear of the cavern. The Brindelwren, as his sisters called it, was licking at the large, charred, area on her side. Wynne chided the creature as they tried to apply the burn salve.

"Now listen here, do not lick the salve off. This is going to help heal the burn. I'm also not sure what it will do to your stomach should you ingest it."

Adda stated, "I don't think she cares. I can sense that it doesn't hurt her as much. That's good."

The Brindelwren watched Bain, the newcomer with the group of travelers. She wasn't sure what to make of him. He carried weapons like the others who had attacked her world.

Adda sensed her questions and looked over at Bain. She touched the flipper of the beast, drawing her attention back to herself. "He's all right, Wren. That is my big brother Bain. He won't harm you. He's one of us, the good guys."

Wren bent her neck to look at Adda, snorting in reply. She then stretched her long neck and shook her head, sending her kelpy looking mane slinging out around her before moving to stand. Everyone stepped back quickly not wishing to be stepped on. The Brindelwren was even more daunting in the standing position, her entire body stretched out behind her. She turned and left, headed back toward the cavern entrance.

Bain asked, "Where is she going, Adda?"

"I believe she's hungry. She's going fishing in the lake."

Jerod stated, "I guess that's our cue to leave."

Bain and Wynne quickly hiked the cavern to the surface, coming out into the still brilliant but waning sunlight. Roamey was still curled up on the rock, his steady gaze still peering out toward the west and the Bleak Mountains. As Wynne and Bain stepped out into the full daylight, Roamey squawked loudly, growing very agitated. Bain and Wynne turned to see what he was carrying on about, only to see several four-legged beasts quickly crossing the rocks, headed in their direction. Wynne and Bain scrambled to climb up on Roamey's back as he screeched and belched a line of fire toward their attackers. Several of them howled in pain, turning in another direction. Roamey lifted off the rocks, flapping his massive wings to pull them upward and away from the snarling Hungerhounds. As Roamey's wings pushed them higher, one of the hounds leaped into the air, gnashing its teeth toward Roamey, and sinking them into his rear claw. Roamey screeched in pain, turning sharply, and belching fire at the offending beast. The creature turned in fear and pain, fire now covering its shaggy fur, blazing in full force as it ran away yelping. Roamey flew higher, the three of them now safely in the air. Bain and Wynne peered down at the snarling beasts which howled in hunger and anger that their most current meal was now flying away.

"Wynne, you don't need to come back this way again. If not for Roamey, we would be dead."

"I understand. Poor Roamey, his paw is hurting him badly. I can feel his pain."

"We'll tend to it when we return to Loradin."

As they flew over Everly Lake toward home, Bain's LSS communicator began pinging alerts one after the other.

"What's going on, Bain," Wynne asked, curiously.

"It says that all of Zanchier is under attack," he worriedly answered.

"What? By whom?"

"Who do you think, Wynne?"

"Quickly, Roamey, we must get home," Wynne instructed as the bird took off as fast as he could fly. She looked down at Jerod and Adda below, telepathically communicating the situation to Jerod.

Jerod instructed Moshi to hurry as well, knowing what likely faced them back at home. Jerod looked back at Adda. He would need to get her safely to Discovery Falls.

Kreelie Rintel barked orders as best he could under the surprise attack of Port Proud. Unfortunately, since Port Proud had the largest population of Scaithers compared to the rest of Zanchier, being Vonder's home-base, the entire city along with neighboring Martanzia was being hit harder than most. The reports coming into the Policing Authority station were from everywhere. They were even beginning to hear such reports from Carpasia and Praxtingen.

Kreelie stated, "Vonder must have a secret and deadly weapons arsenal stored up somewhere south of here to be able to attack Loradin and its surrounding villages."

"Didn't you hear, Captain? Vonder Mortruff is dead. Riglan is in charge now," Caislan stated.

"What? When did that happen?"

"Today, apparently."

"Well, that explains the brutal attacks. Riglan never was very bright. Brutal yes, but intellectual—not even close."

"What do we do, Kreelie," asked Delmar.

"We try to survive this and take out as many of the Scaithers as we can," Kreelie said, grabbing his laser guns and leaving the office. Caislan and Delmar followed behind him as the entire Everly-Sound policing branch followed suit. They left the small peninsula headed into Port Proud, trying to dodge people as they ran in every direction, fear gripping the city. Navigating the streets in the large, armored, module was rough, and chaos was rampant with people scrambling to find a place to hide from the senseless killing spree.

They bounced along the streets, Caislan driving as Delmar hung out the passenger window of the large, sided, transport. Kreelie stood in the back, shooting at Scaithers, and ducking down behind the tall sides of the open-topped module when fire was returned.

Caislan yelled back to Kreelie, "Where are we headed Captain?"

"Wherever the fighting is thickest!" Kreelie yelled in return.

Bain and the rest of the Loradin forces grabbed weapons and headed to the outskirts of Praxtingen, as the Loradin city gates began to close up tightly against the sudden and violent fight. The Animal Brigade ran out in full force to defend and protect the people of the Carpasian territories.

People were seen boarding up their homes and gathering whatever weapons they could find to defend themselves. Impending doom and fear could be felt in the air all around them. People were accustomed to Scaither activity, but this was a whole new level of destruction and death, even by Scaither standards.

Bain had wondered why the sudden attacks now. At first he thought that Vonder was trying to make a point by attacking everyone at the same time. Then he heard of Vonder's death and Riglan's sudden rise to fame. Perhaps Riglan was trying to enforce an anarchic and supreme Scaither rule over all of Zanchier. That sounded like the Riglan he had grown up with.

Bain looked over at his father Wilkins who sat on one of the Bi-mods, racing along the road next to him. Wilkins had voiced his fears back at the LSS office just minutes earlier, saying that with the start of this unchecked onslaught by the Scaither militia, he figured that the future of Zanchier would be a dark one. If those in charge, and the policing authorities, didn't get this sudden war under control, all of Zanchier would suffer greatly. Once things escalated to a certain point, there would be no controlling anyone and no return to their past lives or any sort of law. With the death of Vonder, even though he had been the biggest crime boss around, the man still would have never sanctioned the killing of innocent people, or such a large-scale attack; unless of course it would have benefitted him somehow. Riglan, however, was a whole new type of criminal. One without remorse, empathy, or self-control, and he now had way too much power. He had never feared anyone except his father, and now that Vonder was gone, Riglan had free reign, and was taking it to new heights.

With the news about Vonder and the Scaither attacks, Bain's mother Harper and Aunt Paisley had grabbed the children, the grandmothers, and Nan Trea, and headed out to the still hidden Discovery Falls bunker. They would stay there until this all settled down. Wilkins and Aaric didn't even feel that the Loradin barrier wall would keep the Scaithers out this time. Their reach had stretched too far now that even the once safe city of Loradin was no longer a haven for anyone. The Scaither sympathizers had grown too large in number, whether by forced allegiance or by the simple greed and sin nature of man; men who wanted no boundaries, who called good evil and evil good. The world had changed drastically over the last few years, and now they would all suffer for the foolish inclinations of the unjust.

Bain's thoughts went to Raila. He still hadn't had the chance to speak with her. He hoped to soon get the opportunity to talk to her in person, and if so, he would pin her in a corner if necessary and they would have it out. Life was looking less and less certain, and he wanted to spend what little time they might actually have left, together.

The hoard of LSS agents all in modules and on Bi-mods sped through the closing gates of Loradin and out across the glass sky-bridge connecting Loradin Island to the mainland. The Coastal Guard patrol began falling in line behind them, all racing to meet the Scaither armies on the northern Carpasian roads, as far out from the cities as possible. Unfortunately, since the fall of Overton Colony over the years due to much Scaither occupation of the once strong, walled, city, they also had to worry about attacks from Scaithers on the southern Praxtingen borders as well.

Fort Arvenguard to the north was, fortunately, still occupied by a small force of Sandedge warriors. Rodan Tixtel, village elder of Sandedge, made certain to keep the fort; a very great asset; armed with soldiers continually to keep Scaithers from taking it over. With the alarms signaling all over the eastern side of the lake, Bain figured that Rodan and a large group of his best warriors would have taken the hidden tunnels beneath the Carpasian Pass to the fort to fend off the Scaithers there, getting an early jump on things. At least, that's what Bain *hoped* was happening.

Reaching Praxtingen, half of the LSS and coastal crews split off, some going south to defend the borders there. Bain, Finn, Wilkins, and many others, took the northern road. As they sped through Praxtingen toward the open-air market, Bain noticed all the vendors scrambling to safety. He saw Silus pulling Raila behind his booth, as the city gates began to be overrun with Scaither modules and foot troops, all shooting at anything and anyone that moved.

Bain pulled his pistol from his side, first shooting the driver of a module, then the men standing at the large gun strapped to the top. He managed to clip them both, sending the vehicle careening into a nearby stand. He headed toward Silus and Raila, swinging the bi-mod around and stopping just shy of Silus' booth.

"Raila, get on!" Bain yelled.

She thought for a moment before deciding to listen to him, and then jumped on, wrapping her arms firmly around his waist.

"Come on, Silus, you too!" Bain yelled.

"You two get out of here! I'll be just fine," Silus yelled, pulling a large laser gun from beneath his booth.

"Be careful, Silus!" Bain yelled over the noise of gunfire in the streets.

Silus nodded, donned a protective vest over his chest, and then a helmet. He then slung his weapon over his shoulder and secured the strap firmly across his back, and began firing upon the enemy, calling out insults as he took out evil Scaithers.

Bain and Raila sped through the now fully war-engaged Praxtingen market streets, dodging and weaving in and out of modules, some still in use and others now crippled and on fire. Bain sped past Wilkins and Finn, both on Bi-Mods. Finn's bi-mod was the inspiration for the bi-mod line and was a special edition, and he handled himself and his "Voyager" with amazing expertise.

Both men turned their heads to watch Bain and Raila speed by, now being pursued by several enemy mods. Finn and Wilkins shot at and took out several Scaithers and their modules before turning to pursue the Scaithers now after Bain and Raila.

Bain skillfully navigated the city streets, taking shortcuts and veering in different directions, trying to shake his pursuers. He Dodged bullets and laser fire as Raila pressed tightly against his back. He could feel her flinch each time a bullet rang out. He prayed she didn't get hit and that the flinching was simply fear and nerves and not a sign of a gunshot wound. He didn't have time to stop and ask her if she was all right. He twisted and turned the bi-mod through the narrowing streets, giving them the ability to outrun the larger modules. Bain took the bi-mod off road through the forest of trees on the city's edge. He steered the bi-mod toward Discovery Falls through the thickening forest trees and out across the mountainside. He jumped a small gorge between hills and continued the journey, having to take the lower road around the lake that Discovery Falls emptied into. He glanced back to see where the larger modules were, realizing them to be a good distance behind on the road below. He had to hurry to be able to slip into the underground bunker without giving away the bunkers location. He yelled through his ear-piece, communicating with the control room at the bunker.

"Lower the ramp about a fifth of the way! We're being pursued by Scaithers!"

"Roger that, Bain, the ramp will be ready. How close are you?"

"Less than a mile out and approaching at full speed!"

The control room scrambled into position, pushing the button to drop the large bay door.

Bain yelled back to Raila, "Get ready to lean to the left with me!"

Raila nervously shook her head okay.

As the lowering forest floor came into view, and only about twenty feet stood between them and the dark inside of the bunker, Bain yelled, "Now!" He spun the bike sideways leaning it over almost all the way to the ground. They and the bi-mod slid sideways into the bunker as the floor began to instantly close up, sealing them off from the outside world. The bi-mod, along with Bain and Raila became airborne as they leaned to the right and the bike righted itself. Bain turned the handlebars to the right as the bike touched ground and the two of them came to a skidding halt inside the protective bunker. The whole bunker was now on high alert as detection was very possible now. Raila still clung to Bain as they sat there on the bi-mod trying to catch their breath and take control of their frazzled nerves. Bain put the kickstand down and climbed off the machine while Raila sat there, unable to move. Bain took her shoulders in each hand and looked her in the eyes.

"Raila, are you hurt?" he asked her softly.

She couldn't answer, only shook her head no. The impact of the situation and what she had just experienced took over and she wilted into a puddle of limp, shaking, tears. Bain leaned down and held her as she threw her arms around his neck and clung to him for a little while longer, sobbing as the pent-up fear and relief flooded forth. She knew he had saved her life and she was grateful that he still cared for her so much to risk himself for her.

Aboveground and outside, at the edge of the bunker's bay door, the Scaithers who were in pursuit sat scanning the area, yelling back and forth in confusion about where they had disappeared to.

"They can't be far! I'm sure they came this way. There must be a hiding place nearby."

"Or they just rode that two-wheeled mod into the forest."

"Then why don't we still hear them, you idiot?"

"I hear something. I think I hear them now?" one shooter claimed.

"Look!" another man pointed, "It's two more of those two-wheelers."

Finn and Wilkins approached at break-neck speed, shooting at the Scaither modules and the four men that occupied them. They hit several men in one module, immobilizing the unit. Finn struck the shooter of the second module, as it sped past them headed back toward town. The module stuck to the road as Finn pursued it across the grasslands by the lake, heading to cut the driver off up ahead. Finn and the module merged side by side. The driver of the module pulled out a gun and pointed it at Finn. Finn shot first, striking the driver as the module careened off the road and into one of the large roadside trees, bursting into flames on impact. Finn turned his module around and headed back to Discovery Falls. Once there, Wilkins had already seen to Bain and Raila's condition, the men working at the Fall's bunker were dealing with the Scaither module and bodies, and Finn, Wilkins, and Bain were set to return to the fight in town.

Bain turned to Raila. "When I get back tonight, we need to talk, all right?"

Raila shook her head yes, not sure she wanted him to leave again. "Bain, please be careful."

He nodded as he turned to leave.

"Bain," she said, making him turn to look at her once more. "Promise me you'll come back."

"I promise, Raila. I'll be as careful as possible." He turned and mounted the bi-mod once more as the three of them took the forest ramp up and out of the bunker, back toward town and the war.

Raila stood there watching Bain go until the large ramp closed her in, shutting out the warring countryside and the man who had just risked his life to save hers. A man she suddenly realized that she was still in love with.

Chapter 13

War Efforts

As nightfall covered the countryside, Bain and Wilkins made their way back to Discovery Falls. They were weary, tired, and hungry from the events of the nearly all-day fight. The skilled Loradin army and warriors finally managed to secure the territories borders and send the remaining Scaithers fleeing. The Animal Brigade sending the remaining enemy troops scurrying off toward Martanzia and south to Overton Colony. Bain's father Wilkins, and grandfather Aaric, had been discussing of late the necessity of retaking control of Overton Colony to secure Loradin's southern borders, but they had yet to make a plan to do so. It seemed that every time they got the smallest chance to breathe, the Scaithers would attack once again, and life would stand still for a while longer until the warring settled down.

Bain, directly behind his father, followed by many other men, walked into the secret bunker through the control area, and into the large open bunker area where the modules were kept. He barely got through the door when Raila nearly bowled him over as she flew at him wrapping her arms around his neck. Bain wrapped her in a fierce hug and they stood there silently for a few more moments, just clinging to one another and breathing. When Raila finally began to loosen her grip and lean back to look up at Bain, he placed both hands on either side of her face and looked deeply into her eyes.

"Are you okay?" he asked her, unsure as to her state of mind. He knew the bi-mod ride had been a scary one for her.

She shook her head yes and looked back at him. Tears began to well up in her eyes again and they pooled just on her bottom lid. "I'm so sorry, Bain," she said as her voice began to shake and the tears began to fall freely once more.

Bain took her by the hand and led her to a more private area in one of the rooms. He turned to look at her as she leaned against the wall behind her to hold up her shaking frame.

"Sorry for what, Raila?" he asked her, standing in front of her and leaning down a bit to get her to look at him.

"For the way I've treated you. I didn't understand the significance of what you do. Your job takes so much skill and training. I never knew you were as capable of handling yourself the way you do until today. I was just feeling so unimportant to you. You never talked much about your position at the LSS, and I felt left out, like *I* didn't matter."

"Raila, I know my job takes a lot of getting used to. And there are a lot of things that I'm not supposed to tell you about. It's not that I don't want you to know things, but it's for your safety. You are one of the most important people to me. I never want you to feel like you don't matter."

She began to cry again and said, "I know you care. I realized that today when you saved my life at the market. The way you handled the bi-mod and the things you can do, made me realize that I've been selfish. I'm so sorry," she cried, "I'll never do that to you again."

"It's okay, Raila. I'm sure I could have handled things better myself. Just promise me that from now on, we discuss our feelings instead of letting our anger build until it drives us apart."

She nodded and began crying again, throwing her arms around his neck once more as they stood there holding onto one another.

Bain pulled away, brushed back a stray strand of hair that had fallen across her face, stroking her wet cheek with his thumb. He looked her dead in the eyes and said, "Could you do me one more favor?"

"Sure," she said sniffling.

"Can we go get some food? I'm starving."

Raila laughed aloud, throwing her head back. "I've missed you so much."

"I've missed you too," he said, leaning down to plant a light kiss on her lips. When they pulled apart, Raila grabbed his hand and pulled him through the bunker toward the kitchen.

"Come on. Let's go feed you. With the way all this fighting is escalating, you're going to need your strength."

Bain sat at the table joining the entire group of men who had been out fighting all day, scooping food onto his plate.

Raila sat and watched Bain eat; realizing that the risks he took as an LSS agent and defender of the Loradin territories was who he was. She now completely understood and resigned herself to what life with Bain would mean. She would have to understand his being gone and being in danger more so than most, and she was willing to do her part to support him. Especially now that every citizen of Zanchier was dealing with the same sort of life changes that she had been. Life was uncertain, and each day given to them was even more precious than the last as more and more people died all around them.

The wars continued for months to come, taking them into late Fall and the early snows of the quickly approaching winter season. The death toll on Zanchier rose to extreme heights as men, women, and even some children had perished because of it, either directly or from hunger and poor living conditions. However, many of the now orphaned children were snatched to be trained as future Scaithers, all testing unsuccessfully for telepath abilities. Many families ran out of ammunition, unable to continue to protect their families and homes. The LSS, Policing Authorities, and the Coastal Guard were spread thin. The organizations had taken many losses themselves.

When the Scaither advances would stop for small periods of time; maybe a day or two here, or a week there; the country would have to spend that time burying the dead, many bodies were wrapped in cloth and tossed into the lake for quickness. The colder weather and the war-torn lands made burying bodies for those *not* near the coast nearly impossible with the hardening ground. So, the village leaders instructed the building of burial fires to quickly, and sanitarily, dispose of the dead. This quick disposal also allowed the people refrain from attacks by wild animals that wandered into the villages or hidden campsites following the smell of death. Fighting the Scaithers was bad enough without having to add fighting off wild animals. The rest of the people's time was spent trying to find weaponry supplies and much needed food which was becoming more scarce. Some of the refugees that fled Overton Colony taught others how to fish, clean, and cook the poisonous yet abundant Glowfish. A system of farming the fish for food, drying them, and even using their poison for weapons had become a quick and much needed resource. They even discovered how to use the lumen glands as light sources in and around the glowing Lumens Falls area. The falls lent a greenish glow at darker points at night, making travel in the area easy and undetectable, since many creatures that moved and lived around the falls had adapted a bioluminescent glow themselves.

The Rhe mines in the north territory of Zanchier had all but closed once again; except for Riglan's army; making finding metal weapons and ammunition almost impossible. The small mine in the Xantifal Mountains near the Xantifa Tribe Village had been closed for years. The Xantifa Tribe, with the war being as it was, had reopened the mine and entered the northwestern entrance near their village to begin mining the much-needed minerals once again. The Xantifa were the only people able to access the mine, with a few workers sneaking over from Terra Valley to aid in the efforts. They then had to try to secretly transport the much-needed minerals, Rhenium and Ruthenium. Finding a way to get them across Everly Lake to Praxtingen for processing had been an intricate system to work out. The trickiest part about moving the minerals quietly was getting them out of the southern mine entrance that sat just across Catamount Gorge just below Riverbend Falls. It was plainly visible across the river and lake on the north-western part of Treeline Valley Village. The old mine entrance had been boarded up for many years, showing the mines to be closed. The success of their mission took much cooperation from everyone, including the people of the neighboring villages of Terra and Treeline. The villagers would use whatever distractions or means they had to keep Riglan's men from discovering the operation. Those minerals were all that was allowing the Loradian government to make the ammunition to keep fighting, and so everyone did their part for the war effort.

Even the Gypsies had gotten in on the action, to a small self-preservation extent, and only as it served their own purposes. They were a quiet people who still claimed neutral-ity and avoided the towns and villages much of the time. But they were against the brutality of Riglan Mortruff, seeing much in their travels around Zanchier, and therefore aided those in need more than usual, even as far as lending to the deception of the resistance fighters.

Water-ships were dispersed under the cover of night, back and forth to Loradin, silently navigating the waters in complete darkness so as not to be seen. The captains navigated the ships using only the stars. Captain James Donner often commanded these ships that sailed the dark waters of the lake. They had to set their missions to be made on moonless nights so the ships could make the trip under the cover of complete darkness. The crews were trained to be as still as possible, to not make a sound. Not even so much as an uncontrollable sneeze was ever heard.

The Animal Brigade and the LAPS—Loradin Airship Patrol Services—would often accompany the ships as protection against attackers should they be discovered. The hardest part of the minerals transfer was getting it across the mountains, rivers, and valleys to the shoreline of the lake without being seen. The animals and their riders became the main connection to getting the minerals out. Wynne and Roamey would pick up crates of the minerals, flying them quietly across the rivers and mountains, depositing them in the Xantifal Plains where Oudree and Yar, and Matteo and Tusk, would then pull the wheeled carts loaded with crates across the plains to the ships waiting on the shores. Sometimes, when large shipments were needed, the telepaths and their creatures would work all night. The smaller animals and their telepaths often would run interference by way of distraction for the larger creatures and their riders. When not on missions, Wynne and Adda would sneak off to spend some time with Wren, Adda calling her out to meet up with them in the lake. Wren would even help them to take down Scaither ships trying to sneak across the lake waters to hit Loradin's shoreline. With one flick of her mighty tail, Wren would sink the ships without them even knowing what hit them, and yet they somehow managed keep her existence a secret from most everyone.

Bain, Wilkins, and Finn were often among the LSS agents who worked these transfers, going along to protect the kids, often riding aback the creatures with the children. All of this took great organization and communication which was achieved by Paisley in the LSS command hub. Her connections over the years, and her organizational abilities, made the transfers seamlessly streamlined.

Large transport modules awaited the ships at the Loradin seaports and people volunteered to work unloading and loading the ships so that the armed forces could best be utilized elsewhere. The minerals were then quietly transported to the old Carpasian Millworks in the Praxtingen Mountains near the Airship Academy. The old Millworks ran on the power generated by nearby Lumens Falls, allowing the hum of the machinery and the sounds of the forges to be masked by the roar of the falls.

The people still living in Treetop Village from the wars three years back, grew extra food to supply the troops and people of the neighboring villages. Treetop Village was still undiscovered and therefore its residents lived in peace, but not completely unaffected by the war. Many of their strongest left to help in the fight, and they also had to live with less food since they were supplying the other villages. They also helped to make more primitive weapons for the people who lived inside the warring cities. The surrounding forest supplied them with much material for the making of spears with strong thick vines and branches, the spear-heads made from sharpened pieces of broken rocks or the discarded nails from Pagorinx claws. To further protect themselves, they also decided to set many traps in the forest surrounding the village, knowing that discovery of their Treetop home could become a possibility in the future, especially in the fall months when the trees became bare. Fortunately, the early snows helped to hide the tree village.

Kreelie's father Durger had finally succumbed to his illness and passed one night in his sleep. With this new development, and the increasing strong arm of Riglan Mortruff, Kreelie and the Policing Authority of Port Proud had to move their office south to Fort Arvenguard, taking up arms with Rodan Tixtel's people inside the fort. Riglan had completely taken over control of Port-Proud, Martanzia, and Bakrashan, along with all the smaller villages and towns in and around the larger cities.

Cypress Ridge and Cedar Mills still had control of their cities but were slowly losing the battle against the heavily controlled Scaither occupied cities to their north. Reef Edge helped to conceal the ship movement to the south in the transport of the minerals to Loradin, often sacrificing some of their own ships in the process of coverups. Wickstock, the walled fortress city to the direct west of Bakrashan fought daily battles against Scaither attacks; their walled defenses beginning to crumble against the constant barrage of battering rams and laser cannons. With the mountain being so close, they could quickly rebuild their stone walls if given enough of a break in the fighting to do so, but those breaks were very rare being so close to other Scaither occupied cities, and their leaders often feared losing out very soon. The problem was that with every city in Zanchier under attack by the Scaithers, no one was able to send out troops to aid the cities that were being hit hardest. It was literally every city for themselves, and within every city, the people had to defend themselves, unable to lend a hand to neighbors in desperate need.

Even with the extreme effort that went into the war, the people of Zanchier felt as though they were fighting a losing battle. They all sensed a future of impending doom with each takeover of yet another city or village, a future where the Scaithers would control all of Zanchier along with everyone's lively-hoods. It felt as though life from here on out would be a constant and forever fight just to survive each day.

The coming winter months were colder than usual as people struggled against the brutal winds off the lake and the heavier than normal snows. Or maybe things just seemed worse because life was so much harder now. Some homes were so damaged that heating the inside was near impossible. Some families had to find alternate shelter in the winter months due to the amount of destruction their homes sustained.

Interior cities started to become overrun with refugees seeking hot food and a warm bed. The Loradin Theater and many other public buildings once again became the new homes for those in need. Although the need had been temporary after the war three years back, this war was making permanent residents out of the refugees of Zanchier.

Gracelyn Fenore—Harper Brinley's mother, Neitha Brinley—Wilkins' mother, and Nan Trea—the Brinley children's nanny since early on, took on the position of tending to and running the now boarding house. Gracelynn and Nan Trea moved into the Theater, staying there on site in one of the upper-level, now unused offices. They organized anyone willing to help feed, cook, clean, run-errands, and tend to the children of those serving in the other areas. Gracelynn, being theater director and a talented actress, organized plays to help involve and distract those who were stuck inside the theater due to the war. When not putting on plays for the commonwealth, they would also spend their time growing food in the city park, gathering donated clothing, and helping to repair homes for anyone who needed it. They would also put together daily food bags for people who ventured into the city looking for something to eat.

Harper helped Dr. Barrister with the running of the Discovery Falls Academy, and since the Praxtingen Market had been destroyed months back, Silus Aersor now spent all of his time at the Fall's command center communicating with leaders and running missions. His Vindaper farm was now handled and tended by volunteers. They would breed, butcher, and skin the Vindaper, using the meat to feed the people and the troops, and the hides for clothing and blankets.

This new way of life on Zanchier was becoming familiar, even though there was always the threat of a Scaither attack; the island of Loradin was still the only true refuge for most people. Life in the barrier protected city resembled more of the old way of life than anywhere else in Zanchier, and people throughout Zanchier's Scaither infested territories, bartered whatever they had for passage across Everly Lake to the Loradin territories.

Because of the hard ways, and desperation, a new breed of people arose from the tyranny. The people of Zanchier labeled them as pirates; those that preyed on the desperate and took people for nearly everything they had just to ferry them the sixteen-to-twenty-hour boat ride across the lake. Most Pirates were simply people hiding from the Scaithers as well, just trying to make it in this new existence. Desperation made once good people into some of the vilest cut-throats around. Some of these pirates even took people's passage money, and then handed them over to the Scaithers instead of providing the agreed upon purchased passage across the lake. Finding a trustworthy soul in Zanchier these days was as rare as seeing the now daily talked of sea-beast, which no one ever truly got a real look at, only a glimpse here or there. The rumors of the creature, which seemed to strike down Scaither ships with stealth-like ability, drew the attention of everyone. And many children, for purposes of amusement, would risk Scaither capture and sneak out of their lakeside village homes to venture out to the shoreline in hopes of seeing the elusive creature that seemed to be championing for the good people of Zanchier.

Chapter 14

The Last Stronghold

"Kreelie," Bain said through his com-call, "how are things going at the fort?"

"It's rough, Bain, and getting tougher every day. This early winter makes it hard living here."

"Then come to Loradin, its tough here as well, but it's better than Fort Arvenguard."

"I can't buddy. We're short on men here as it is. I can't just leave my men."

"I hear you, Kreelie. We're short of fighting forces everywhere. I know you can't leave."

"Yeah. It seems like our people are being killed or dying of hunger or extreme conditions, and the Scaithers are just thriving.

"Riglan must have some sort of food or supplies bunker stored up," Bain stated.

"No," Kreelie said, then went quiet for a moment. "He just has control of all the harvest fields, the mines, and the lives of the people who can't fight back. He forces people to do what he wants. I always knew that Riglan was a slime-ball during our academy years, but the things I've seen him do, witnessed with my own eyes, goes beyond simple slime-ball. He's evil incarnate, Bain. The sooner someone takes him out, the better we'll all be."

"Maybe the LSS can lead a secret mission to do just that. I'll talk to my father and see what he says."

"I wouldn't chance it, Bain. Riglan is always heavily guarded. He never leaves the safety of the warehouse offices. Reports from spies say he never even steps out of the building. He's a spineless coward, with the propensity for great evil, as long as someone else is doing his dirty work."

"Then why do his men follow his every direction and order?"

"He threatens to shoot them where they stand, and they've been conditioned over the years by first, Raif, then Vonder, to not question the authority of their leader. Not to mention they have the freedom to do whatever evil they wish, with no repercussions. They all see him as supreme ruler and basically worship the ground he walks on."

"Whew," Bain exhaled. "I would have never guessed that Riglan was that bad. He's only twenty years old. What could have possibly happened in his lifetime to make him this coldblooded?"

"Privilege and having the biggest crime-boss around as a father. That and the sudden thrust of ultimate power and an army at your fingertips can all lead to a pretty inflated view of yourself and what you think you want."

"Well, keep safe and warm, Kreelie. We'll try to get some more soldiers to the fort to help you all there."

"If you can spare them, it would be great. Rodan's warriors have basically been depleted. They have a very small group that has stayed at the village to keep the youngest of the children protected. Even the village kids of Sandedge know how to sharp shoot by age eight."

"I don't doubt it. I'll let you know about the troops as soon as I can. Talk to you soon Kreelie."

"Later Bain."

Bain searched out his father Wilkins in the command room of Discovery Falls. Bain and Wilkins had both given up life inside the Loradin walls and had taken to staying at the Falls. Harper, Adda, often times Wynne, and of course Raila were all living there now anyway. Bain often wondered about Seadon and how he was doing. He would give him a call later after speaking to his father.

"Morning Bain," Wilkins said with a slight grin and a nod, a grim expression tightening the features of his face and causing worry lines around his eyes and forehead.

"Father," Bain acknowledged.

"Good morning, Bain!" a boom came across the room as Silus approached.

Bain smiled at his large friend. Silus was always in good spirits, no matter the situation.

"Morning Silus," he smiled and nodded.

Silus stopped beside Wilkins and Bain. "So, whose rear-end are we kicking today, Wilkins?" he asked with a broad smile.

Wilkins couldn't help but smile at the man's tenacity. "We need to send reinforcements to Arvenguard. The men there need food, warmer clothing, wood for burning to keep warm and extra help, though finding people to go is hard. Conditions at the fort are rough. They get pretty much constant onslaught from the north, and now the south as well as Scaither control is seeping its way into northern Carpasia, probably from Rhamadon."

Silus sighed and smiled, "I'll go and take my old troop with me. These fella's are itching for a good fight. We may be old, but we still have a lot to give. There's a lot of fight left in us."

"The living conditions are rough Silus," Wilkins warned.

"I've lived a long, good life, boys, and I've lived through things a lot tougher than this. We'll manage."

Bain stepped up, a worried expression on his face. "Silus, please be careful."

"Now you listen here young fella'. Old Silus has lived a good, long life. If I give up my life for the people of Zanchier, the people I love, then I can die no better way. But, I don't plan on dying, so there's that."

Bain grinned and chuckled lightly at the man's reasoning and words. But as Silus saluted them and turned to leave, Bain's smile faded. He felt like it was the last time he would ever see Silus Aersor.

Back at the LSS headquarters, the very pregnant Paisley was in the process of organizing agents and troops for Loradin when she was suddenly struck with pain. She began having small contractions, trying to not pay too much attention to her already busy schedule. She stood at her desk, realizing that they were getting closer together each time.

"Kinley," she spoke into the intercom.

"Yes, Paisley," Aaric's former secretary replied.

"I may have a bit of a problem," she said, just as her water broke. "Never mind. Make that an affirmative. I definitely have a problem. My water just broke."

"Oh! Yes ma'am. I'm informing the medical floor now. They'll send up a wheelchair for you ASAP, and I will be right in."

"Thank you, Kinley, you're a life-saver," Paisley finished, just as a massive contraction hit, almost sending her to the floor. She slid into her office chair to await the arrival of the medics, breathing deeply to try to control the quickening and forceful contractions.

Kinley quickly entered the office. "Are you all right, Ma'am?"

Paisley nodded quickly taking deep breaths. "Have you notified Finn?"

"Oh! No, but I'll do that right away." She picked up the office comm and dialed Finn's number.

Finn felt the vibration and looked down at the LSS issued time-piece strapped to his wrist, recognizing the number on the other end to be Paisley's office, and picked up the call through his earpiece.

"Good morning beautiful."

"Um…good morning to you as well, Mr. Mobely," Kinley stoically stated.

Finn laughed. "Sorry, Kinley, I assumed you were my wife."

"Yes, sir. About that, Paisley is in labor, Sir."

"What! Now?" Finn asked, a bit surprised. "I thought she still had a few weeks?"

Paisley yelled into the intercom. "Sorry to burst your bubble, darling, but you can't time these things."

Finn could now hear her controlled breathing exercises over the com. "I'll be right there."

"Meet us on the medical floor, Sir. The medics have just entered the office and are preparing Paisley for transport."

"Thank you, Kinley." Finn ended the call and turned his Voyager in the streets, quickly heading back toward the LSS offices.

"Rodan!" yelled Kreelie over the noise of gun and cannon fire, "You need to call for more troops! I don't see us being able to stave off this advance of Scaithers with what few fighters we have left!"

Rodan, who was ducking down behind the upper walkways of the fort replied, "Discovery Falls and Rhamadon are sending some, but I don't know how many. We're just running out of people to fight!"

Kreelie turned back to the advancing Scaithers on the ground outside the fort. "Wait! Rodan, do you see that? What do you think that contraption is?" Kreelie said motioning off to the northern road as a large, strangely-built module came into view from behind the tree-line. It was slowly driven into place and parked, the top part of the module moving and spinning into place, taking aim at the fort. Everyone on the upper walkway of the fort stopped firing for a moment to take in the monstrous looking weapon. It looked to have been built with an armored hull with a long, massive, cannon-type frame on the top, but it didn't appear to shoot the archaic balls that the ones at the fort used. The part of the cannon where ammunition fire would come from had a smaller round hole than typical cannons; much like the laser powered cannons on board the airships.

Then they heard the whine of an engine as the cannon powered on and quickly generated enough force to shoot a line of laser fire, blowing off one of the corner turrets at the top of the wall.

"Run! Off the wall!" Rodan yelled, just before the cannon module let loose another beam of destruction. People ran for their lives, trying to get lower behind the sturdier walls of the fort. Some of the men were leaping off the walkway, trying to not get hit by the deadly beam which began a long turning sweep of fire across the whole top part of the fort, sending stone flying in all directions.

The Scaithers then pointed the beam at the large wooden doors of the fort, blowing the massive doors to bits with one hit. The wood splintered and flew throughout the inner courtyard as Scaithers came running through the now obliterated gate, shooting, and killing anyone in view.

The few soldiers left in the fort fought with valiant effort, taking out as many Scaithers as they could, but soon the massive laser module rolled into the fort and all firing ceased as it pulled to a stop and powered down.

Kreelie, Rodan, and thirteen others, were all that were left of the resistance force inside the fort. Many Scaither soldiers came running in behind the rolling, man-driven, laser weapon which was now trained on the fifteen remaining men. The laser's cannon pointed directly at Kreelie and Rodan stopping its movement. About thirty Scaithers stood around the laser module's base, weapons pointed and ready to fire, yelling at Kreelie and the others to drop their weapons.

Kreelie asked Rodan, "Why aren't they firing?"

"I don't know. It isn't like them to take prisoners."

At that moment, the door on the side of the armored module opened up and out stepped Riglan Mortruff himself. This surprised Kreelie and Rodan, who looked at one another. Riglan didn't normally venture outside his protective home.

"Kreelie Rintel," Riglan said, jumping down from the module and walking over to stand directly in front of him, but far enough away to not be taken over by him. "Well, well, the turncoat is finally caught."

"I'm no turncoat, Riglan. I fight for the people of Zanchier. The same ones you yourself grew up with. The people you murder and victimize every second of every day."

"You used to work for Raif Martray, who also worked with my father, Vonder. Which means you and I used to fight for the same side. Therefore, turncoat!" Riglan sneered.

"Let's just say I was young and foolish. And like so many others, we were misled to believe that Raif Martray was a good man; which he quickly proved to be anything but."

"But you worked for the Port-Proud Policing Authority. My father had most of those station-leaders in his pocket. Was Father's money not good enough for you and your father? You've always been worthless; just like that brainless friend of yours, Bain Brinley."

"There are more important things than money and power, Riglan."

"That's what I hear, but I tend to disagree."

At that second, Riglan raised his gun and shot Kreelie in the head. "Proof right there that power is everything. I'll give Bain your regards," Riglan stated coolly and without feeling.

The rest of the resistance was then shot down where they stood. No one was left standing. Only two of the people fighting at the fort escaped death. Delmar and Caislan both watched in horror as Kreelie, their friend who had taken them in and tended to their needs like an older brother, was executed. They had both been fighting from beneath the main structure of the lighthouse—from the large room which held the secret tunnel entrance—when the laser cannon mod broke through the fort doors. They climbed through the secret passage door, closed it off barring it from the other side, and ran in fear toward Sandedge Village through the secret tunnels of Arvenguard Pass. They would send word to the others that Fort Arvenguard was now under enemy occupation, taken by force with a large, transportable, laser cannon. And that all who fought and served there were now dead; killed in cold blood. Kreelie Rintel executed by Riglan Mortruff himself, and Rodan and the remainder of his men then executed by Riglan's troops.

Riglan Mortruff's laser cannon machine rolled south down the road, followed by the large troop of Scaither soldiers, meeting up with the relief troop for Fort Arvenguard between Praxtingen and Carpasia.

Riglan had decided to stay back at Fort Arvenguard and let one of his troop leaders take over the operation of the laser module. He and Everin, his lead man, listened through their radio, as the laser module and his ground troops plowed through the lesser advancing Loradin army. If only his father, Vonder, would have lived to see his and the Professor's invention come to fruition.

Silus Aersor and the group of several hundred men didn't stand a chance against the laser cannon. Only a few of them got away with their lives, but none of those men were Silus. He and his old-timer troop led the advance bravely, taking many of the ground troops out with them. The radio operator called frantically over the communications system for backup, describing the horrific slaughtering of the Loradin troops before him, and the seemingly indestructible power of the laser cannon.

Finn slid the Voyager to a stop in the parking garage of the LSS building. He ran through the hallways and instead of waiting for the slowly descending elevator took the steps, two at a time, all the way up to the tenth floor where the medical area was located.

By the time Finn reached the tenth floor of the building, he was so tired and out of breath that he had to lean against an obliging wall to rest briefly.

"What in the Creator's name was I thinking," he mumbled aloud and between great gulps of air. "I'm too old for stunts like that anymore." He took a few more deep breaths, and went in search of Paisley, finding her already prepped and pushing as the doctor gave instructions.

"Aaaaahhhhh…!" Paisley screamed in pain as she pushed.

"I'm here, honey, I'm here," Finn said, still breathing hard himself and scrambling to Paisley's side and planting a kiss on her forehead.

She panted quickly and deeply a few times, as she looked confusingly at his perspiring face and labored breathing. She pushed hard once more, yelling during the effort.

At that moment, Kinley—who never shows emotion or excitement—squealed in delight. "She's here!" she announced as she jumped up and down with joy.

Paisley fell back against the pillows in exhaustion as Finn watched the doctor prepare the baby and hand her over to him. He gazed down at the tiny girl in his arms. "She's beautiful, Paisley." Finn marveled at the little miracle as he handed their daughter over to her mother. His comm beeped relentlessly the entire time with alerts of enemy movement all over Zanchier.

Paisley held their daughter and looked at Finn. "I know you have to go, just be careful and make sure you come back. You have two beautiful girls who need you in their futures."

"Make that, *three* beautiful girls that I'll be returning for," Finn stated, leaning over to kiss his newly born daughter and then his brave and fearless wife.

"Take care of my girls, Doc; you too, Kinley. Where's Joslyn?" he asked a tad worried.

"She's in the nursery and is just fine. Don't worry, I have safe houses in place should our walls be breached."

"Thank you, Kinley, You really are invaluable."

"I know," she stated matter-of-factly.

Finn smiled broadly at her remark and left hurriedly. This time waiting on the elevator and taking it to the ground floor. He straddled his Voyager and sped out into the city, heading toward the border to aid in the fighting.

The Animal Brigade and the airships were deployed in response to the call; Wynne and Roamey being the first on the scene. She flew over the chaotic battle below, Roamey breathing hot molten fire at the laser cannon module, doing minor damage, but heating up the interior of the operations seat. Roamey and Wynne circled time after time, laying fire to the laser cannon, soon joined by Seadon and the airship fleet. They too began an intensive fiery onslaught of the machine and the advancing Scaither troops. Eventually, the operator of the module threw open the door burning his hand in the process on the hot metal. He gasped for air as the air inside the machine was hot and the oxygen eaten away by the heat. As the operator fell to the ground, gasping for air, Roamey and Wynne flew lower as Roamey belched a line of fiery breath inside the machine, lighting the interior ablaze. The driver of the laser cannon module now running for his life, was hit by a bullet in the process and dropped to the ground.

As the remaining Scaither troops turned to retreat back to Fort Arvenguard, they were slowly taken out by the Animal Brigade and the airships. Unfortunately, as they got closer to Fort Arvenguard, another line of Scaither troops and five more laser cannon modules began their advance toward the fort. Several of the laser cannons began firing on the airships, taking several of the ships down, falling from the sky into exploding balls of fire as they hit the ground or careened into the eastern mountainside. They called for more ships as back up, and the Loradin water-ships answered the call to action, sitting just offshore and firing toward the fort to try and penetrate its thick stone walls to crumble the now Scaither stronghold.

Scaither ships sailed quickly from Everly Sound and Port Proud to defend against the Loradin army, a battle at sea now taking on a full-scale war as the Loradin ships had to turn away from taking down the fort to defend themselves from the Scaither attack by water.

The battle was a long and arduous one, as Scaither airships soon joined the fight. The battle was fairly even for a while, but then Loradin began to lose ground. Roamey and the airships managed to take out two more of the laser cannons before their forces became too few to withstand. Several airships were damaged and had to turn back for repairs. Moshi and Jerod were able to take out one of the laser cannons with Moshi's lightning producing abilities. He emitted an electrical pulse toward one of the cannons that shorted out and shut down the entire system from an electrical overload.

As the fight continued in full force, Wynne and Roamey noticed the last two laser cannons veering off the battlefield followed by a group of Scaither troops headed straight toward Discovery Falls. One laser module veered south toward Praxtingen and the other kept its course toward the falls, the ground troops splitting up as well. Wynne tried frantically to communicate with Adda through mental telepathy. Adda hadn't learned to speak that way yet, but Wynne willed her to hear.

'*Adda, can you sense me?*' Wynne waited for a reply as she and Roamey flew full speed toward the falls, hoping to head the army off and draw their attention. '*Please, Adda, can you sense me?*'

Adda sat in the bunker's sleeping quarters with the other children all playing games when she felt like she could hear her sister calling to her. "Wynne?" she asked as she searched the rooms and adjoining areas, still hearing Wynne calling to her. Then, in her mind's eye, she could suddenly see Wynne on Roamey's back. "Wynne, I can hear you," she said audibly.

'*Adda, warn Father and Mother that Scaithers are nearing the falls! They're headed to the entrance to the underground bunker at the forest's edge.*'

"Yes, of course!" Adda ran to the communications room to speak to her father, Wilkins.

She grabbed his attention and told him about what Wynne had communicated to her.

Wilkins and Harper exchanged looks. "How do they know about the bunker?"

Harper asked Wilkins, "Are you certain that's why they are headed this way?"

"Why else would they take the dead-end road? Sound the alarm. Get everyone out of the bunker and into the underground tunnel toward Treetop Village," Wilkins said with urgency.

The alarm system in the underground bunker blared over every intercom within the underground system. Parents grabbed children and what little they could carry as people worked to direct them quickly through the hidden tunnel that would take them beneath the river, the forest floor through the mountain, and out to Treetop Village. It took about thirty minutes to get the last of the people into the hidden tunnel as the men, women without children, soldiers, and guards all stayed behind to fight where needed. Wilkins and Bain led the group that was ready to head out of the secret pass near the mouth of the falls to come up behind the Scaithers.

"Bain," Raila yelled to him.

"Raila, what are you doing here? You were supposed to go with Dr. Barrister and the students to Treetop."

"I want to stay and help," she defended.

"Raila, you've never fought on the front lines in a war before. You have no idea what you're doing."

"I'm a quick learner. Besides, I have learned to shoot a gun over the last three years."

"Raila, marching into foot battle is different. We're about to engage in an actual face to face battle with the most ruthless people in all of Zanchier. These guys won't kill you. They'll take you as a prisoner and do horrid things to you. I've heard how they treat women and girls alike that they capture. Please, go with everyone else."

"No! I want to fight, Bain. I feel useless just sitting around waiting on you to come back. I'm just as capable of fighting as the other women."

He sighed heavily, knowing it was no use arguing, and knowing they didn't have the time to spend doing so. "Here," he said, taking off his LSS issued hand-laser, and strapping it onto the back of her right hand, quickly explaining how it worked. "Stay as close to me as you can, understand."

She nodded her understanding, taking a deep breath. They waited for a few more seconds before Wilkins gave the signal to exit. The large group of people quietly and quickly exited the hidden vine-covered entrance near the waterfall's cascade, scurrying up the embankment behind the unsuspecting troops.

Chapter 15

The Disappearance

The laser cannon module stopped just twenty feet in front of the dead-end road and the edge of the forest beyond. The operator of the module swept the cannon's laser beam along the forest edge, cutting through the smaller trees like butter, as large tree trunks exploded, shooting pieces of wood in every direction. The tops of the massive, old, trees, fell to the forest floor, crashing down amongst the still standing trees as creatures of all manner rushed in all directions to escape the noise and the falling forest around them.

The Scaithers standing and watching had to run to avoid being hit by debris as it flew out, taking down a few of the men. As they tried to rally themselves and gather their senses, the Discovery Falls team advanced and attacked, taking those in the rear by surprise.

A battle ensued, as Scaithers and the resistance fought fiercely.

Wynne and Roamey swooped down from the sky and laid fire upon the cannon module repeatedly, dodging bullets in the process, and the resistance fought to protect themselves and the girl aback the Kabihanxu.

As the man inside the module jumped out from the intense heat inside, he was struck down by Bain. Bain looked at the now empty laser module as an idea came to mind. After a few minutes of fighting his way toward the module, it had cooled enough for him to leap inside, the controls cool enough to touch. Leaving the door open for further ventilation and being technically minded, he made a quick study of the operation system. Before starting the machine, he quickly scanned the battle still taking place, looking for Raila, seeing her safely hunkered down behind a large tree, firing at the enemy.

They locked eyes and he yelled, "Raila, stay here!"

She only looked at him, wondering what he was up to.

He then turned the large cannon which spun all the way around and put the module in gear to travel back down the road toward the falling cities of Carpasia and Praxtingen, leaving the rest of the resistance to continue the ground level fight at the falls.

Raila watched Bain take off down the road. She had decided to support him in his lifestyle, and she would also be part of the fight. No more sitting and waiting. She took off, running back inside Discovery Falls and the Bunker. Bain had allowed her to drive the bi-mods enough over the last few years, that she knew enough about the mods extra features and functions for the built-in weapons system. She slung her weapon over her shoulder around to her back and opened the bunker door. As it slowly laid down into the ramp position, she threw on a helmet, straddled Bain's bi-mod, and took off up the ramp speeding past the battle still taking place at the forest's edge. Thankfully, the resistance fighters were winning this fight and were rounding up what few Scaither soldiers were left standing, as prisoners of war.

Wynne and Roamey had turned back toward the city of Carpasia, following Bain as he moved as fast as the large, heavy, module could travel. Certain thicker parts of the interior of the laser mod were still a bit hot, and he burnt his fingertips a few times as he operated the controls, making a further quick study of how the device worked. With the door of the machine open wide, the interior cooled off much quicker. By the time they had reached the outskirts of Carpasia Bain could see that there were many dead resistance fighters and Scaither's alike laying along the road.

Bain pushed the module as fast as possible toward Praxtingen, hoping he could reach the city before the last laser mod left to the Scaither army could level the city. As he sped along the road, he noticed a bi-mod come up alongside him. He looked over expecting to see his father Wilkins but was confused to see someone else. It took him a minute to realize who it was from the clothing and the body size.

"Raila!" Bain yelled in agitation. He had told her to stay at the falls. He was worried for her. She wasn't used to the fighting and wasn't that skilled. She could shoot all right but wasn't a tough type of woman. He didn't understand what was driving her to take to the front lines to fight.

As they got closer to the Praxtingen city limits, Bain reached over to close the door to the armored module to protect himself from any sharpshooters. Wynne flew above with Roamey, and Raila was still to his left side as they passed through the city gates. The last laser module was just ahead of them, laying waste to the city buildings that made up the older market section of the city. As the laser module moved ahead of him, burning everything in its path, Bain fired into the module with a blast from his laser, sending sparks like a welding torch bouncing off the metal in all directions. It continued on through the streets, dodging blasts that Bain sent toward it. The laser module headed toward the glass sky bridge and the Loradin gates and barrier. Bain followed behind inching closer to it. As the module crossed the glass sky bridge it began firing on the Loradin gates, slowly melting the thick metal doors, eventually cutting a huge hole into the gate, now leaving Loradin vulnerable. Bain laid into the module again as his laser cannon began to penetrate the hull of the module, finally cutting through the metal and blazing a whole through it. The laser lit the interior of the module on fire causing an interior explosion and stopping the module in its tracks. The Scaither army blazed forward in their machine gun modules and on foot, ready to storm the city of Loradin in a kamikaze style attack.

Loradin's city alarms blared as hordes of Scaithers moved through Loradin killing anyone in sight. They split in all directions, attacking every part of the city, being met in the streets by the LSS, Coastal Guards, and Policing Authority. War broke out everywhere in Loradin, as the cities defenders fought to save the city and its people. The cruelty of the Scaithers was even more vicious than normal. As people ran for cover, screaming in fear, they were struck down from behind without thought or feeling. The Loradin Theater was attacked as those taking shelter there ran for their lives. Gracelynn and Neitha were both on the fourth floor of the theater when the attack took place, allowing them to find a place to hide from the invaders. Nan Trea, however, had been on the ground level and in the direct line of fire. She was shot by several invaders, collapsing to the floor. The Coastal Guard came rushing in behind the invaders, taking them out one by one, finally securing the theater, but only after many lay dead.

By the time the resistance got the city secured and either captured or killed the Scaithers, almost every major building in Loradin had sustained damage and the city had many casualties, including the LSS building. The Scaithers didn't get past the second floor, but they did destroy the entire tech department and several other offices.

When the chaos settled and the casualty list began to be tallied, the names added to the list for the hour-long battle was extensive. As Bain stepped out of the laser module to scan the streets for any sign of Raila, the devastation he saw everywhere was overwhelming. Many homes and buildings burned and fell into rubble. He walked the streets at first, taking in the destruction. As his anxiety built he began to run, scanning every avenue and street as he passed, fear taking hold as he looked for her. He turned a corner near the Loradin city gates and that's when he saw the bi-mod lying on its side in the middle of the street. He took off running faster toward the bi-mod, screaming her name as her body came into view. He ran to her as fast as he could, falling to the ground beside her. He grabbed the helmet and pulled it off her head, tossing it aside. He cradled her body in his arms as he spoke to her.

"Raila, please baby, wake up," he begged her. But as he looked her over, he suddenly felt something wet on his hands. Blood. Raila's blood. He looked down at the blood on her side just beneath her heart.

"No! Raila, please wake up. You can't die on me, Raila!" Bain yelled down at her unresponsive form. He sat in the street, her lifeless body in his arms as he mourned her loss; still begging for her to come to.

As he sat there rocking her lifeless body, a hand lay on his shoulder as a voice broke through his sorrow. Finn Mobley spoke to him with sadness in his voice.

"Bain, I'm sorry, but she's gone, Son."

Wynne and Roamey had finally touched down and she ran to her brother, kneeling beside him and laying a hand on his arm, tears for his loss and the loss of her friend streaming down her cheeks.

Bain wiped his eyes with the back of his sleeve, laying Raila gently down on the concrete. He stood up next to Finn and Wynne, Finn comforting him with a reassuring hand on his shoulder as Wynne hugged her brother.

A few other LSS agents came over and picked her body up with a gurney, carrying her to an area where they were taking all the bodies of the deceased for recording and burial. As

Bain, Finn, and Wynne made their way back to the LSS building, reports of the death toll began to come through, and they began to mark off the names of friends and co-workers who were listed as deceased. Among the LSS employees were Winnie and Cranston, two of the tech geniuses Bain had come to call friends over the years. Also listed among the dead being called in over the comms was Nan Trea, Silus Aersor, Rodan Tixtel, and Bain's life-long friend, Kreelie Rintel.

Bain's world spun out of control as grief overwhelmed him. So many of his loved ones were now gone forever. Anger filled him replacing his grief. He left the LSS building in a hurry, unable to handle the extent of loss he felt. He grabbed a bi-mod from the parking garage, straddled the machine, and took off at high speed through the burning streets of Loradin, out across the sky bridge through Praxtingen and toward Discovery Falls. He needed to lay eyes on his father, mother, and sister Adda. He needed to know that Seadon was all right as well.

When he reached the falls and ran inside, he found his father in the communications room talking to the people at Treetop Village. Another person was on the radio with the airship academy, getting statistics from them. Seadon Brinley was not listed on the injured list so Bain assumed that meant he was fine. He turned to his father and asked about Harper and Adda.

"They're fine, Son. What about Wynne and Raila? Do you know where they are?"

Bain filled Wilkins in on the situation with Raila, the LSS in Loradin, and the losses at Fort Arvenguard as well.

"I'm so sorry, Bain."

"I tried to tell her not to come, Father, but she just wouldn't take no for an answer. If she'd have just listened, she'd be safe with Mother and Adda. I should have made her stay here!" Bain argued.

"You couldn't have made her do anything, Bain."

"But I didn't try very hard to stop her either," his words ground out, his voice cracking with emotion. "I should have tried harder, Father," Bain said, as Wilkins reached out to embrace his son in a comforting hug. Bain pulled away from Wilkins hold.

"I'm sorry, Son. You can't blame yourself for this wretched battle. Riglan Mortruff is to blame for this. He hasn't an empathetic bone in his body. He killed so many people today, Bain. The reports keep coming in of the devastation from all over Zanchier, and many are still fighting off Scaithers. No one could have foreseen what was to take place today. No one is responsible for anyone else. Everyone did what they could and what they thought was right. Remember that Son."

Bain swallowed the lump still sitting tightly in his throat and looked up at Wilkins. "She shouldn't have died, Father. None of them should have. I'm so sick of power-hungry idiots with control and money, who care nothing for anyone other than themselves! I just…need to get away for a while."

Wilkins asked worriedly, "What do you mean, Bain. Where are you going to go? The Scaither's reach is everywhere. You can't hide from this war, Son."

"I'm not hiding, Father. I just need to think. I'll com-call when I can. Tell Mother I love her, and everyone else too."

Bain turned toward the bunk rooms, gathered a bag of clothes and necessities, some food, weapons, ammunition, and travel supplies, and straddled the bi-mod once again. He struck out down the falls side road turning south, and rode through Praxtingen toward Sandbar Beach. He'd take the gypsy trailway, if he could find it, staying as far from people as possible. He needed to be alone, to get away from all the reminders and the fighting, to mourn for his friends, and for Raila. He didn't know where he was going yet, but if he could make it to the Xantifal Mountains and his mother's old treehouse, perhaps he could stay there for a while until he had some control over his anger and his emotions. He couldn't fight another battle anytime soon. He couldn't bear to loose anyone else he loved. Solitude was a necessity, at least for a while.

Chapter 16

Is Hope Lost?

Wilkins and several of the other men with families left the hidden bunker beneath the falls, traveling the long underground tunnel out into the forest toward Treetop Village. He wanted to see Harper and Adda with his own two eyes. Plus he needed to inform her of the deaths and her son taking the news very hard. When they reached the camouflaged door that led them out into the thick forest, they carefully looked around. Scaithers were everywhere now, and they couldn't risk being seen. Treetop village was the last and only safe place now for the people of Zanchier to hide out and live in some semblance of peace. Wilkins warned the men behind him to be extra careful and watchful as they walked toward Treetop.

Getting to Treetop took several hours. The village was well hidden and very far up near the mountain top. The only real dangers this far out and up were the wild animals; the massively large Pagorinxes and Kabihanxus to be exact. But Wilkins figured with the LARS students now hiding at Treetop Village, they would likely have the entire forest trained before too long.

As Wilkins and the men came into the area of Treetop Village, he whistled a bird call to alert of their approach. After surviving the harrowing battle they just fought, he certainly didn't need to be taken out by friendly fire.

Harper and Adda were peering down over the railing of one of the huts when she spotted Wilkins. She and Adda ran across the rope bridges that linked the huts and treetops together, headed to the village's center main tree that was hollowed in the middle. Instead of taking the twirling staircase they jumped on the elevator pulley system and were let down to the ground by the men on guard. She and Adda didn't have to run far before they met up with Wilkins at ground level. They both threw their arms around him and were welcomed with the same enthusiasm.

Wilkins pulled his wife and youngest into his arms, wishing with all his heart that his other three were there as well.

Harper looked up at her husband, "Thank the Creator you're all right. Where are Wynne and Bain, and have you heard from Seadon?"

"I spoke to Seadon just before I left the communications bunker, he's fine. And Wynne is with Finn and Paisley at the LSS offices, along with Father, Mother, and Gracelynn."

"What about Bain, and I haven't seen Raila. I'm not sure where she went."

Wilkins took a deep breath and released it. He looked at Harper and began to explain about Raila, Kreelie, Rodan, their friends at the LSS, Silus, and Nan Trea.

"Oh Wilkins, so much death," she stated between tears. "How's Bain? Where *is* Bain?" she insisted, worry beginning to take hold in her chest at what her husband wasn't saying.

"He's fine, Harper," he quickly said, seeing the worry and agitation beginning to build in Harper's demeanor. "At least physically anyway."

"What does that mean?" Harper urged, confused.

"He isn't handling all the death very well. I think he blames himself for Raila's death. Kreelie and Silus were close to him, as well as all his tech friends dying and then Nan Trea, the woman who basically helped raise him; he just said he had to get away from all of it for a while and then took off."

"He didn't say where he was going?"

"No. Just to tell you and Adda, and everyone else, that he loves you and he would contact us when he could."

"Oh, Wilkins. This war, these Scaithers," she spat out, "they've destroyed so many lives with their greed and lust! I don't see life returning to normal. I'm afraid nothing will ever be the same again."

"You're right there. Zanchier is forever changed. Loradin's defenses are destroyed. The defense barrier's mainframe uplink server is fried. The Scaithers took it out when they attacked Loradin. It was like they knew exactly where and what to hit. Someone else inside with privileged information had to be an informant for them. Treetop Village is truly the last safe place for anyone. Let's just hope we can keep it that way."

Harper looked up at the swaying rope bridges, barely visible from the ground. "And there is no way it can support many more refugees. It's overcrowded now."

The three of them followed the rest of the men up the stairway into the treetops for a momentary rest from the ever-encroaching war.

As they were making the climb up the stairway, they heard hurried crunching in the forest below. They all stopped as Wilkins ran back down the stairs, his weapon raised to take out whoever or whatever was headed their way.

Wilkins stood at the base of Main Tree; his weapon ready. The bushes out to the left of him rustled loudly like a herd of Raisedback Vindapers were about to break through. Then suddenly, out popped Delmar Bamerly and Caislan Harrington. They stopped abruptly; their hands rising in the air. "Woah, it's just us!" Delmar yelled.

Wilkins hung his head in relief and disbelief. "Boys, don't you know the signal, and to be quiet when going through the woods? You're lucky I'm not a nervous shot."

"Sorry, Mr. Brinley. We're just tired. We've been running for the last thirty minutes trying to outrun a Pagorinx back that way, chasing us from the treetops." Delmar pointed behind them.

Wilkins quickly looked up, scanning the branches overhead. "Well hurry up you two, into the trees. Let's get camouflaged for a while. Where did you two come from anyway? Weren't you stationed at Fort Arvenguard?"

"Yes sir," Caislan answered. "We were the only two to get away with our lives. We took the tunnels to Sandedge, but we were only there a brief time before it too was attacked. Our ammunition ran out, so we took off toward the Carpasian Mountains, and here."

"Yeah," Delmar interjected, "we're starving."

Wilkins grinned and slapped them on the shoulders. "Well let's get you boys fed then."

They all ventured up into the trees for a meal and a little down time. Wilkins would not stay for long, as many of the warriors would not. They would have to get back to the bunker and the fight if Zanchier had any chance of winning against the Scaithers. Hiding out forever was not an option. The rest of Zanchier still suffered greatly at the evil destructive hands of the Scaithers and their leader Riglan Mortruff, who was proving to be the most ruthless in the history of crime bosses.

After a night of rest and being with Harper and Adda, Wilkins and any warriors that Treetop could spare, went back to Discovery Falls. What they didn't expect to find when they walked in was the total destruction of the place. The dozen or so people who had lived at the bunker were dead. There were also several dead Scaithers.

Wilkins shook his head at yet more losses.

Caislan asked, "How did they know about the bunker?"

"I'm not sure. But they knew something was out here because they sent that laser module out to the forest edge yesterday. They knew we were hiding somewhere; it was only a matter of time before they discovered the bunker. We need to keep a lookout from now on. The bunker is compromised and that means that Treetop Village could be as well. We must be extra careful from now on when traveling back and forth. We're going to have to switch to night travel only."

One of the village men stated, "But that's deadly. The carnivorous forest creatures could kill us all."

Wilkins looked at the man. "That's the chance we're going to have to take. It's either that or risk exposing Treetop, our families, and all the others who shelter there."

Everyone agreed Wilkins was right.

Wilkins looked around at the devastation. "All right everybody, let's get the dead buried and this place cleaned up. I want lookouts stationed at every exit, except the village tunnel. We also need to find someone who is good with technology to repair the smashed consoles and control panels. And let's make certain there is nothing in here anywhere that could lead any future invaders to think there is another hide-out nearby."

Bain crossed the Lumens River Bridge, taking a hard left to follow the gypsy trails. Few people knew which directions they traveled, but he had noticed their caravans several times while out exploring Praxtingen over the years. He had even had a few conversations with Aliyah, the old leathery healer woman, and her granddaughter Natalia who he guessed was in her late thirties. Natalia was the leader of the gypsies and a tough woman to boot from what he gathered the few times he had interacted with them.

The trail led into the southern part of the Carpasian Mountains near Overton Colony. He would have to be extra careful because he knew Overton had been one of the first cities taken over by the Scaithers a few years back. But the good thing about Scaithers, once settled in their debauchery, they grew lazy, drunkenly, and careless. Hopefully, the ones living it up in Overton were just that. The gypsy trails were well hidden and masked, but they often passed by cities all over Zanchier for trading purposes. However, the Gypsies had a way of disappearing quickly if needed. Bain didn't know how they did it, just that they could vanish suddenly without a trace. Something he hoped to learn quickly.

Night was falling and he needed to find a secure safe place to make camp. If he could find the gypsy camp in the Carpasian Mountains then he could build a fire for warmth, otherwise he wouldn't chance being found out. The quickly approaching winter weather was growing colder by the week. He needed to make it to the Treehouse in the Xantifal Mountains before the heavy blue snows of Zanchier set into full drop mode or he might not survive the trip. He traveled the trail as best as he could make out in the growing dark, found the presently deserted gypsy campsite, hunkered back underneath a rock ledge for protection, and built a fire for warmth. He snuggled down into his sleeping sack, grabbed a piece of Vindaper jerky as a quick meal, and soon drifted off to sleep.

Bain woke four hours later to the sound of distant howls in the night. His fire had fortunately stayed burning to ward off any wild animals, and to keep him warm. It had snowed during the night, blanketing the ground and trees in a light blue sheen. He stoked the fire a bit, adding more wood to it to keep it burning longer. The chill in the air had a bite to it so he broke out the small coffee tin he had brought, put the small kettle of water on the fire to boil, and waited for the strong brew to seep. Since he was fully awake, he would have a quick breakfast and coffee, then pack up and head out again. He had no idea how long it would take him to get to the Xantifal Mountains going the long way around, but he had no desire to be captured by Scaithers. Crossing Everly Lake would have taken him about twenty-four to forty-eight hours in total. Going around the Southern Carpasian, White, and Bleak Mountains would likely take him a week. He didn't even know anyone who had ever gone in that direction. No one ever went into or passed by the White Mountains. In academy, they were always told that there was nothing but death out past the mountains. He wasn't even certain that the gypsies had ever traveled that way, and they knew practically everything there was to know about Zanchier and its geographical mysteries.

His coffee was brewed and his food warmed so he ate his breakfast, doused the fire, and waited for the sun to break over the horizon of the mountains. Once the sunrise lit the sky he straddled the bi-mod and took off once more headed southeast along the gypsy trailway. Once he reached the end of the mountains, the trail turned back northeast. He knew that would take him near Sandedge and Rhamadon. He stopped the Bi-mod, looked around and decided to travel along the base of the White Mountains. There was nothing but desert to his left and the eerie white landscape of the mountains to his right. He drove for an hour before coming to a stand of green trees that sat by the edge of a massive body of water. Bain was glad to see it, he could fill his canteen. He remembered the gypsies telling stories to the children as entertainment when they would visit the villages, long before the wars broke out. They often spoke of large water, so blue you could see through to the bottom. They also would bring these things called shells with them and tell the children that creatures from the big water lived inside some of the shells at one time. Bain had always thought the stories to be fictitious; made up to entertain. At least that is what everyone would tell the children once the gypsies left. All the children would be excited and want to venture out to see the big water and find shells for themselves. The adults told them the shells likely came from south of Sandbar Beach since many had been found out that way over the years. And that there were more to be found closer to the Marshlands, but no one ventured there for fear of death, and certainly not to look for shells.

Bain went to the edge of the big water, watching the waves roll in and crash against the shoreline. The cool breeze that blew off the water brushed against his face. It was warmer this far south than it was in the colder interior of the mountain surrounded lake. Bain leaned down and cupped the water, bringing it to his mouth. He quickly spit the water back out, surprised by the extremely salty nature of it.

"Well, I can't fill my canteens here," he said to himself. "I wonder if this is where the brackish water of the Marshlands comes from? That would explain why that part of Everly Lake is partly salty; which means, there must be some waterways that link to the lake."

Bain walked around a bit, looking for some fresh water in amongst the scattered trees in the sand but found nothing. He straddled the bi-mod once more and took off, staying closer to the mountains and the firmer sand there which made traveling easier.

He headed southwest knowing that the Xantifal Mountains lay in that direction. Nearly seven hours later he came upon a large waterfall at the edge of the mountainside which fed into a small lake. He got off the bi-mod and walked over to the lake. Freshwater! Bain excitedly filled his canteens with the cool tasting liquid, then decided to sit by the water for a while and have a late lunch. He wanted to make suitable time but needed a break from the constant riding and driving. The bi-mod could be a rough ride, but a regular module would have never been able to traverse some of the terrain he had come across. He figured he only had about five more hours of daylight before he would have to make camp. He would have to start looking for a safe place to bed down. This was unfamiliar territory; one the gypsies apparently didn't even dare to travel.

While he sat resting, he looked around at the lush greenery that flourished near the lake and the small river that flowed from the south end of it. He noticed some small spots of color in some of the trees and decided to walk around and explore the area. He soon realized the spots of color were some sort of fruit growing in amongst the bushes and trees. He plucked one of the low-hanging fruits from the tree and turned the oval shaped, reddish-yellow fruit over in his hands. He bit into the flesh noticing its sweet, yet slightly tangy flavor as juice ran down his chin. He spit the tough, bitter hide out but savored the flesh of it. He had never tasted anything like it. He picked several from the bushes, gathering various kinds and wrapping them in a shirt, trying not to smash them, and stowed them in his pack. He even saw some coconuts like the ones back in Port Proud laying on the ground. He gathered some of them as well for the sweet liquid and pulpy sweet flesh.

Bain went back to the bi-mod and traveled south along the river from the falls, hoping to find a way across or around the river. Strangely enough he came to where the forked river merged into one stream, finding a small bridge which spanned the river. This surprised him because that meant that at some point someone had lived here. Bridges didn't build themselves. This comforted Bain some, but also made him a little nervous as well. He wasn't sure who or what he could run upon out this way, and he decided he would have to be cautious.

One of the ingenious things about the bi-mods was their ability to switch into a stealth mode. Being an LSS operative's piece of equipment, the tech team had made certain the machines could be as quiet as possible, switching off the noisier engine and over to a battery that allowed it to run quietly on the power of the sun. This made it super quiet and travel efficient. It didn't have the same power as the fuel driven engine, but since Bain doubted he'd be able to find any fuel out this far, he was grateful for the technology.

Bain was surprised to find that the lush greenery continued west and he noticed another river that ran along the base of the mountains; which were no longer white but turned brown with hints of life part of the way up. Bain wondered if the change meant he was nearing the Bleak Mountains.

The scenery stayed the same for several hours until he came to another freshwater lake, likely fed by the same falls. He traveled thirty minutes south finding that the lake did not feed out to another river. As he rounded the lake headed west, traveling another thirty minutes, he came upon some ruins; fragments and large pieces of once whole buildings. The area looked to have once upon a time, been a large and flourishing city. Now, it was reduced to nothing more than someone's memories from long ago, buried in the desert sands. He traveled further into the ruins, finding a large walled city, the once massive wooden gates now laying in front of the opening, half buried in the sand. Bain rode inside the courtyard and looked around. There definitely wasn't anything living here. This place had long been forgotten. Bain wondered what had happened here, and why no one else in Zanchier knew about it. Or if they did, it was a very well-kept secret.

After looking around, Bain decided this was the best place to make camp. He chose a tall portico on the wall, made sure there was nothing else taking up residence inside, and made a fire for warmth. Although it was warmer here in the south, the night began to take on a chill, and the fire would hopefully warn off any curious creatures.

Chapter 17

The Forgotten Coast

Wynne and Roamey flew over the mountains and trees of the southern Carpasian Mountains searching for Bain. The sun was just breaking over the mountain ridge bathing the landscape in warmth, a contrast to the chilly winter air. Last night's snowfall made tracking anyone or anything near impossible.

"Roamey," Wynne complained out loud, "how could Bain just leave like that without telling anyone where he's going?" Roamey squawked his reply, which didn't help her at all.

Her father had no idea where he had gone, and the only clue she had was the few people who saw a bi-mod traveling along the southern road toward Sandbar Beach. There wasn't much else out that way. Unless he had joined up with the traveling gypsies, what else was there?

She knew the gypsy roads well. Being on sky patrol nearly every morning and evening for the past three years, she saw a lot. She knew where several of the gypsy's hidden camps were, along with their hidden trailways, and even how they could sometimes just vanish without a trace.

She and Roamey followed the trail past Overton Colony. The once beautiful walled city was now home to mostly Scaithers who cared for nothing, so the city had slowly fallen into ruin. They continued their flight southeast along the trail but found no sign of Bain. She had been searching for hours and decided to give Roamey a rest and return home. She needed to check in with Jerod and Moshi anyway since the LARS Animal Brigade had to make some serious decisions now that Loradin had been compromised.

Her grandfather Aaric, the newly appointed governor of Loradin and its outer territories, was working around the clock trying to get the Loradin Barrier repaired. Unfortunately, many of the people who knew how to fix it had perished in the recent Scaither attack. Kamsten Whitsler and Maubrey Vanderpol were the only two tech geniuses left in Loradin and were doing what they could to fix the barrier, but again, parts were scarce as the metal from the Rhe Mines was now under complete control by Riglan Mortruff and his Scaithers.

Wynne remembered Riglan from her earlier academy years in Port Proud. Though he was six years her senior, his reputation as a bully went all the way down the chain. Everyone had known him as a mean prankster who picked on anyone he could, but never alone. He always had his cronies with him. But nothing would have ever made her think that he could be capable of such cruelty. At the early age of twenty, he had already cemented his reputation to become known as the cruelest and most tyrannical crime lord to have ever lived. This alone made her fear for Zanchier's future, her future. What kind of world would they have left to live in if Riglan Mortruff's rule continued? She shuddered to think of it.

Because of the state of Zanchier, and the uncertainty of anything, her father Wilkins had requested she come to stay at Treetop Village with the rest of them. They even sent for Seadon too, but he was so involved with LAPS that he had told father no. He said he was needed there. Many airships were destroyed in the last fight over Everly Lake, and even more with the most recent Scaither attack. After several crashes and the deaths of a few students, some of the students were now too afraid to fly and had left Airship Academy and the LAPS Corp, but Seadon was determined to stay and tough it out.

Wynne and Roamey flew back across the Carpasian Mountains headed north. She would com-call Jerod later after settling in at Treetop Village. Roamey would likely enjoy living in the forest again. He could hunt for his dinner and play in the trees and learn to build a nest; all the things that wild Kabihanxu do. Teaching him to do these things herself might be a challenge, but perhaps they could find a wild firebird to observe and learn from it.

A few hours later, Wynne and Roamey carefully and as quietly as possible, landed in the forest near Treetop, looking around for Scaither activity before moving toward the village. She and Roamey walked leisurely through the thick underbrush, coming upon the small clearing where the main tree of the village sat. Upon their arrival, several of the LARS students staying at Treetop came running out to greet them, Dr. Barrister following quickly after them.

"Wynne," Dr. Barrister greeted, "good to see you. I didn't know you were coming out here today."

"I've come to stay. Father asked me to." Just then, she heard her name called from somewhere in the treetops. Her mother Harper came running down the main tree's spiral staircase. Her mother enveloped her in her arms, squeezing tightly.

"Mother," Wynne said, squeezing her back. Right behind Harper was Adda.

"Adda, it's good to see you," Wynne stated with a hug.

"Oh Wynne, I'm so glad you're here to stay. I've missed you terribly, and Roamey!" Adda excitedly said.

"We've missed you too, Adda."

"Although, I must admit that I miss Wren more," Adda stated, her demeanor suddenly turning sad.

Wynne understood her feelings. She didn't know what she would do without Roamey. "I'm sure she misses you too."

All the children, including Adda, quickly hurried to Roamey's side, playing with, and petting the massive bird. Roamey loved the attention and squawked and stomped in excitement. Wynne looked over her shoulder at him and gave a small warning.

"Roamey, behave. No rides without my permission, got it?"

Roamey squawked and nodded his head a few times in agreement. Wynne and Harper walked arm in arm up the main tree steps to get her settled in.

Harper asked, "Wil said you went in search of Bain this morning. Any luck finding him?"

"No, sorry Mother. There was no sign of him."

Harper's worried expression made Wynne quickly add, "But, I'm sure he's fine. He is an LSS agent and quite capable of handling himself, and stellar at hiding. He'll let us know where he is when he wants to be found."

Harper grinned at her. "When did you become so wise?"

"I've always been like this, remember? Your little adult?" Wynne giggled, causing Harper to laugh too.

Harper hugged her sideways. "Oh, how I've missed you and your humor."

"Oh! Not to change the subject, but Aunt Paisley had the baby."

"What? Already? Are they all right?"

"Yes, just fine. They named her Reesa."

"I'm glad all is well with them," Harper stated.

"Yes, as am I. Goodness how I've missed you Mother. And Father, and Adda. I just wish Seadon would come to stay as well, and I hope Bain figures out what he needs to soon and comes back to us, which I'm certain he will. He never was one to run from a fight."

"Well, he isn't exactly running from the fight. More like running from his feelings. This war has been especially hard on him losing most of his friends, and then Raila too."

"I know. I really miss Silus as well. He was one unique person. And Raila and I had become pretty close too while working at LARS together over the years. I hope this war will end soon."

Harper's heart ached for her children. "I do too, sweetheart, but I fear it never will."

Bain woke early the next morning, remaking the fire that had gone out sometime during the night. He had slept hard last night. Better than the night before. Perhaps the long hours on the bi-mod were taking their toll. He stood up and stretched, strapping on his gun. He then grabbed several of the fresh fruits he had picked, and his canteen, deciding to walk around to explore the ruins a bit.

He headed back out the southern gate of the walled courtyard and walked south toward the large body of saltwater, finding an old dock-house with wharfs that stretched out into the water. Several of them were broken and falling apart from years of neglect and likely storms. He walked north back toward the exterior of the abandoned city. As he walked around the walls, he came to a large bridge that spanned a wide river that stretched from somewhere south of the mountains to the saltwater behind him. The bridge was wide like it had serviced many modules passing side by side. Much too large for just foot traffic, which led him to believe that whoever once inhabited this city, also had some other form of transportation.

Bain looked at the matter arranging device on his left wrist. Apparently his MAD had been damaged somehow in the last fight, or he could just use the MAD to get to the treehouse. Perhaps it had been damaged when he and Raila had slid into the bunker on the bi-mod?

A sudden pain hit Bain's chest as thoughts and images of Raila flew into his mind. This sudden onslaught caused him to double over a little, falling to the ground as hyperventilation took over his breathing. He leaned against the side walls of the bridge and spent the next several minutes trying to get his breathing under control. Thoughts of Raila, Kreelie, and all those he lost were doing strange things to his body, and he needed to try to manage that. He couldn't afford to lose control out here in the wild. He could take the time to mourn their loss later when he got to the treehouse in the Xantifal Mountains.

Once Bain got his emotions under control, he walked partway over the bridge and scanned the area around him from the higher vantage point. He could see another large, dilapidated, structure to the west, and another one to the northeast behind the larger walled structure where he slept last night. He decided there was too much to explore on foot and went back to get the bi-mod. He straddled the module and went through the western gate of the courtyard. He followed the wide river north passing the smaller broken buildings. He came to an area of the river where large boulders came into view and blocked the passage beside the river. Bain parked the bi-mod, scaled one of the large boulders, and stood viewing what was on the other side. From his place high upon the rocks he could see that the Marshlands bordered the strange forgotten city. He could also make out what appeared to be Cactus Valley far to the west, which meant Rock City was just beyond that. Directly to his west was the Bleak Mountains. He knew from lore, and more importantly his recent experience, that Hungerhounds dwelt in the Bleak Mountains and ventured out to Rock City when food would happen to appear. Meaning, Bain had best be on the lookout, and avoid the mountains as much as possible. He certainly didn't want to fight off a pack of Hungerhounds, especially not alone.

Bain quickly slid back down the boulders and headed back to the walled courtyard. He had already spent the morning exploring the outer city area and so decided to spend one more night here. He'd take the rest of the day exploring the many interior buildings and doorways which led inside the rock walled structure.

He grabbed a quick lunch and set out exploring once again, deciding to com-call his father to let him know what he'd discovered on the south side of the White Mountains.

Wilkins picked up the call quickly. "Bain? Where are you Son?"

"I'm fine, Father, don't worry. I just wanted to tell you about this place I've found."

Wilkins exhaled loudly. "Thank you for checking in. Your mother and I have been worried sick."

"I know and I'm sorry. But did you know there used to be a pretty large city southwest of the Southern White Mountains?"

"How did you get back there? And what are you doing that far south?"

"I'll explain later. Anyhow, did you know about this city?"

"No, actually. I've never heard of anything being outside the mountain ranges that surround Zanchier. We were always told as children that the mountains went on forever and if they did end, it was only into desert, which also went on forever. The White Mountains and the Dune Seas that surround the lake and cities were also so desolate that no one ever dared to try to cross them."

"No one ever ventured through the marsh either?" Bain asked, surprised.

"I've heard that people tried long ago but were never heard from again. People assumed they died in the Marshlands or were killed by Hungerhounds. You need to be careful out there on your own, Son. I wouldn't want a similar fate to befall you."

"I'll be all right, Father. I'm being very cautious."

Wilkins took a moment before replying. "So you say there's a city there?"

"Yes, a large one, just between the Bleak and White Mountains. The desert sands have ravished it mostly, but it could be made livable again. It could be the answer to escaping the Scaithers. It's obvious that no one knows about this place, or if they do, they're not concerned with returning. There are a lot of fruit trees and plants here too, about thirty minutes to the east. They're even still loaded with fruit. The weather is much milder here as well. It's cooler for a desert climate, but there is no frigid wind or snows. The night gets quite a bit colder, but it warms up quickly with the arrival of the sun."

"Maybe we can get Wynne and Roamey, or Seadon and the airships to check things out."

"Maybe," Bain replied growing quiet. "Well, I'd best let you go. I'll check back in when I can."

"Bain, can't you at least tell me where it is you're headed?"

"Not yet, Father. But I promise to check in every day to let you know I'm still alive."

"Please do, Son. It will put both mine and your Mother's minds at ease."

"Yes sir."

"Bain, we love you."

"I love you too, Father. Give Mother my love as well." Bain disconnected the call and continued his exploration of the interior of the thick walls of the city.

Night began to fall quickly and the chill in the air made him shiver. He went back to the area on the southern wall where he had made camp and lit a fire. Just as the fire began to grow and light the area around him, he heard a noise. It sounded like a low growl from somewhere within the city walls. Bain pulled out his torchlight with one hand and his laser gun with the other. He carefully scanned the inner courtyard of the ruins, following the light with his laser poised and ready. Then, he saw them walking through the western gate. Looking his way were several large Hungerhounds.

Bain stopped moving, his breathing escalated to a small panic. He hoped the fire that stood between him and the hounds would deter them from approaching. He quickly glanced around the interior of the walls, looking for an escape. He noticed a flight of steps that led up to the top of the turret. Sudden movement from the corner of his eye caught his attention as the Hungerhounds began their approach in his direction.

Bain took off up the turret, taking the narrow steps two at a time, passing the safety of the narrow second level entryway.

He could hear the snarling and barking of the Hungerhounds as they got closer. He barred the heavy wooden door after running through, sliding the still solid bolt into the cut-out hole of the rock. He hoped the hounds wouldn't fit through the staircase, and if they could, maybe the door would hold them off long enough for him to find a secure hiding place. Bain ran as fast as he could, scanning the area as he went. He went up another flight of steps that led to the open ledge of the walls top walkway, which led around the entire length of the courtyard walls, although parts of it were crumbling and broken. The only problem was, there was nowhere up here to hide. He hoped the Hungerhounds couldn't climb the tall stone walls. As he stopped to glance around to determine his next move, he captured the attention of a hound still standing in the courtyard below; the other two snarling and scratching at the wooden door, which sounded as though the wood wouldn't hold much longer.

"What to do, what to do?" Bain said aloud. He fired off his laser gun at the Hungerhound who was now trying to scale the wall after him. He hit it on the side, making it fall and yelp in pain. It got up and continued leaping and jumping toward Bain, gnashing its blood-stained teeth, and yipping in hunger and pain as it pawed at the wall, scratching off pieces of aged and weakened stone.

"I need some help here!" he said loudly to the sky, hoping the Creator would hear his plea.

The other two hounds that had been busy tearing at the door gave up their quest and returned to the courtyard. The yip and cry of the now injured hound grabbing their attention. They both spotted Bain and began leaping and biting at him. The injured hound tried to do its part, but only aggravated the other two. One of the hounds turned on the injured one and began fighting with it, tearing at the bloody flesh of the beast. Bain thought that he only had to worry about the one hound whose attention he could not shake, but the hound attacking the injured one killed it, then turned its attention back to Bain to help the other one in the attack.

"Anytime now!" Bain yelled in expectation, waiting on divine help from above.

As the hounds leaped and pawed at the wall, with Bain running along the top, headed toward another turret to get out of the open air and their line of sight, one of the hounds managed to jump up on the wall behind him. Bain shot his laser at the one following and running along the ground below. He missed, and tried again, trying to stay ahead of the hound now chasing him along the top of the wall. This time he hit the beast in the head, stopping it and making it whine and circle in pain as it pawed at its own flesh, trying to scratch off whatever was burning its head.

Bain ran as fast as his feet would carry him, unable to turn and fire at the beast chasing him without stopping completely. Just as the Hungerhound stretched out its long, shaggy-haired, neck to snatch Bain up for dinner, the Brindelwren appeared, slamming into the side of the hound with its large head, and knocking the hound off the wall, slamming its body into the desert sand as it slid to a stop halfway across the inside of the courtyard. The Brindelwren bellowed a loud throaty call as if warning the creatures not to try and attack again. The hounds limped away yipping in fear, turning to snarl one last time before disappearing through the south gate into the dark desert beyond.

Bain looked up at the massive creature. It looked even larger than it had the day he saw it in the bio-luminescent world beneath the Marshlands.

"Thank you, Wren!" Bain yelled up to the creature. The Brindelwren turned toward him, stared at him for a moment, then lifted its head in the air giving a mighty shake, sending its kelpy mane flying all around it. It then moved its head closer to Bain and snorted a small blast of air in his direction, poking him in the torso with her nose. Bain wasn't certain how to react, but if she was this close to him, she must not be frightened, or hungry. He reached out and stroked her nose as she made an undulating purring sound with her throat.

Bain asked the beast, "Do you remember me?"

Wren nodded her head up and down.

Bain smiled broadly. "Thank you, Wren. You saved my life." He knew he couldn't communicate with the creature the way his sisters did, but he knew she understood his words. She purred again, making another soft reverberating noise before turning back to the river behind her. She slowly slid into the water, turned once more to look at Bain, and then disappeared below the surface, headed in the direction of Everly Lake.

"I knew Everly Lake had to connect to the saltwater somewhere. And boy am I thankful it does." Bain offered a quick thank you to the Creator, then stood there, watching the large water ripples in the moonlight on top of the river until he couldn't see them anymore. He decided to grab his pack items and find a higher point to sleep for the night. One that was more protected. After quickly putting out the fire he had built earlier, he chose the highest point with the most walls and fewest windows, kept his weapons near his body, and drifted off into a broken sleep for the next eight hours.

Chapter 18

A New Home

Wilkins, Harper, Wynne, and the entire village of Treetop woke in the early morning hours to the clang of the warning bell as the night guards rang the alert.

"Invaders!" yelled the night guards over and over as they clanged the bells as forcefully as possible, one taking a bullet for his efforts and falling to his death over the balcony railing.

People scampered in every direction, as flamed arrows flew across the railings and through hut windows. Men carrying flamethrowers walked beneath them, lighting up the entire forest.

Roamey squawked in protest as he walked the ground below, defending the village from the Scaithers. He blew fire from his beak, screeching in anger as he did. Many men ran in fear, not having the prized Rhe armor as protection. Only those in the highest commands received such luxuries.

The men fired at Roamey with their guns, the bullets bouncing off his armored skin beneath the colorful feathers. He fought against the invaders, picking them up and throwing them through the trees, and lighting fire to anyone within proximity of his powerful breath. People ran as Roamey fought, the village warriors breaking out weapons in the dim morning light to fight back against their adversaries.

Treetop Village began to burn in many areas as families took to the escape routes. Main Tree was packed with people descending the staircase and the elevator, as the men working it pulled it up and down as quickly as possible.

The stronger refugees used the rope and pulley systems that hung from the trees in many various places; the weighted sandbags acting as counter-weights for a safe descent from the huts above. Wynne called to Roamey who flew up to the railing near one of the huts and hovered there until Wynne and Adda could climb on his back.

Wilkins urged, "Wynne, take your sister to safety."

"Where Father? What place do you consider safe?"

"I don't know, Wynne! Just find someplace!"

"What about you and Mother?"

"We have to stay and fight. Someone has to help the others."

"That's what Roamey and I am for, Father. We stand a better chance at fighting than you do."

"Your sister…"

"Is fine! We will protect her!" Wynne yelled. She turned to Adda. "Hold on tightly, no matter what, understand?" Adda shook her head in understanding. They flew down, lighting the ground on fire around the approaching invaders.

Roamey flew higher so that Wynne could assess how many more invaders were coming. It was hard for her to make out the extent of the invasion for the trees below, but there looked to be hundreds.

The other forest creatures came to the aid of Treetop Village as LARS students called them into action. Tribhons swung from the trees, slicing at the men with their long razor-sharp claws and stinging them into temporary paralysis with their tails. Trefells bowled people over while others quickly chewed through smaller trees, dropping them on the men. A few young Pagorinxes that the children had been studying and interacting with while at Treetop were called upon as well, quickly dropping down on the enemy or scaring them into retreating. Wild Raisedback Vindapers sliced at men's legs with their protruding tusks and trampled them underfoot. Woodstrikers slithered their way into the men's clothing and bit at their ankles, poisoning many and frightening even more.

The battle to save Treetop was a long one. Men and woman tried putting out the fires in between fighting to save the village. Those that had left the safety of the trees and ran along the ground were cut down by enemy fire and blades. Men, women, and children were either slaughtered, or the women and children were stolen away and placed in ankle chains and secured to trees to prevent them from running away. Scaithers stole that which they desired; taking what they wanted with no apologies and no care for anyone else.

People tried to free those that were chained but were captured themselves for their efforts. The animals, their bond-mates, and the armed men and women, were so busy fighting off the attack that they couldn't rescue the others. Women screamed for their children and the children cried in fear as they were pulled from their mother's arms. The snatched children and women were then thrown into modules modified for mountain travel and hurriedly whisked away to some unknown location.

The fighting lasted for almost thirty minutes before the creatures that protected the village eventually killed or ran off the last of the invaders. Less than a hundred people were all who remained compared to the many hundreds that were living at Treetop Village. Many were injured, but not mortally. Many had been killed, and others captured. Men who had lost their wives and children to Scaither kidnapping were trying to form plans to get their loved ones back, most knowing it was a lost cause. To go after the Scaithers with so few men would be suicide.

Wilkins and Harper met with Adda and Wynne in a small clearing near the base of Main Tree.

Wilkins looked at Wynne. "We need to see who all we can round up in the forest that might be injured and bring them back up into the treehouses. There are several huts that are damage free that should be large enough to house the survivors."

"Yes sir. Roamey and I will check the forest around the camp."

"Those of us who can, will search closer to the village and clean up here."

Wynne and Roamey took to the canopy of the tall trees to search for any injured or lost Treetop refugees.

Wilkins turned to Harper. "Tonight, we'll discuss what needs to be done. The Scaithers will be back. We need to find a place where we don't have to fight everyday of our lives just to survive."

"I agree. But, Wilkins, where in Zanchier are we going to be able to find such a place?"

"Remember when I told you I spoke to Bain yesterday?"

"Yes, but what does that have to do with Treetop Village?"

"He told me of an ancient city that he found south of the White Mountains. One where fruit trees grow prolifically, and there is another saltwater lake, more vast than Everly Lake. Perhaps it's time that we do what's best for us instead of everyone else."

"You mean leave Zanchier?"

"Perhaps. If that's where this journey leads us. It's better than staying here and losing people we know and care about nearly every day."

"Is there a way we can find out more about this place? Does it even have a name?"

"Bain just called it a forgotten coastal city."

"Well, it's certainly worth a shot, but what about everyone else?"

"We'll offer to let them come along, but it's ultimately their choice. And we won't tell anyone where we're going just in case they get captured. Only we will know where and how to get there. We can send Seadon out with an airship to scout the terrain as well as Wynne and Roamey."

"If you think it's worth a shot then I'm game. But perhaps before we just take off blindly, we can inquire of the gypsies. They know just about every place around or near here. Maybe they'll know of this Forgotten Coast?" Harper stated.

"It's worth a shot, but that's telling them where we're going," Wilkins warned.

"Perhaps even Riglan isn't brave enough to mess with the gypsies for fear of being cursed. I know his father Vonder was very superstitious, and I'm hoping Riglan is as well."

"All right. We'll see if Wynne knows where they are at this moment or can track them down. Either way, by this time tomorrow, I hope to be headed out of Zanchier and out of the reach of the Scaithers," Wilkins stated bluntly.

Bain struck out early the next morning, hoping to ride as far as he could without stopping. The attack by the Hungerhounds the night before gave him enough sense to not stop until he got past the Bleak Mountain range and into the southern part of Xantifal. He would ride hard and fast. He figured, and hoped, that the bi-mod would outrun the hounds if they pursued him. And if he stayed closer to the edge of the Dune Sea, but close enough to the Bleak Mountains to have firm soil to ride on, then he should be all right and able to travel at top speeds. He had enough fuel on board to run the powerful engine most if not all the way. He figured he had at least a fifteen-hour ride at full throttle before he could consider himself safe from the beasts. Maybe he should call his Father to let him know of the dangers? No. He would tell him when he reached the Xantifal Mountains, when he knew he would be safe. No sense in worrying his parents when he knew he was still in danger.

He prayed to the Creator for protection, strapped his hand laser to the back of his right hand, wrapped his gun around his torso with it facing his chest for easy retrieval, stuffed his left jacket pocket with some jerky and smaller fruit, and made certain that his canteen was easily accessible so he wouldn't have to stop for hydration. He would eat and drink as little as possible to prevent having to stop to relieve himself since such a stop could very well end up being his last.

He pointed the bi-mod toward the west and took off out the gate of the ruin city. Fifteen minutes later he hit the large expanse of bridge going so fast the bi-mod became slightly airborne for a moment. As he traveled out across the sand, trying to decide on the firmest route to take, he could hear the distant howls of the Hungerhounds. He throttled the bi-mod even more and sped out across the packed sandy ground, hoping that he hadn't made the wrong decision about disappearing for a while.

Wilkins had spent the entire morning on com-calls with everyone he could think of about the attempt at seeing what lay beyond the White Mountains, just south of the Marshlands. From every angle that they knew of, the brown dead landscape of the Bleak Mountains collided with the White Mountains just past the Marshlands. But according to what Bain said yesterday on the com, there was a definite pass between the two. Whether or not that pass was able to be traveled was the question.

Wynne sought out the gypsies to question them about the Forgotten Coast, as her mother took to calling it. Fortunately, she came across the caravan headed north toward Sandedge not too far from Treetop Village.

Madame Aliyah, now accustomed to seeing the girl Wynne and her firebird Roamey, slowed the Yarequu pulling the wagon to a stop just shy of where Wynne and Roamey had landed.

"Madame Aliyah, thank you for stopping to talk with me," Wynne stated, still sitting aback Roamey.

"Certainly, young Wynne. What can I do for you?" The Yarequu spooked a bit standing so near a creature they often avoided in nature. "Woah, old girl, that creature will do you no harm with Miss Wynne nearby."

"My father bid me to ask you about a ruin city south of the Marshlands. Do you know of it?"

Aliyah took a deep breath, looking at Wynne sideways, unsure she wished to retell the tragic story. "Are you certain you wish to hear this tale? It's not a happy ending; full of darkness and pain," Aliyah cautioned.

Wynne nodded. "Yes, please. If you don't mind?"

Aliyah set the brake on the wagon, laid down the reigns, and turned to face Wynne.

"My ancestors told us of a place on the coast that was called Miracle City, like the waterfall that once, or perhaps still does, exist east of there. But my story begins in the lesser city to the west of Miracle City and the Salt River called, Meribow."

"What happened to the people that lived there?"

"I know the story well. Our ancestors hail from there, and what transpired in that cursed place is a truly tragic tale. The city and its people fell under a cursed moon, many, many years ago. There was a family—my great, great, great, grandparents to be exact—that was different than everyone else. The man worked hard for his family and was a pleasant, quiet fellow. The woman was an herbalist, like we gypsies. She often created tinctures and healing potions for people who were ill. Even though she helped people, this made them whisper about her. Some even called her a witch or said she was possessed by evil spirits. They had a son and a daughter, both of whom could communicate with the creatures around them; like you and the others at LARS do. The children were both gentle and kind at heart, helpful to anyone who needed it. However, their abilities frightened the people of Miracle and Meribow Cities, and they often shunned and chastised the children, calling them witches as well. The family ignored the taunts of the ignorant people, until one fateful day when things escalated and the taunts and jeers from the villagers could no longer be overlooked.

Some young boys were picking on the girl; becoming quite violent. The girl was playing with a young Hungerhound—likely known as something else back then. The creatures were docile in those days; for the boy and girl at least. Anyhow, the boys became violent with her, and she became frightened. Her pleas for them to stop, and her cries for help, were overlooked by the people of Meribow City as they passed by, ignoring what was happening. The hound pup growled and snarled at the people, who also beat the creature. Her brother heard her cries and rushed to her side to help, but he too was overtaken by the growing group of people who were joining in against the two children and the juvenile hound. As the children's fear grew, the agitation of the creatures that dwelt in the Bleak and White Mountains grew as well. The creatures sensed the children's fear and pain and heard their cries for help. Many creatures came down out of the once lush and fruitful mountains, rushing into Meribow City, frightening the people. The creatures grew sad and angry by what they witnessed. The two children who had befriended them, helped them, and understood them, lay dead in the streets; killed by their own kind; along with the hound pup. The creatures turned and attacked the people of Meribow; slaughtering the entire city; the taste for human blood filling their senses. The chaos could be heard across the twin city bridge on the other side of Salt River. The inhabitants of Miracle City came to the aid of Meribow. Many of them perished trying to fight off the creatures, and many of the creatures died as well. When the woman, my grandmother, found her children lying dead in the streets she wept bitterly for them. They say the moon that night was a full, blood moon. And in her pain, she made a pact with the evil one; the dark angel cast out of the heavens by the Creator himself. She cursed the cities and all of Zanchier, sentencing everyone locked inside the borders of the now desolate and cursed mountain ranges. The creatures turned cold, bitter, and distant from all humans. Their tortured souls living in anguish and pain to this very day as their hunger for human blood still torments them. The horrible stench of death lingered over the entire city for months to come, bringing more and more wild and hungry creatures to the city, cursing those creatures as well. The people who survived that first attack soon perished from increased attacks. The cities fell to ruin and became uninhabitable as the last of the people were killed."

"Goodness, that's quite a sad tale. Why don't your people return to your native lands?"

"Oh, no, girl, we don't dare do such a thing. We fear the curse and the creatures of that place. We're quite content living our lives as we do now."

"But the Scaithers..." Wynne stated, Aliyah interrupting her.

"Don't bother us none. We can handle them well enough, and we have our own little secrets that aid us when necessary."

Wynne sadly grinned at the old gypsy woman. "Thank you, Aliyah, for the story. It's not one I shall ever forget or wish to retell unless necessary."

"Just heed my warnings girl. If you and your family choose to venture to that cursed place, be careful that the curse doesn't take root in your hearts as well. I beg you all not to stay there for long. Find another place to call home quickly. That place isn't fit for any sort of life."

Wynne nodded her understanding as the old gypsy woman clicked the reins to start the Yarequu to walking again. Wynne watched her go, replaying the entire tale over and over in her head. It wasn't something she wanted to forget. The pain caused by greed, hatred, and fear, just like what was happening now in Zanchier with the Scaither takeover, caused people to do horrid things. Only, this affected everyone, not just the people like herself and the other LARS students. Thank goodness people hadn't reacted to her gift in the same way. She looked to the heavens, thanking the Creator for his protection. She would retell this story to her parents at a later time and needed to remember all she was told.

Aliyah traveled the gypsy trails as the wagon swayed from side to side from the rocky dirt road. The light blue snow was falling heavier now; blanketing the forest in a shimmering layer. Just as she passed a stand of large boulders that jutted out from the bottom of the mountainside, she heard someone sneeze. She pulled the wagon to a stop and listened intently.

"Who's out there?" she questioned, knowing that if it were Scaithers, they would not fear speaking to anyone. "Come on now, show yourself to old Aliyah."

At her last request, two young men stepped out from beneath the cover of the deep, shadowy, rock cave. They shivered in the cold, wiping their running noses on their torn and battered jackets. Their faces were red with the cold, and dirty and smeared with soot.

"Come on over here you two. I won't bite you," Aliyah said with a beckoning wave of her hand. The boys walked over to the wagon and she asked them. "Who might you two be?"

The boys looked at one another. "I'm Delmar Bamerly, and this is Caislan Harrington, Ma'am."

"And who do you belong to?"

"No one, Ma'am. Our families are all dead. We've been orphans since we were nine. Then after the wars three years back, we took up with Kreelie Rintel until he was killed just a few days ago. Then Treetop Village was attacked, and now, we don't have anybody or anywhere to go."

Aliyah looked them over. "Well, if you don't mind a life of traveling around and living off the land, and avoiding them nasty Scaithers at all costs, then I'd be glad to have you as part of the gypsy family. Would that suit the two of you?"

"Yes ma'am," they both readily agreed.

"But it's work I tell you. No slackers in our family. Everyone does their part."

"We aren't afraid of work ma'am," Caislan stated.

"You two can call me Tatik, it's what the family calls me; it means grandmother in our ancient tongue. Now, hop on up here beside me and we'll head back to camp and I'll introduce you to the family."

Caislan and Bamerly both eagerly climbed on board the wagon seat and Aliyah shared her lap blanket with the partially frozen and shivering boys. She flicked the reigns and the wagon slowly ambled along the forest path, disappearing beneath the low hanging branches of the snow laden trees.

Chapter 19

The Expedition

Seadon and Captain Matt both agreed to fly over the Marshlands later that morning while Wynne and Roamey tagged along. Wilkins had wanted to fly over with Wynne, but she had said the extra weight might tire Roamey too quickly since they are flying so far with nowhere to land to rest. So instead, Wilkins, Harper, and Adda, along with Finn, Aaric, and Captain James Donner of the Coastal Guard hitched a ride on the airship with Seadon and Captain Matt.

Everyone, except the captain and crew, stood at the glass-wall viewing deck as they quickly floated across the sky.

"Mother," Adda giggled, "it feels and looks like we're hardly moving at all."

"Well, it's because we are so high up from the ground. Do you remember the last time you were in an airship?"

"Yes, well, a little. It was when you found us again!" Adda answered excitedly. "But I don't remember it looking like this."

"Well, you were only five," Harper grinned down at her. They stood at the glass, pointing at things, and talking about what they saw.

Adda said, "Look, Mother, that's where we discovered Wren!"

"When were you ever near the Marshlands?" Harper asked curiously.

Adda's shoulders went up in defense as her head shrunk into them. "With Wynne," she shyly answered.

"What?" Harper asked surprised.

"Well, I made her take me. We were on Brigade patrol one day when we saw the Brindelwren in the water below us." Adda stopped talking like it was the most natural thing of all.

"Adda, continue please," Harper instructed. Adda began telling her all about her falling into the water, meeting the Brindelwren, then her, Wynne, and Jerod taking Moshi through the underwater caverns. How they found the bio-luminescent world, the Brindelwren injured and how she and

Wren had bonded, and then she mentioned the smashed underwater modules made by Vonder Mortruff. By the time Adda had finished, Harper's head was spinning and she had taken to falling into a chair that had fortunately been nearby.

"My word! What an adventure! I'm just curious as to why I was never told before now?"

"Wynne said that you would probably kill us both," she stated matter-of-factly.

Harper nodded her head in agreement. "You're probably right." She grinned down at Adda with a look of warning that said not to keep such things from her again.

Adda beamed back at her mother, and the two of them continued their search for strange and unusual things outside the windows of the airship.

Just on the other side of the airship Wilkins and the other men talked about tracing the river that curved, turned, and twisted through the Marshlands and the mangrove swamps like a striker's long, thin, body. Captain James made a quick sketch and map of the rivers, laying out a possible path that could possibly allow ships to sail through the mangroves and marshes to wherever this ruin city sat.

Wilkins looked out the window to see Wynne flying nearby on Roamey. He would never get over the abilities that his beautiful girls held. To see his once shy, unsure, and slightly timid Wynne on the back of one of the deadliest creatures in Zanchier took his breath away. The kinship they shared was truly remarkable to witness. The afternoon sun bounced and glinted off her hair as it blew out behind her in the wind. Roamey's striking colorful feathers in teals, purples, red, yellow, oranges and golds, made it look like she sat upon a throne of fire as they streaked across the sky. He then turned to look at his youngest, Adda. She too possessed these same remarkable traits as her sister Wynne. One day, she would likely be doing the same. He thought about the creature, the Brindelwren, and how Wynne had explained it and Adda's bond. She was so young and already had found her bond-mate. The largest creature ever seen commanded by the tiniest of girls. Wilkins sometimes worried about that fact, but watching Wynne over the years with Roamey, reminded him to take it in stride. He then turned to watch Seadon at the controls of the airship. He was so proud of the people his children had become.

The airship continued to float along as Wynne pointed down toward Rock City off to their right. Wilkins followed where she pointed. A pack of about five Hungerhounds stood on the tops of the rocks, watching them fly by, the large beasts curious as to what they saw, but more than that, they were hungry.

"I've never seen one of those in person. It's kind of hard to make them out. They just look like fuzzy dots on the rock tops," Finn stated.

"Neither have I," Wilkins replied.

"I would think this to be a first for all of us," Aaric put in as they all stared at the beasts, trying to make out what they could from such a distance.

Adda looked at her mother and shook her head no. Harper's eyes widened in shock as Adda whispered in her ear about Wynne and Bain's narrow escape and the injury to Roamey's foot. Harper sank further into the chair's back, suddenly needing the support. She decided she would need to have a chat with her, apparently reckless, daughter as soon as they set down on the ground again.

"Just the simple fact that we can see them at all should attest to the size of them," Captain Donner stated. They all nodded in agreement. Again, his statement did not settle well with Harper.

Wilkins turned to look at Harper who sat with her elbows perched on the chair arm and both hands holding her forehead.

"Harper, are you all right? You look a bit peeked."

"Harper waved him off. "I'm fine, just sorting through all the new information," she stated, trying not to say too much right now.

Wilkins shrugged and his attention returned to the conversation about the appearance and size of the Hungerhounds from what they could make out. An hour later they were flying as low as possible through the pass between the Bleak and White Mountains. It wasn't long before a large structure came into view. Everyone grew quiet as they watched the large ruin city rise up from the sands.

Wilkins asked, "Is this part of the southern Dune Sea? Or is this city located in the Deadman's Desert to the east?"

Aaric replied, "I doubt anyone has ever made that determination before now. We can chart that after we have more of a look around." They all nodded their consent in reply.

Finn said, "This is one, large, walled city. Or at least it was."

Captain Donner replied, "Most of the walls seem to be intact from what I can tell. I just wonder if those Hungerhounds come out this far?"

Harper put in, "From the looks of the Bleak Mountains and the lack of vegetation; meaning the lack of a food source; I'd say they'd go as far as needed for a meal. That could very well be what happened to the civilization that once inhabited this place. Perhaps they couldn't survive against the creatures of the Bleak and White Mountains? Maybe this place isn't such a good escape after all?"

Aaric reassured her, "With the advancements in technology now, I'd say we have a good chance at holding our own out here. I'd rather take my chances against the beasts than the Scaithers any day. I'm getting much too old for all this fighting."

Wilkins went to the ships control room. "Captain Matt, can you head east? I'd like to check out a stand of fruit trees and plants that Bain told me about."

"Certainly, Mr. Brinley," the captain formally stated, as was his way.

As they flew over the ruins below, they could see the large expanse of water off to the south. It seemed to stretch out forever to the west. They could see a small island further east, as they came upon a large waterfall at the base of the White Mountains to the north, with rivers that stretched all the way along the sands to the water in the south.

Wilkins pointed out the large grove of trees that sat beside and between where the rivers split.

"I believe those are all fruit bearing trees. Captain Matt," Wilkins stated, "can we put down here?"

"Certainly," the captain replied.

Harper grew nervous. "Wil, do you think that's a good idea?"

"We'll be fine, Harper. We have plenty of weapons, a battle airship, and a firebird."

Harper inhaled deeply, letting loose a slow sigh. "All right. I admit, I kind of want to explore myself."

"That's my adventurous girl," he smiled down at her.

She cocked a crooked grin at him.

The airship found a small clearing to set down, between the two rivers at the south end of the waterfall lake. Captain Matt pointed its nose west, cannons facing forward, just in case the Hungerhounds they saw earlier decided to come exploring as well. Everyone filed out of the airship, making certain they had weapons and stayed in groups of two or more.

Harper sent Adda along with her father while she made a beeline for Wynne; who at the moment was dismounting Roamey; determined to have a chat before her angst left her.

Bain was making good time; at least he thought he was. He sped along the base of Bleak Mountain, some Hungerhounds lending chase across the jagged rock ledges up the mountain-side. Fortunately, he had been right about the speed of the Bi-mod. The hounds were no match for it and could not catch him, even though several did try. One even leaped out in front of him and he had fortunately shot it, knocking it out of his path. He looked back to see the other hounds that were in pursuit attack the now wounded hound. They cared not for their own. He supposed hunger could do that to a body, especially one without reasoning. At least they no longer chased after him. He looked at his timepiece and noticed the hour was into mid-afternoon. He had been riding for ten hours now and had about another five to go before he would be in safer territory. At least he hoped so anyway. There was nothing to go by geographically as far as he knew. No one had ever made this trip from the southern side of the Zanchier mountain ranges. He would definitely map the area and all he had seen and experienced for future reference once he stopped for the night. He was growing a bit tired and hungry. But his life expectancy and his future spurred him on further. He wasn't certain what he would face ahead, but he knew what lay behind and along the Bleak Mountains where he still traveled. He was beginning to notice a few actual living trees dotting the landscape the further west he went. That was a good sign. A sign of life up ahead.

"Wynne, we need to have a chat." Harper stopped beside her and Roamey, who now lay on the ground, rolling in the coolness of the grass. Trying not to be too overbearing, she kept her voice on an even keel.

"Yes, Mother?"

"What's this about underwater caverns, a creature called a Brindelwren; which Adda can apparently speak to, and having a run in with Hungerhounds?" She stood there with her hands on her hips, waiting for an explanation.

Wynne grinned nervously, clearing her throat. "This is why I told Adda not to tell you. I knew you would freak out and get mad. Besides, Adda was not exposed to the Hungerhounds. That was just Bain and I."

Harper rolled her eyes; like Adda not being there for that one made it any better. She exhaled sharply. "Wynne! This stuff you're doing is dangerous!"

"No more dangerous than fighting in Scaither wars Mother. Besides, we're both just fine. All of us are. There's more danger from going to sleep in Zanchier than any exploring we do as Animal Brigade Scouts. Besides, I have Roamey."

Harper sighed hard, "Maybe, but your taking Adda…"

"She left me no choice. Besides, we found her bond animal. Wren is a beautiful creature. Silus, Creator rest his soul, said the old-timers called her the sea-beast in legends. She's actually quite gentle you know and has helped tremendously in keeping Loradin's shorelines safe from Scaither ships."

"Well, good to know," Harper said incredulously. "What about Vonder Mortruff? She said something about seeing the underwater module he was building."

"Wren took care of those, destroyed every one of them. Apparently they attacked her and the underwater bio-luminescent world. I think that might be how Vonder got killed. We never saw anyone when we returned; well, anyone alive anyway, just the destroyed ships."

"Would you *please* inform me of these missions before you take off? Just so I know where you are in case something happens. You know, like if we need to look for you," Harper stated, irritably.

"Yes ma'am," Wynne stiffly saluted her mother.

Harper cracked a smile at her daughter's stoic face. "Sorry, I don't mean to be so tough on you, but our lives are up and down all the time and I am just so stressed by it all. I'm tired Wynne, and I just want something better for you and your siblings."

"I know Mother; isn't that why we're here in uncharted territory? Well, sort of uncharted."

Harper linked arms with her daughter and smiled, giggling slightly at her answer and demeanor. "Let's go join the others and have a look at our possible new home." They joined Wilkins and Adda, tasted of the fresh fruit trees and discussed how many people they thought could live here. They also discussed how many water-ships and airships it would take to get them all over and through the Marshlands, all while avoiding Hungerhounds and other possible dangers of the Marshlands in the process.

Chapter 20

The Scaither's Kingdom

Riglan Mortruff stood on the fourth-floor balcony outside his office looking down over the people gathered below. The docks and loading areas that jutted out over Everly Lake just north of Everly Sound were packed with Scaithers, all waiting to hear what their new, very permissive leader had to say.

Riglan pompously stood at the railing, his arms raised, waving, and motioning for the people to get louder, basking in the rousing applause and cheers of his followers.

After several minutes of this, Riglan quieted the people so he could speak.

"People of Zanchier," he began, "I have experienced remarkable success in my takeover of the lesser cities of Zanchier. Port Proud will now be the epicenter of all the lands. I no longer have any adversaries that can stand against me!" More cheering from the rowdy crowd erupted. Riglan raised his hands to quiet them. "I supremely decide what's right and wrong. My commands shall be followed. My rules will be supreme law, and frankly, I don't have many!" More cheering erupted. Riglan raised his hands for quiet again. "My one and only rule is not to cross me," he smiled cockily as the crowd got quieter. "You cross me, you die. Other than that, do as you will and bring me the proper cut; sixty percent of all your spoils. You do that, and I'll have no problem with you, unless of course you challenge me. So, let's hear it for your new supreme ruler of the Scaither's Kingdom," Riglan said excitedly, raising his hands high in the air to bask in the raucous glory of all the evil people of Zanchier; people who wanted no law, and no rules. Ruthless people who would take whatever they wanted, would cheat to keep more of what they steal, and who would hurt and pervert the innocent.

Several LSS agents, who stood in that crowd pretending to be Scaithers, mourned the loss of Zanchier and the once fairer justice system. Now, there *was* no justice system. It was literally every man for himself, and if you couldn't defend yourself, then Creator help you. They slunk their way out of the crowd, turned on their MADs, and disappeared back to Loradin. They still had a little control within the city now that the barrier had been restored and the sky bridge gates repaired, but they had nowhere near the manpower that Riglan now possessed. Zanchier would for the foreseeable future, live in an archaic state of being.

Bain pulled up to the base of the Xantifal Mountains six hours later. He was tired and sore from sitting on the bi-mod for the last sixteen hours without stopping. He now shivered in the intensifying cold of the mountain range. The engine of the bi-mod was extremely hot, and it popped and cracked as it cooled in the cold, dark, winter night air. He found a large Weeping Giantrush Tree with drooping branches which, synonymous with the Xantifal Mountains, would allow him to climb out of the dampness of the night. He pushed the bi-mod beneath the thick branches that touched the ground, and up near the trunk of the massive tree. He made a pass all the way around the base to make certain he wasn't sharing the space with any wild creatures. While walking the circumference, he noticed a hole on one side that was quite large, enough to lie down in, build a fire, and store the bi-mod. He pushed the machine inside and placed it in front of the opening to deter any creatures from entering while he slept. He built a small fire on the ground inside the tree to get warm and heat up some food. His hunger outweighed his exhaustion and he ate quickly, passing out almost immediately after finishing his dinner.

The next morning, Bain woke refreshed. He slept soundly all night and for nearly ten hours. The long night's sleep was good because the trip up the Xantifal Mountains could prove to be deadly. Just as deadly as passing by the Bleak Mountains and the Hungerhounds; plus making it all the way up to the ridgeline would prove to be a long and arduous trip. He remembered his mother telling him it had taken her four or more days to travel up and down the mountainside when going for supplies to the villages below, which sat on the opposite side of the mountain from where he thought he was now. He believed he was further south and even though he wouldn't necessarily be walking up the mountain the way his mother had, the trip would likely still take him several days. Not to mention, trying to hide from the Kabihanxus and Pagorinxes who were abundant in these mountain ranges where food was plenty, and humans were all but void except around the mountain's base.

Bain chose a path — likely one used by a large animal — and began the climb up into the mountains. The higher he got, the colder the air became. The presence of snowfall also would hinder his climb as the bi-mod wasn't necessarily designed for off-road mountain climbing, especially in Winter. Fortunately, winter had just begun so the presence of snow on the ground would likely be thin. He hoped he wouldn't get lost and could reach the top and find the tree before the heavy snowfalls began. He wasn't at all familiar with these mountains, and heavy snow would make finding his way even more difficult.

The airship floated back into Loradin after a long day exploring the Forgotten Coast. Wilkins, Aaric, Finn, and Captain Donner, finished planning the steps to take whoever wished to escape Zanchier's interior and Scaither rule out to the Forgotten Coastal cities. The airship descended and set down at the airship field on Loradin's northwest shore, and everyone stepped outside to finish discussing last minute details. They would send word to every trusted leader in every city, having them to discretely announce the move to an undisclosed location, and if anyone wished to make the move, they would have to notify their leader by midnight. They needed a head count to know how many transports they would need, and everyone going would have to be at the Southern Coastal Guard stations and docks, or at the Loradin Airship field by two a.m. the day after tomorrow for loading. The water and airships would leave first thing in the morning two days from now, before sunrise, so as not to be seen by the Scaithers. Anyone not there by then would miss the ships. To make transporting more balanced, they instructed anyone from southern Praxtingen, Sandedge, Rhamadon, or Overton to meet at the Coast Guard stations. Anyone in western and northern Zanchier and Carpasmere to go to the airship fields for transporting.

Finn stated, "I hate to say this, but we could be causing ourselves a massive issue here by opening this to every citizen of Zanchier."

Aaric replied, "You're right, but it wouldn't be fitting to leave anyone behind looking for a better life. There will be no quality of life for anyone here who doesn't pledge loyalties to Riglan Mortruff. Therefore, we must give anyone who wishes it the chance at a better life."

Wilkins asked, "What do we tell people where we are going if they ask? Surely someone will want to know before climbing on board."

Captain Donner put in, "My guess is most people will be too frightened to chance it if they know where we are going. They've all grown up with the stories and legends of the Marshlands and the Bleak and White Mountains. I figure most will simply stay here and take their chances with the Scaithers."

Wynne stepped up, clearing her throat for attention. "I didn't know any of the true legends about the area before today, just the relative dangers. I don't think anyone does, by that I mean to say, that I did find the gypsies this morning Father as you asked me to. Madam Aliyah, the old gypsy healer, told me the story surrounding the ruin city."

"Let's hear it," Wilkins responded.

Wynne told them all the entire story that Aliyah had related to her, trying to remember and not leave out any of the details. Everyone was surprised by the gruesomeness of the tale and the origins of the curse that had allegedly been laid upon the area.

"I don't believe in curses," Aaric stated.

"You might not, but the majority of the Zanchier people do," Harper put in. "When I was in Vasalage prison four years back, you would be surprised to know just how many educated, scientific-minded people actually believe all of that. Those beliefs have been drilled into them from birth. Many won't go willingly, or happily. Those fears might even end up giving our escape away."

"But we haven't told anyone where we're going," Wynne stated.

"That's true, and takes us back to my earlier question," Wilkins added. "We could have a lot of people show up."

Aaric said, "Well, we'll tell them it's imperative to keep it a secret for safety reasons and they will see soon enough. If they wish not to go, they can turn around and go back to their homes. And let's offer up some prayers, and hope that the Creator leads and guides us here."

They all went their separate ways, Aaric went home to Neitha, Harper com-called her mother Gracelynn with the news, Wilkins, along with Finn returned to the LSS offices and Paisley and his two girls, Wynne returned to LARS to explain to Jerod and the others, and Captain Donner went back to his last days on shift at the Coastal Guard station.

The next two days were spent with plans being implemented for the escape of the people of Zanchier to the ruin city. People gathered supplies, things they could carry and easily transport inconspicuously by module or cart. Aaric used what money and power he had left to secure supplies for as many as he could, buying grains, meat, and animals for food and having them loaded onto the water-ships. All over Zanchier, the hundreds of people that actually chose to make the journey, silently and carefully prepared for the trip, leaving their homes under the cover of night to sneak across the lake or mountains, trying to make it to Loradin in time.

On the opposite side of Everly Lake, Bain was still scaling the mountainside of Xantifal.

Bain's trip up the mountain was brutal as there were no roads to follow. And he had learned the first day, not to take the worn pathways that existed, for there were large animals hunting along those paths. So, he had to break out and make his own way. Sometimes, there were fallen trees lying on the forest floor that were so massive and large, he spent at least thirty minutes trying to navigate around them. One particular afternoon while struggling to get up the mountain he felt the ground beneath him begin to shake. At first he was confused, until it dawned on him what it was he felt.

"The Shifts!" he yelled aloud. He had no idea what to do or how to avoid being swallowed by the earth. Bain pushed the Bi-mod as fast as he could, no longer concerned with anything but the shifting of the mountainside. As he sped along, trees fell beside him, cracking and falling into nothingness as a ravine opened up to his right. Bain steered the bi-mod toward the left, hoping to avoid running off the edge of the quickly disappearing ground. Being this close to the Shifts meant one of two things. Either he was going to die, or he would be deposited elsewhere in Zanchier. As far as the Bakrashan mountains, near the northern territories of the Carpasian Mountain range. He surely did not need that.

As the rumble got louder and the ground shook violently, Bain did what he could to navigate the earth below him, making certain he still saw earth beneath him. After ten minutes of shaking, the tremors began to subside and eventually stopped all together. Bain stopped the bi-mod, out of breath himself and completely shaken. He wondered how far he had been put off track. As the dust settled and he dismounted the bi-mod to have a look around, he noticed a village down the mountain at the base. He was still pretty far up which was good, meaning he didn't have to start all over again. Now to figure out which village it was. He stood there a few minutes taking in the landscape and trees, the bodies of water that were present and any other geographical landmarks he could make out. There were only two villages that were graced by the enormous Weeping Giantrush trees, and they were Terra Valley and Treeline Valley. The village below had a large lake, and it appeared the mouth of a wide river emptied into it. That meant that he was just above Treeline Valley and very near the Xantifal Mountain ridgeline.

"Whew, at least the Shifts didn't send me too far north." Bain gathered his bearings, now knowing the tree-house his mother once sheltered in four years ago was southwest and straight up. The Shifts may have given him another hour of travel, but the trip would likely be an easier one. He would just have to find a way to get across Catamount Gorge's smaller side rivers to reach it.

It was the morning of the escape and people filed onto Coastal Guard ships and airships in droves. They only had a few hundred people confirm the wish to leave, but at least several hundred more showed up than were expected.

Wynne commented to Jerod, "There are an awful lot of extra people. I hope they have room for all of them."

"I overheard your grandfather and Captain Donner speaking earlier. Donner said they were sending over another water-ship and crew to transport the excess."

"I wonder if they are having the same sort of problem at the airfield."

"More than likely," Jerod replied. "People are desperate to escape. Everyone knows that things will never be the same again. I just wonder about all the people to the west that wanted to come but couldn't get here."

"Every village leader was given notice. Even those that were our enemies in the war three years back. Grandfather was reluctant to send that invitation, but we are all Zanchieths in his eyes, and he said everyone should be given the chance to leave. That's likely where the extra people came from. I only hope the Scaithers didn't find out about our trip because of the inclusion of the western villages."

"Well, we only have a few hours to go before sailing orders are given and we haven't seen any Scaithers yet, so that must be a good sign."

"Let's hope so."

Wynne and Jerod got back to their jobs of loading necessary supplies onto the ships as people came in and dropped them off. The animals made quicker, easier work of lifting the heavy crates on board the vessels over the small slit of water between ship and dock.

Several hours later, every ship was loaded with refugees and supplies. Wynne looked to the sky, wondering if the airships were already sailing above them. They would begin the journey in darkness in hopes of avoiding being spotted. The water-ships would have to tread carefully not to collide into one another on the water, as the airships would have to do the same in the sky. No lights meant little visibility, but it was a chance they would have to take. Fortunately, the moon was in the waning stage and the fullness had decreased significantly over the last several days, lending darkness to aid them.

The trip across Everly Lake was a long one. All the captains maintained the same speed to avoid collision. They could at least communicate with one another via radio, calling out way points to communicate their current positions. The radio system had been their only way of undetectable communications during the wars three years back. Because of this the Coast Guard and airship captains had the systems installed to make communications easier instead of using code words.

By the time the sun began to peek over the horizon, they were nearing the Marshlands and far from any sort of detection. Jerod and Moshi checked the winding waterway out first to make certain the ships could pass. The waterways were narrow, but deep enough. Captain James Donner led the first of the four ships through the mangroves, making the journey as slowly as possible. When Jerod and Moshi found an obstruction, they worked to eliminate the blockage, tying ropes around mangrove plants, and throwing a rope up to Wynne and Roamey if he and Moshi couldn't free it themselves. Once again, the animals proved to be invaluable. Wynne thought about the story Aliyah had told her. If only the people then had been more open-minded, everything would have been all right. The once large cities of Miracle and Meribow might have been grand by now.

The twisting, turning trip through the mangroves, and then the Marshlands, was taking a long time. The airships, being able to fly over directly, would be there by late that afternoon. The sailing ships, having to use the overgrown canals, and moving at the pace they were currently traveling, would likely take days to get to their destination. The ships continued their agonizingly slow pace through the mangrove marshes. As people slept through the night, the captains, crew, and creatures and bond riders worked to clear enough space for the ships to pass. The night grew dark and cold, and Jerod and Moshi were all but frozen. They slipped onto a bit of dry ground to rest while Roamey set some of the dried mangrove bushes nearby ablaze for them to warm themselves.

The ships were stuck for a while until Moshi and Jerod were rested. As they sat in limbo, resting while they could and taking turns taking naps, they could hear the distant howls of Hungerhounds. Everyone began to grow nervous as those that stirred from their sleep scanned the inky darkness out across the barely lit marshlands; glowing eerily in the dark. The orange and green bio-luminescent creatures stirred in the

Marshlands, leaping about, and croaking their strange songs as a deep roar emanated from beneath the dark waters.

Wynne looked at Jerod excitedly. "Do you think that was the Brindelwren?"

"I hope so," Jerod answered tiredly, bundled in a blanket Wynne had thrown down to him from off Captain Donner's ship. The howl of the Hungerhounds split the night air once more.

Jerod stated, more awake now, "They sound closer."

Wynne looked at him, a bit alarmed. "Perhaps the sound just travels better on a clear night like tonight."

"Sure. We'll go with that answer." Jerod stood up, moving closer to the fire. The desire to dry off and warm up faster suddenly becoming more important.

The low, muffled, roar from somewhere deep below shook the area causing the water to ripple against the bottom of the ships. Jerod watched the water in front of the first ship begin to stir more rapidly.

"Um, Wynne," he pointed, rushing back to Moshi, and stirring the slumbering beast from his sleep. He climbed back up on Moshi's back as the beast slowly stood up on its two hind legs to stretch, nearly tumbling Jerod to the ground.

"Moshi, heel boy!" Jerod commanded in a loud whisper.

He and Wynne watched as the Brindelwren's long slender neck broke the water's surface just in front of the first ship. The men on board began to yell, "Sea-beast", tripping over one another and those asleep in their efforts to flee to the back of the ship, or scamper below deck to safety.

Wynne tried to calm the men, a tad unsuccessfully. Just as one man was about to fire on the Brindelwren, Captain Donner grabbed the gun out of his hands.

"Attention sailor!" The young man stood at a saluting position, as did the rest of the Coastal Guard crew on board. Captain Donner bellowed, "If the beast had wanted to hurt us, don't you think it would have by now! If you men had bothered to pay attention at all instead of letting superstition rule the good sense the Creator gave you, you'd have recognized the beast's gentle nature and how the creature is interacting with the other two creatures and their riders!"

Now that the crew and their passengers were calm, he gave them the "at ease" order. "Go about your business," the captain ordered once more. He looked over at Patrice and tipped his hat in her direction.

Dr. Patrice Barrister tried to hide the smile forming on her lips at the forceful nature of the captain. He might seem somewhat like an overbearing brute, and even she had thought so when they first met almost four years ago, but he had grown on her over the years at every *chance encounter* they had. James Donner had made certain to be one of the guards on rotation at Discovery Falls to escort the children to LARS. She recognized that he seemed to linger when she was near or make an effort to seek her out for some unimportant question that only she could answer. However, he had never gotten up the nerve to ask her out. Of course, luxuries such as dates and forming loving relationships had been put on the back burner over the last several years with her job as surrogate parent to over twenty children, and the more recent problem and escalation of Riglan Mortruff's ego and his sudden, unfortunate leap to power. Perhaps in this new world they just might have the opportunity to see where their relationship could lead.

The Brindelwren gave a throaty hello to Wynne and Jerod, nodding and calling excitedly. Wynne giggled at her antics and then tried to calm her a bit.

"Wren, how did you get here? The river is blocked with mangroves and silt."

Wren telepathically replied to her question, saying *'beneath mangroves, through caverns that lead to ocean.'*

"Ocean?" Wynne questioned her. "Is that what the big water is called on the outside of the sand and city?"

The Brindelwren nodded her head up and down and snorted.

"Wren is there a way you can clear a path for the ships to pass easily? My friends have tried all day and half the night and are tired now."

Wren lifted her head and dove below the surface of the water. She began to thrash her mighty tail at the sides of the mangroves as water stirred violently and the ships rocked back and forth. This form of clearing continued on and off for the next six hours, the ships now sailing more easily through the broken, floating, limbs of the mangrove trees. The rocking of the water from the thrashing of Wren's tail caused many people to get sick, a few leaning overboard to retch. There was one particular area where the water wasn't deep enough and the silt and marsh grasses were thick. In these areas Wren, Moshi, and Roamey, were hooked to ropes and they pulled and tugged the boats through the sludge until they were set in deeper waters and could move on their own. People cheered loudly for the creatures, reaching out over the ships railings — when the opportunity afforded them — for a chance to pet the Brindelwren as she passed by. She seemed to revel in all the excitement and attention. Wynne noticed how animated she became every time she heard people cheering and clapping at each hurdle they passed with her help. Wren's head bobbed up and down and her flippers slapped the surface of the water. The children on board were giddy, giggling and playing in the water that splashed over the railings and onto the ship's deck. The adults grumbled and complained, although still grateful for her assistance in clearing their way for faster travel. Not only had she helped in that manner, but the howls of the Hungerhounds were not heard again once Wren had made her appearance, making them all assume that the hounds feared the Brindelwren. Wynne was truly grateful to live in a time where her kind got to live in peace instead of being tortured for their gifts.

Chapter 21

The Prophecy

Over at the ruin city, the airships were unloading people and supplies. The courtyard was large enough for two of the airships to land inside and the other two landed just on the outside of the walls and western gate.

Seadon asked the captain as they let the ship down easily, "Captain Matt, sir, do you think we should go and load the people on the sailing ships onto the airships and bring them the rest of the way?"

"I don't see how that would work," Captain Matt answered. "There's nowhere to set down and therefore no way to get them on board."

"Perhaps Wynne and Roamey could lift people up and inside the airships as we hover?"

"I'm afraid that would be quite difficult, and maybe even dangerous. No, as long as the ships are able to make it through, the people on board will be just fine. We'll just make certain that when they get here, everything will be ready to make them comfortable."

Seadon nodded his understanding, and they set out about the village helping people get settled, putting supplies in storage areas, and whatever else needed doing. By the next morning, thanks to the Brindelwren making easier work of breaking through the overgrown mangroves, the four sailing vessels arrived at a deeper and wider part of the river that ran near ruin city. People stood at the ship railings and peered out at the strange land they never knew existed.

Captain Donner, having seen the docks on the earlier expedition days ago; though some were in poor shape; decided to sail out into the saltwater that Wynne had told him was called the ocean. The four ships made the trip from their position near the Marshlands to the shore of the ocean in an hour, pulling alongside the more stable of the docks, checking for soundness and allowing people to unload.

They made the short walk to the ruin city with each family being given a place to rest until they could figure out living accommodations for the four-hundred-and-sixty people who chose to make the journey. Everyone who wasn't exhausted from the trip through the marsh was busy setting things up or helping someone else. There were many elderly people who chose to escape, knowing they would never be able to survive another Scaither attack.

The younger people were assigned to help some of the older ones with setting up temporary shelters until proper housing could be built. Most of the men went out looking for wood that could be used to repair the walls and build homes inside the rock-hewn walls. Many of the women and younger children walked the hour-long distance to the freshwater lake to collect drinking water and another hour to gather fresh fruits. People were happily exploring their new home. A home of peace where they could make decent lives for themselves and their families. Although they did not have to deal with Scaithers, they had to be careful, and many took weapons with them to defend themselves; to make certain the Hungerhounds did not surprise them.

The sailors and ship captains set sail out into the ocean a little way and set their fishing poles into the water. The massive fish they pulled from the ocean would feed many in Ruin City; which is the name everyone had taken to calling it.

The lively hood of the people increased daily as their fears were soon replaced by contentment and joy. Life was good for all for the next two months with little to no problems arising.

The Hungerhounds, not certain of all the people in the old city watched and waited, whining for the ready meal just off to the east, but uncertain their few could overtake so many humans and the creatures that protected them; especially the Brindelwren which they already feared. However, one fateful night a few of the teenagers grew too brave and ventured too far out from old Meribow City, and too near the base of the Bleak Mountains. Four boys and five girls sneaked by the old man who had fallen asleep while on guard duty. They knew not to go too far from the city, and not to venture past the guard stations, but with nothing to fear any longer, their senses being lulled into a false sense of security, their thoughtless bravery turned to complete foolishness and disaster.

As they joked and played with each other in the desert sands, daring one another to risk a closer look at the Bleak Mountains, tragedy struck.

Back at the cities where people peacefully and joyfully milled about, blood curdling screams and the vicious snarls and growls of Hungerhounds split the night air, carried on the breeze from somewhere in the northern desert. A city alarm was raised as people took to gathering their loved ones, many not realizing their children were nowhere to be found.

"Captain Donner, Mr. Brinley, my daughter and son are missing," one woman anxiously announced.

"We'll do what we can to find them," Wilkins replied.

"Everyone stay inside the city's walls!" Captain Donner yelled. He, Wilkins, and Finn, and as many others that would fit, jumped into the two modified, open-topped, modules that had been created and built by Kamsten Whitsler and Maubrey Vanderpol, and struck out over the large bridge and out across the dark desert. They were followed by many of the village men and woman, armed with weapons. Many flowed out into the desert sands searching for the screams that could still be heard on the wind.

As they ventured further out, they came across three teens running back toward the city. The fear that filled their eyes and body language was evident as they cried hysterically, pointing, and jabbering about Hungerhounds and their friends. Several of the men jumped out to help and protect the distraught teens as they led them back to the city. Further out about another quarter mile, they found another boy covered in blood lying in the sand, his body severely wounded from a scratch or bite to the abdomen.

Several more men leaped out of the modules, hoisting the unconscious boy up and placing him in the back. The rest piled into the module that would continue on. As they got closer to the Bleak Mountains, they could see the hounds and their kills. As the modules approached, the beasts snarled and growled at the intruders, taking a fighting stance. The men fired their weapons, unloading everything they had into the creatures, killing two, but the other four turned and ran back into the mountains.

The men carefully approached the beasts, poking them to make certain they were dead. They then turned to try to identify the bodies of the teens. Several of the men grew sick by what they witnessed, retching in the sand where they stood. Captain Donner made the decision to bury the bodies of the teens in the sand where they lay rather than return them to their parents in the horrid state they were in. The men radioed back to the city with what they found and the names of the few people they could identify from the remains. Several parents collapsed in pain at the loss of their children. Others paced and worried, wondering if the unidentifiable was their own since they were nowhere to be found.

The injured boy who had been taken to the city was treated, but in an unstable condition. The men who had returned with the boy earlier, took the module and some shovels out to where Captain Donner and the six other men waited. They worked through the majority of the night, cleaning up the area and marking the graves as best they could. Hours later, they returned to the city, exhausted physically and emotionally by the things they had seen and what they had to do. Upon returning to the city, one of the men realized he had buried his own daughter as his wife asked if he knew where she was. The next morning, just after daybreak a crowd began to gather in the center of the courtyard. The despair that was felt through the city the night before was nothing compared to the anger and resentment of the parents whose children had been lost.

"We have to go back! We can't stay in this horrid place any longer!" a woman shouted in anger and remorse, as people yelled in unison with her.

Captain Donner tried reasoning with them. "People, we haven't had any problems until now. Look, I understand you're in pain, but if the kids who were killed last night had obeyed the rules then they would still be alive."

"You're blaming our children for this!?" another distraught parent yelled and the crowd became more agitated.

Captain Donner sighed heavily. "I'm not blaming anyone! Look, people, please, give it a few days or weeks. Things will get better. Do you all really want to return to Zanchier's interior and deal with the Scaithers again, and the violence and oppression that comes with that?"

"Better that than being eaten by the wild animals out here," someone yelled and the crowd jeered.

Wilkins replied to the crowd this time. "The same thing can happen to anyone back home. Wild animals have always been an issue, even there. Here, if you just stay away from the Bleak Mountains, I don't think we'll have any problems."

"What's going to stop the Hungerhounds from coming into the city?" another asked angrily.

Wilkins replied, "They haven't so far and we've been here for two months without any problems."

"I have another child. I will not lose this one to those beasts. I wish to be taken back to Carpasmere," one of the distraught parents yelled, weeping for her loss.

Aaric raised his hands to quiet the crowd. "Please, everyone, just give us a day or two to figure this out. We may be able to find another solution instead of returning. Please just go back to your homes or whatever it is you need to do and we'll let you all know more tomorrow."

"We're not changing our minds!" a man yelled, pumping his fist in the air. As the people disbursed they were still mumbling and threatening to leave on their own, the mothers and fathers still mourning the loss of their children.

Bain had found the tree-house to still be in decent condition after four years of not being used. He had com-called his parents shortly after arriving to let them know where he was. The quiet and wild beauty of the ridge-line helped to soothe his tortured soul while he learned to live off whatever the mountain provided. The winter on the mountain top was cold and harsh, but wood for fires and cooking, and food were both plentiful. The black, white, and teal color of the Pagorinxes and the colorful plumage of the firebirds, were easy to see against the light blue snow; making them easier to avoid.

Often, late at night while he stood in the massive split that traveled up one side of the tree-house, he would watch the strange lights that would appear and disappear in Storm Valley a mile below. He decided that tomorrow he would check out the lights to see exactly what they were. Bain thought about his family; his mother and Father, brother Seadon, and sisters Wynne and Adda. His father had told him that they were all now living in the ruin city that Bain had found on his trip out to the treehouse, and they were all doing very well. Maybe he would go to the city to be with his family? His time alone had given him the peace he needed to heal from the losses, but it had also taught him that he valued his loved ones and missed them terribly. He would get up early and pack, then satisfy his curiosity about the strange glowing lights in Storm Valley, and then continue southeast to Ruin City.

The next morning, Bain woke early before the sunlight could dim the glowing lights of Storm Valley. He rode the bi-mod the mile or so down the hillside, stopping in front of the glowing light that just sat in the center of the field. There was literally nothing behind or beside to create such a light. He had watched it come and go over the last few months, his curiosity growing with each new appearance.

Where does it come from? Bain's technical mind wondered. He adjusted the pack on his back to a more comfortable position, and in the process didn't notice his compass fall to the ground. He reached forward with his hand and put it into the glowing glittering light. He figured it to be some sort of portal, much like the MADs that they wore on their wrists; which he had managed to repair during his solitude. He stepped through to the other side into a completely new and different world unlike anything he had ever seen before. He stood there looking at what stood before him, amazed that he was no longer in Zanchier but somewhere else entirely. After a few moments of being mesmerized by the bustling city, he turned back to the portal deciding to get the rest of his family and return. But when Bain turned back, the portal was gone. There was nothing but the city in which he now stood.

Hours later, the people of ruin city gathered in the courtyard again, not waiting for days to hear from Aaric and the other leaders of the city. Aaric, Captain Matt, Captain Donner, Finn, Paisley, Harper, Wilkins, and Dr. Barrister all gathered in the center of the growing crowd.

"Are you taking us back or what?" someone yelled, spurring the crowd into complaints, and bickering.

Aaric begged once more, "Look, if you'd just give us until tomorrow to come up with another solution."

"We're not waiting! We'll not spend another night in this cursed place. I remember the old forgotten legends about this city. Now I know them to be true! You've led us all to be slaughtered!" The crowd became loud and agitated again.

Aaric looked at Captain Matt who nodded his agreement. Aaric sighed. "All right, all right, please, settle down. If you wish to return then you may do so, but many have decided to stay. Some of the captains and crews have agreed to return you all to Loradin but you will have to make your own way back to your old homes from there. But, please, if you return, you must promise to not tell anyone else where we are or how to get here. On pain of death, your word must be kept," Aaric stated.

They all readily agreed, but those staying knew that the weak would talk at first threat, and their world would once again be threatened by Scaithers.

"When can we leave?"

"As soon as you can be ready. Three of the airships will be prepared and waiting for you on the western gate. They'll leave in an hour. Be here by then or you'll have to stay."

The crowd dispersed as people hurriedly left to pack. One hundred and sixty people returned for the journey back to the interior of Zanchier. The families of the kids who had perished all chose to return, except for one. The boy who was injured still clung to life and couldn't be moved so his family also stayed behind, as well as one of the families of the kids who had returned from the desert alive. After the airships were loaded, the people staying to stick it out sadly watched the airships lift and sail away back toward Loradin and their former oppressed lives. One of the captains and crew of the airships stated they would not return, but the other two would be back by nightfall, and would also bring back more fuel for the modules and airships, and any other necessary supplies they could manage to find. Kamsten and Maubrey had been working hard, with very little technical equipment, to design a solar powered device and rechargeable battery to power the machines when fuel was scarce and had asked the returning pilots and crews to procure a few items for them. Everyone slowly departed as the airships sailed out of sight. They went quietly back to their homes and duties, as they waited to hear what those in charge had decided to do about their futures and the Hungerhounds.

That evening, before the airships could return, the people of Ruin City had to fight for their lives once again as the Hungerhounds grew more daring and aggressive. The hounds from the night before returned with even more of their pack. They approached the outskirts of Meribow city, now unoccupied as everyone decided to move over to the higher walled city for greater protection. The Hungerhounds slowly moved into the area, going as far as crossing the Salt River Bridge.

Jerod and Moshi took a stand as Moshi bellowed his deep reverberating song. The beasts yipped and yelped in pain as the sound pierced their eardrums, causing some of the younger hounds to turn and run.

Oudree and her Yarequu, used the creatures camouflaging abilities to disappear, riding through the pack as Oudree sliced at their hides with her long, curved, swords.

The commotion above water, stirred the Brindelwren from her night fishing out in the saltwater, and she hurried to return to Ruin City and the Salt River. She swam up quickly and leaped from the water onto the eastern riverbank, taking everyone by surprise and making a stand against the beasts. She fought off several as they dared to attack her, biting at anything they could get close enough to.

Wynne and Roamey took to the sky to warn off the creatures with Roamey's fiery breath, laying a ring of fire around several of the beast, trapping them for a brief time. But with nothing but sand to adhere to, the fire quickly burned out.

While in the air, Wynne heard a strange screeching noise that seemed to grow in intensity. She turned just in time to see something large fly at her from above, knocking her from Roamey's back. She fell to the ground hard, landing on her back in the sand which knocked the wind out of her. She lay there trying to regain her breath when she noticed several large birds soaring through the sky from the direction of the White Mountains, descending on ruin city and snatching people up into the air and carrying them off. She knew then that they fought against more than just Hungerhounds. At that moment, when she was getting her breath back and was trying to stand, a hound menacingly approached. She figured this was the end, until the beast was snatched into the air and flung a long distance away by non-other than Roamey.

Wynne sighed heavily, "Thank you, Roamey! Your timing couldn't be better," she said, climbing on his back. "Well, maybe a little better. That was too close for comfort." They took to the sky again, taking aim at the creatures in the air. There had to be a dozen or so of the wretched looking birds, which Wynne took to be the giant Harpies of lore and legend. The ones the gypsies told stories about when she was small. Roamey laid fire to many, turning them back to the White Mountains, their feathers burning, their screeches of pain filling the evening sky with a frightful sound.

The Brindelwren bit at anything that got close to her, using her spiked tail to wound and kill the hounds as she snatched Harpies from the air, slinging them out toward the ocean waters several miles away.

Just when it seemed like they might be losing ground in the fight, the two returning airships began firing on the Hungerhounds and Harpies, killing some and deterring others. Soon, with the remaining animals running in fear, the city settled down once again. It had been a hard, gruesome battle, one where more lives were lost and many others injured.

As the people rested for a bit, and mourned yet more of their friends, the leaders decided to talk.

Aaric began. "Perhaps those that left were right. We have no idea what else is out in those mountains, or when they'll decide to come calling for dinner again."

Wilkins stated, "I agree to a point. I don't think we can stay here but going back to fight Scaithers every day is just as bad."

Paisley added, "Yes, but at least our opponents aren't wild, massive, hungry, beasts. I'm beginning to think we stand more of a chance with the Scaithers."

"Or," Captain Donner stated, "we can take to the open ocean and see what other worlds we can find?"

Harper replied, "What if there are no other worlds? What then?"

"There must be other places. The day of the expedition I saw another island not too far out, maybe three or four miles at best."

They all looked at one another and Finn said, "I'm game. I say we give the ocean a try. Paisley and I would like to find somewhere less menacing to raise our girls."

Wilkins and Harper looked at one another. "We're game as well. I'd say after tonight, that most people will be." They continued cleaning up and burying the dead once again; a thing that seemed all too normal over the last few years of wars and now animal attacks. They gathered everyone in the city center to discuss the plans to vacate Ruin City all together the next morning. Everyone who was left agreed heartily to the move.

Wilkins pulled his family aside to talk. "Harper, we need to go get Bain. If we're leaving Zanchier, then he needs to come with us. We all know the location of the treehouse, so we can use our MADs to make the jump. Quick and easy."

"I agree. Shall we go now?"

"No time like the present."

Wilkins explained to his father where they were going and that if they weren't back by the time the ships were to depart, to leave without them. Aaric, Neitha, and Gracelynn bid them all farewell, safe travels, and a hope for returning.

Wilkins, Harper, Seadon, Adda, Wynne and Roamey, used their LSS issued MADs to open up their tree house destination and exited at the base of the massive tree. They searched for Bain, inside first, not finding him, but seeing signs that he had definitely been there.

Harper thought for a minute about where Bain would have gone, then remembered the lights in Storm Valley that had gotten her attention several times before. She and Wilkins had the same revelation at the same moment and they all took off for the valley below. Roamey followed them, flying down into the valley to wait. While there, another Kabihanxu stepped out of the trees and looked at him. The two of them studied one another as their natural instincts took over. Roamey realized that the other Kabihanxu was a female. The two of them bonded as the Brinley clan finally arrived in the open valley. Seeing the bi-mod parked beside the portal, they desperately looked for Bain. The night was beginning to fall heavily as Wilkins stepped up to the glowing light. It was the same sort of portal that he had walked through five years back and disappeared, until one day when he found a portal to return home to Zanchier and his family.

Harper asked nervously, "You don't think he went through it do you?"

At that moment, Wilkins looked down and saw a glint in the snow. He bent over to pick up the compass that he recognized as Bains. He held it up for Harper to see. He knew that Bain was likely lost to them forever. Out of all the men who had walked through the portal with him years ago, only he had returned.

Wilkins turned to look at his family. "We have a decision to make. We return to the ships and leave with everyone else, or we can walk through this portal and hope to find Bain, which I tell you now, will prove to be near impossible."

"We can't just leave him behind, Wilkins," Harper stated, unnerved.

"Bain's family Father," Seadon said.

"So through the portal it is?" Wilkins asked and they all nodded in agreement. He turned to com-call his father Aaric to explain their decision.

Wynne turned to look at Roamey. She watched him happily courting the female Kabihanxu. Her heart ached with sadness knowing she couldn't bring him along. He turned toward her, sensing her sadness, and approached. He bent his head to nuzzle the girl who had been his friend his entire life.

Wynne stood there, crying into Roamey's feathered face, sniffling as she tried to compose herself. She looked up at the large firebird.

"I have to go now Roamey," she said, her voice cracking with emotion. "You take care of yourself up here in the wilds of the Xantifal Mountains. I'll miss you terribly." She choked back more tears as he pushed at her, nuzzling her lovingly.

Harper reached over, took her daughters arm, and pulled her into a hug. The Brinley clan locked hands and disappeared into the portal and into another world altogether, unsure where they would end up or where Bain could have gone.

The four sailing vessels and the three airships loaded with people and supplies, set sail for another world early the next morning. The Telepaths decided it would be best to say goodbye to their creatures and send them back to the wilds of the Zanchier Mountains, uncertain about what sort of world lay ahead. The children and some of the adults all gathered around the old-timers who motioned them forward. They often liked to tell stories for entertainment and to lift the spirits of the people.

The old-timer began, "There's a prophecy the gypsies used to tell, back when I was just a young boy, much about your age," he said, pointing at some boys around seven years old, happily seated at his feet, grinning in delight. "This prophecy told of some heroes; men and women; who would one day restore balance to all the realms and all of Zanchier. These people were known as The Twelve..."

The story continued as the vessels sailed out across the bright blue waters and hopefully onto a better future for them all.

THE END
(Or perhaps, a new beginning.)

About the Author

SG Boudreaux is a stay-at-home mom who has home-schooled her children for the last twenty years. Two have graduated, and her youngest is an eighteen-year-old, special-needs child. She and her husband of twenty-seven years live in the country, in a small rural area, just outside of Lake Charles, Louisiana. She was born in West Virginia, lived in Florida for many years before moving to Louisiana with her mother and youngest sister. She married a local boy and has lived there ever since. She loves the culture, the people, the sense of community, and definitely the wonderful Cajun food. You can find out more about her and her books on her Facebook, Instagram, Twitter, or her website at www.sgboudreaux.com

Her previous series of books are clean-reading, fiction, fantasy, and time-travel.

You can write to her at the address in the front of the books.

Look for new books by S.G. Boudreaux titled the *Stormwalker, Series*. This series will be the continuation of the Brinley's stories to be released sometime in 2024.

Other Books by SG Boudreaux

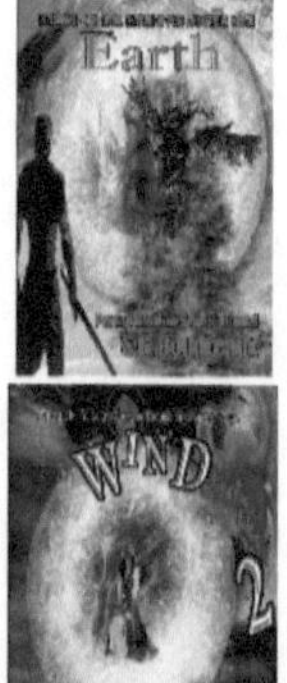

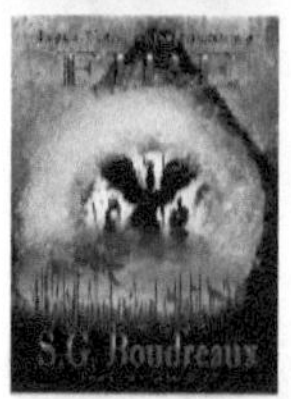

Non-fiction titles by Shawna Boudreaux

SG Boudreaux is also writing another book titled *The Barter*. This is a dystopian, survival/romance story based upon life after the collapse of the world. This novel takes place on the Louisiana coastline, just south of Lake Charles in Cameron. Also releasing in the summer of 2023 is a Bestiary entitled The Keeper's Book of Unusual Creatures and Other Pertinent Information. This book is based on creatures created for the Peregrination and Zanchier Series of books.

Thank you for your continued support, and I truly hope that you enjoy my line of clean reading, fiction, fantasy, novels.